The Summer Camp Uprising

a novel by

Arthur Sharenow

(author of: 37 Summers: My Years as a Camp Director)

Zorba Press
Ithaca, New York USA
https://zorbapress.com/

ISBN: 9780927379526

Book cover design by Susan Krevlin

For more information about this book
and other books published by Zorba Press
contact the publisher by email:
books@zorbapress.com

Release date: 2021-July-04

Printed and bound in the United States of America
Printings: scu-inp-016, scu-cov-001
0102030405060708091011121314151617181920

Published by Zorba Press
https://ZorbaPress.com

Dedication

To my daughter, Susan Krevlin,
who played an enormous role in the final version of this story.

To my son, Robert Sharenow,
whose example as a writer inspired me to make a serious attempt at writing.

Thank You to

Susan who volunteered to do copy editing, but turned out to be not just a copy editor, but also truly an editorial consultant. I came to appreciate and value her suggestions on choice of language, most of which have been incorporated. In addition, she designed the book cover, which appropriately reflects the turmoil of the story.

Robert, whose work ethic as a writer, inspired me to sit down at my computer and start writing. He has written several wonderful novels, while at the same time holding a very demanding full time executive position. I thought to myself "If he can write novels while working full time, it is time for me, a retiree with few competing time demands, to sit down and start writing."

Michael Pastore, my Editor and Publisher of this novel, who demonstrated incredible faith in my ability to turn out a novel he would be interested in publishing. Michael has made important suggestions along the way as well as the doing the important final edit before bringing the novel to publication.

Quotes from The Summer Camp Uprising

"Most of our campers are returnees and many of the counselors as well. They know the rules. There has never been a problem, and, as long as the lines are clearly drawn and everyone knows the rules there never will be."
— Nelson Cohen

"Nelson thinks he can run this place without help, but he just doesn't understand times are changing. He doesn't get what's going on in colleges these days. He doesn't seem to understand the stress these kids are under, worrying about the war and wondering what they'll do if and when they are drafted. I'll bet some of our counselors have spent as much time attending protest meetings as they have classes during the school year. How can they take these rules that seem so petty to them seriously?"
— Vico Leoni

"I'll show him. Imagine him calling me self-centered and dishonest. I'll show him who had ideals. I'll show him how a camp should be run. I'm going to make this place the happiest camp in the country these next few weeks."
— Joey Katz

Characters in the Novel

Camp Adventure Administrative Staff

Nelson Cohen ... Owner and Camp Director
Cindy Cohen ... wife of Nelson
Harriett ... daughter of Nelson
Vico Leoni ... Head Counselor
Dotty Leoni ... wife of Vico (married 5 years)
Celia ... daughter of Vico
Paulette ... Girls' Head Counselor
Joanne ... Girls' Senior Unit Leader
Roland Samson ... Waterfront Director
Bob Weinberg ... Assistant to the Waterfront Director
Evan Spielberg ... Assistant to the Waterfront Director

Unit Leaders and Counselors

Joey Katz ... Senior Unit Leader
Kerri ... counselor and girlfriend of Joey
Jeff Saunders ... Junior Unit Leader
Gloria ... counselor and girlfriend of Jeff
Randy Daniels ... Unit Leader
Tubby Brown ... Unit Leader
Shari ... new girl counselor
Cozy Martin ... counselor
Rachel ... counselor and girlfriend of Cozy
Major Goldblatt... counselor
Bob Weinberg... counselor
Dick ... counselor
Richie ... counselor
Jim ... counselor
Sammy Samuels ... Junior Unit counselor

Unit Leaders and Counselors (continued)

Fred Sweeney ... Junior Unit counselor
Mike Budd ... Junior Unit counselor
Harry Enfield ... Nature counselor
Dick Reback ... counselor with issues
Tim Brownstein ... counselor

Medical and Support Staff

Dr. Bob ... Camp Doctor
Daisy ... Camp Nurse
Dr. Clarke ... doctor in the Hospital
Bob Benson ... Chef
Anna Benson ... Dining Hall Manager
George Hall ... Head Maintenance

Campers

Liz Aronson ... sick child
Stevie Himmelman ... camper of counselor Dick Reback
Billy Massotti ... camper of counselor Dick Reback
Russ Segal ... senior camper
Jake Newman ... senior camper
Bobby Nason ... senior camper
Danny Sundberg ... senior camper

Characters from Joey's Childhood

Abe Katz (father of Joey)
Mommy
Johnny Greene ... best friend
Ezra ... friend

1

Deciding On A New Career

Vico

The students should never have held such an election, but they did, and I was the winner. It was embarrassing to be named the most popular teacher at Hewlett High School. My wife Dotty said she wasn't surprised, "I'm sure you got the votes of all those teenage girls. There are only four male teachers in the whole school, and I've seen the other three."

"Thanks a lot, Dotty. I like to think maybe my teaching had something to do with the vote. Besides, it was the boys, not the girls, who voted for me. The boys never stop asking me questions about my baseball career. You'd think I made the Majors."

"I'm sure it didn't hurt that you are also the youngest teacher in that school by at least ten years. Were any of the other teachers upset when the results were announced?"

"Most of them looked amused not upset, and a few went out of their way to tease me with their congratulations. They were just having fun. None of it sounded mean."

By any objective standard, I know I am considered a success. Dotty and I have been married five years and we are very much in love. Our daughter Celia is the second love of my life. Between Dotty and me, I know we spoil her perhaps more than we should, but she is so adorable it is hard to resist. Our master plan calls for one more child, hopefully a brother for Celia in a year or two. We have a wonderful two-bedroom apartment, sunny and bright and an easy commute to my school. That's all we need at this point in our lives. Of course, I wish my salary was a little bigger, though it is certainly more than enough to put food on the table and pay the rent. We are lucky in that we can also afford a few of the luxuries that make life worth living because of a modest steady income I get from my grandfather's trust fund.

I've been told by more than one friend that I seem to be a man without problems, a well-adjusted human being; that I have everything going my way. I have to laugh. Obviously, I have succeeded in keeping my insecurities to myself. I have been dogged by the ancient saying: "Those who can, do. Those who cannot, teach." For years, my father espoused this classic cliché. To his credit, he has refrained from repeating those words since the day I started teaching, but I'm convinced he looks down on my profession and feels that I'm wasting my talents.

Those words were impressed on my brain as a youngster, and they remain there as though printed for eternity. What is there, after all, to this teaching business? I've been at it for six years now, and I know everything there is to know. There are no hidden facets, no mysteries, no new avenues to explore. It is what it is, and it will never be anything more. Will I be satisfied to spend the rest of my life trying to get a bunch of teenagers to appreciate a language some of them can barely speak, let alone read with appreciation or write with any sense of clarity?

I sometimes hear them in my sleep as they converse in their version of English, "I was walking down the street, right, when I see this girl right... so I says to her...."

I admit there are satisfactions. Every so often I see a kid who entered my class at the beginning of the term not even slightly interested in being in school, when suddenly he or she begins to light up with a thirst for learning. Then there are times I wonder why I even try. Can I delude myself that I am getting better at my job from year to year? Sometimes I question if I'm as effective a teacher now as I was my very first year when everything was new and exciting. Sometimes I wonder how I ever got into teaching at all.

My childhood was lonely. Our house was always very neat and completely respectable. Beneath the surface it seethed with tension and anxiety. I never brought friends home. I didn't dare. I visited their houses, met my few friends on designated street corners, but never at my house. My house was a house of sorrow, a house of the unexpected, a house of shame.

Memories of that childhood household will always be a part of who I am. As much as I might like to repress them, the incidents and my own horror at them remain vivid to this day. I will never forget my mother's rages and furies, the stomping on the floors, the banging on the walls, the secret warnings and messages she received. Things always seemed a little better for a while after she came back from one of her "rest homes." That wouldn't last long. Soon enough, the cycle would start all over again. She would scream at the living room radio because evil forces had taken over the broadcast studios, inserting messages directed at her. I remember the sad times when she would lie in bed all day moaning and crying. Then there were the worst times of all, the violent times when she threw dishes, lamps, and ashtrays or whatever was handy against her invisible enemies. On those days I retreated to my room, pulled a pillow over my head and cried in terror. It was usually right after such incidents that she went away for one of her rest periods. I'll never forget the time she cut off all of her hair, or the day she lit her dress on fire, and the hysteria that followed. Nor will I ever forget the parade of grimly efficient steely grey housekeepers my father hired to look after me and the house when mother was "away for a rest." The memory I would give anything to forget was when I discovered her on the bathroom floor. My most lasting image from that day was of blood and her lying there on the floor. The ambulance came and rushed her to the hospital. I was alone in the house for hours, waiting for my father to return home from a business trip.

I hated the priest who stood by the open grave and recited "We all come from dust, and to dust we must all return." There was never a kind word, never a word about mother, the sad lady who lost the final battle against her demons. The priest knew nothing of my smiling loving mother who hugged and laughed and played with me when I was very little. That priest never knew her, never mentioned her. She was a suicide. She was a sinner. All he could think to say about her was "dust returns to dust." What a terrible thing to say. What a terrible way to sum up a life. Is that what life is all about; dust to dust and nothing in between but sorrow and pain?

I have spent the years that followed rejecting that terrible notion. I have also spent years convincing myself I am not my mother and I am not destined to wind up as she did. The day she was buried I resolved to be strong, to be independent. I resolved to always stand on my own two feet. I know now that every decision I've made in life has been based on my need to keep these resolutions.

As a teenager, baseball was my emotional life saver. I discovered early that I had the ability to throw the ball harder and faster than any of the other boys my age. When I was twelve years old I went to the library and found a book about pitching, studied the illustrations carefully and taught myself how to throw a curve ball. I practiced throwing that curve ball against the garage door every day after school. I mastered the art so successfully that when I tried out for the Junior High School team, I could see the coach was impressed. He called people over to watch me throw my phenomenal curve ball. When we started playing games, I struck out everyone in sight. In school and around our neighborhood I could tell people heard about my successful pitching, and they were impressed. I kept pitching and winning all the way through my junior and then senior high school years. I was suddenly a minor celebrity and had a lot of new friends. It was through baseball I proved to myself I was strong, that I would never collapse like my mother.

When I was invited to come to a tryout camp sponsored by Major League scouts I was floating on air, but my Dad warned me that "every boy there will be a great player and will have had the same kind of success" I had experienced in high school. He said they would all be much better than the boys I was used to playing with and against. The very first day of camp I quickly discovered that in this case my father knew what he was talking about. The boys trying out came from all over the country, many from the southern states. Some of them had such strong accents I could barely understand what they were saying. Most of them were big guys, some well over six feet. My mouth dropped open when I saw that first batting practice. I was slightly in awe as balls were slammed over and against the distant fences in batting practice. I did my warming up while at the same time looking over to see what the other pitchers could do. Some of them could throw the ball as fast and some even harder than me. I was pleased to discover none of them showed a curveball anywhere as good as mine.

By the end of the three-day tryout camp, I knew I had made an impression. One of the scouts called me aside.

"Hi kid, my name is Johnny Pytlak. I scout for the Philadelphia Phillies. You looked pretty good out there. Where did you ever learn to throw a curve ball like that?"

"I studied a book called *Let's Talk Pitching*. It showed illustrations of how to throw different pitches. That's where I learned how to throw my curve."

"That's amazing. I never yet met anybody who told me he learned how to play this game from a book. However you learned it, kid, that curve ball could be your ticket to the majors. What do you think? Are you really interested in making your living playing baseball?"

"You bet I am!"

After high school graduation, and with my father's reluctant permission, I signed my first professional contract. My first team was the Greensboro Rockets in the Carolina League. I soon learned that baseball was not just a game. It could be hard work when played day after day in the blazing hot sun. On the positive side, I was striking out batters and winning games, and had confidence that I would eventually make it to the big leagues. I got used to my arm being sore the day after I pitched, and I decided to ignore the pain and play through it. After a few games, the pain in my elbow never went away between games. It was worrisome, but I didn't want to miss a start so I didn't say anything to anybody. I didn't want to be thought of as a complainer, or worse, a weakling. I pitched every five days, and each time the pain became sharper and harder to ignore. One day as I started my pre-game warmup, I was wincing with pain on every throw. My manager Skip was watching from a distance. After watching me for a couple of minutes he walked over to where I was warming up and took the ball out of my hand.

"Kid, if it hurts that much, we'd better get you to a doctor."

My father insisted I see a doctor in New York City. At Mount Sinai Hospital we met with an Orthopedic surgeon. X-rays showed bone chips in my elbow. I had surgery to remove the chips and the surgery was proclaimed a success. The surgeon advised me that I'd be able to pitch again in a couple of months. "But," he said, "seeing what's going on in your elbow I wouldn't recommend it. In my opinion if you keep throwing a ball the way you throw, the same thing will happen again. The cartilage where the humerus and the ulna meet at the joint is all worn down. I've worked on the arms of a lot of ballplayers, most of them Major Leaguers. You're eighteen years old, but your elbow looks just like what I would expect to see in a thirty-five year old who'd been pitching for fifteen years. My advice to you is to go into some other line of work."

That was a blow. I wanted to ignore the doctor's advice, and go back to the team. The doctor smiled sympathetically, and made a suggestion.

"I don't blame you for not wanting to give it up. Before you make a final decision, why don't you take the X-rays to a couple of other Orthopedists in town, and get their opinions on whether or not you should keep pitching."

Dad and I went from doctor to doctor with the post-surgical X-rays, and they all shook their heads and agreed I would just be sentencing myself to future surgeries until finally, I would have to give it up. They made it sound helpless, and I reluctantly understood my baseball career was over.

My father suggested I join him in his business. I knew Dad's business was solid and I would be able to earn a good living at it. I also knew I didn't want to accept the invitation. It would be a surrender of my sense of independence, my need to prove I was strong enough to be a success on my own. Also, I had absolutely no interest in manufacturing or selling women's dresses. I questioned my own motives, wondering if I turned the offer down primarily because I couldn't see working side by side with my father. I loved my father, but with that love, there was always an irrational resentment. Even though it wasn't true, I always felt my father was at least partially responsible for my mother's craziness.

Was it independence or cowardice that led me into teaching? Was it the easy way out? I will always be secure as a teacher. Then again, I will never have to prove anything to be a success as a teacher. "Those who can, do. Those who cannot, teach." I was never entirely free of doubts about my decision. I was always looking for something fulfilling that might also be compatible with teaching. I decided to write a novel. I always enjoyed writing when I was in college and writing is something entirely compatible with teaching. I could write regularly through the school year and then would have a huge block of time in the summer to complete my masterpiece.

Like so many others, my ambition was to write the Great American Novel. Two years have gone by since I started my novel and I've been mired down since page one forty-seven. What happened was that I wrote my protagonist into a corner, and my creativity abandoned me as completely as I subsequently abandoned my hero. It seems hard to believe two years have gone by since I sat down so confidently and with a powerful sense of purpose. I remember that day I sat myself down at the typewriter, resolved to write twenty pages before I would allow myself to call it a day. I locked myself in and turned out twenty pages, confident I would accomplish at least that much every free day. In fact, after the first few days, the remaining pages were eked out two or three at a time, with weeks and occasionally months between writing sessions. I have finally faced the fact I might never finish. What a bitter pill that is to face.

I could become a school administrator. That's another possible avenue for a teacher. For that I knew I would need a special degree. I applied to NYU and CCNY and was accepted by both programs. With the reality upon me, I have decided not to register. The thought of going back to school three nights each week defeated my ambition.

My next thought was a career as the director of a children's summer camp. I was aware many school teachers seemed to supplement their teaching income by working in camps. I asked a few of my friends who regularly went off to camps every summer. Some worked at Day camps. Others at Overnight camps. They were universally enthusiastic. The Overnight camp counselors even more so.

My friend Cal was a math teacher, and I had never known him to sound excited about anything. On the subject of camp, he had unbridled enthusiasm.

"It's great. You live right there at the camp, no expenses, no worries, and you're playing ball with kids. What could be bad?" Your own kids have a place to go swimming every day, and when they get a little older, they get to be campers, and be a part of the camp program too. You save a fortune because you get paid and you don't spend a penny all summer. I think you ought to give it a try, Vico. If you don't like it you don't do it again. I'm betting you'll love it."

By the time I came home from school that afternoon my mind was made up. Now I just had to convince Dotty. I gave her all of Cal's persuasive arguments in favor of going to work at a camp, and then added my own additional agenda.

"Look, if we don't love it the first year that will be the end of it. Assuming that we do love it, we go a few years, gets some experience, and then we buy a camp of our own. That will be our business. When the time comes, I'm sure my father will lend us the money to buy a camp and get started. First we have to be certain that's what we want."

"Vico, you know I want you to be happy, but this is not a small decision. This is a big step, and you're already building castles in the sky. Now you're buying your own camp. We have such a beautiful house here, and we know all of the neighbors, and Celia has playmates here. There are lots of good reasons to not think about going away for the summer. Knowing you, you'll never be satisfied until we give it a try, so I'll go along for one summer, and then we'll see."

"That's all I ask, honey. I think we're all going to love it."

I did in fact love it. I had a job as a group leader in a large sleepaway camp operated by The Jewish Federation. After that one summer I was sold. Dotty was happy too. I tried hard to explain to my father what I found so appealing.

"The religious part doesn't matter. Kids are kids, and the chance to work with kids out of the confines of a school is a genuine pleasure. And these kids are so happy. At school only a minority of the kids look forward to each day's classes. Sometimes it's like pulling teeth just to get them to pay attention. At camp it's just the reverse. A huge majority love it while a small minority finds it challenging. Everything about camp is more intense and inherently more fun. You get to know so many people so well, in a way you would never get to know them in the city."

Dotty chimed in, "I have to agree. I was skeptical and I know it's only been one summer, but I'm convinced."

My second summer at camp was even better than the first. I was group leader for a larger group with older, more interesting (interesting-to-me) campers and a larger staff of counselors to supervise. I felt myself truly free at camp. There was no time for nagging doubts when coaching kids at baseball, leading a hike or running a campfire program. I was the leader and both the campers and the staff who I worked with were unquestioning and enthusiastic.

By the end of that summer, I was sure I had made a truly excellent choice. Now I had to construct a plan for the future. By my reckoning this meant two things: first, I have to work in a private camp for at least one or two summers because that's the kind of camp I want to buy and run in the future; second, it's time to find a camp administrative position, preferably as a Head Counselor or Program Director.

One day I spotted the ad in the classified section of the Sunday Times. "HEAD COUNSELOR, Dynamic young man with camp exp. For well established Maine Brother-Sister Camp...."

2
Facing Challenges at Camp
Fall 1968

Vico

The Long Island Expressway is never a joy, even at the best of times. It has been described by some as the world's longest parking lot. Though that was an exaggeration, I knew that I needed to allow more time than the distance would seem to warrant to get to my interview in the town of Roslyn. I was not mistaken. It took almost an hour to cover less than twenty-five miles. Finally, getting off the expressway, I threaded my way among quiet tree-lined streets of a solid upper middle-class neighborhood, one that reminded me of the houses where I grew up in Brooklyn. Nelson Cohen was waiting for me and greeted me at the door with a big smile and an outstretched hand. As we shook hands, I did a quick appraisal of the man who I hoped might be my future employer. Cohen was in his late thirties and carried a few pounds more than his five-foot ten height would warrant. He had a round face, still tan from the summer sun. He had horn-rim glasses resting loosely on his nose. His brown hair was neatly clipped, but with a receding hairline and a small round bald spot on the crown.

"Come in, Vico. I've been looking forward to your visit since our chat on the phone."

That was the beginning of a wonderful meeting that stretched through the afternoon. Midway through, he called a time out for coffee and cake. By the time we shook hands again and said goodbye, Camp Adventure and Nelson Cohen had a new Head Counselor. I came away convinced I was about to start exactly the right job, with a wonderful camp and an extraordinarily understanding camp director.

"Dotty, he's a wonderful man, and I'll bet he runs a great camp. He really understands kids and he has much more creative programming than anything we saw going on at the Federation camp. I didn't realize until today how much there is to learn about camping. This summer will be a real education for me. The living conditions sound good too. We'll have our own cabin, near the boys' waterfront. Nelson said the cabin was rustic, but it does have electricity, running water and a refrigerator. And Celia will be a day camper, spending a few hours each day with the youngest bunk of girls. She'll love that. And Nelson said if you want a job, he has a few available that might interest you — strictly optional."

On that October day I could not imagine how much of an education I would get in our first summer at Camp Adventure.

Nelson and I had a number of telephone conferences during the bitter cold winter months. In the middle of April, the weather suddenly went from winter cold to summer hot, and it made everyone ready for the camp season to begin.

"Vico, I know I told you about our New Camper Party, but I may not have given you the date...It's Saturday May 12th. I hope you'll bring your wife too. I'm looking forward to meeting her, and it will be a chance for both of you to meet some of the staff as well as about twenty new campers and their parents."

I pulled into the parking lot and found a space. The party was held in an enormous modern bowling alley in Queens. Some kids were already bowling when Dotty and I arrived. Nelson introduced us to the kids and parents who were there, and then made sure we met everyone, as children and their parents streamed in during the following few minutes. Bowling turned out to be a great success. It was a fun way for kids who didn't really know one another to interact easily. I was able to help some of the younger kids who clearly needed help. Nelson formally introduced me, and Dotty too, to all of the parents and campers during refreshment time after the bowling. While everyone sat around eating pizza and having soft drinks, Nelson gave an inspiring sales pitch. I was an included part of the pitch. Of course, the kids were already enrolled for the summer. Nelson explained later, "I never miss a chance to reinforce the positive image of camp for the parents and the new campers. It makes them feel more confident about their decision."

After the new camper party, the rush to summer seemed to speed up. The finish of the school year seemed to telescope. It was almost time to pack up and go when I received an unexpected call from Nelson who was already at camp.

"I'm not sure whether I ever told you it would be good for you to get to camp before the start of staff orientation." He hadn't. "I need you to be at camp tomorrow or the day after at the latest. Can you manage that?" This news did not please me, and I was sure Dotty would be upset.

"Today is the last day of school, and I have a few things I have to finish up before I'm really free to leave. Of course, if you need me I'll be there. It would have been easier to arrange if I had a little notice."

"Yes, I understand. I'm sorry about that, but it's really important that you get your bearings and learn your way around before the whole staff gets here."

Dotty and I had planned our own timing pretty carefully, and though I knew she would be upset, I agreed to be there late the next day. I wanted to get off to a good start with my boss and my new job. We hurriedly packed the car, including Celia, and we took off for Central Maine. Dotty was fuming. She wasn't as angry at Cohen for his no-notice demand that we appear, as she was upset at me for agreeing without consulting her. Once Celia fell asleep it was a long very silent ride. Not a good start. As we reached the town line of Pottsville, I could see Dotty's interest and excitement rise to match my own. As we drove in on the dirt road and saw the camp spread open before us her anger melted completely. "It's really beautiful, Vico. I have a feeling this is it. We're going to be happy here." I leaned over and kissed her, and the anger between us evaporated as we arrived at Camp Adventure.

The camp property was surrounded on three sides by the pine forest we had just driven through. Straight ahead I could see a crystal clear lake, green ballfields and red tennis courts. Roughhewn cabins stretched out in front of the lake and extended off to the sides, disappearing into the forest. The overall impression was rustic but well maintained. The facilities were not at all like a fancy resort, however they were miles ahead of what we had been used to both at the Federation camp and at our camp last summer.

Dotty was delighted by our cabin. It exceeded both of our expectations. There were two bedrooms, a living room with a fireplace, a bathroom, a small screened porch and a nice play yard. The refrigerator in the living room was already stocked with milk, juice and fruit. I noted a neat stack of firewood on the porch. "Jesus, Dotty, this guy understands the importance of details, particularly for families. I'm impressed."

We met with Nelson and his family in the camp dining hall at six o'clock. The dining hall seemed cavernous with just one lonely table set for the seven of us. We hadn't met Nelson's wife and children in the Spring. Cindy Cohen was very thin, spoke rapidly, ate rapidly, and as soon as we all finished our main course, pulled out a pack of cigarettes and smoked with an almost desperate intensity. She stubbed her cigarette out as soon as dessert arrived. I had hoped she and Dotty would become friends, but now I rather doubted it. She was a high energy woman, the kind who would be bound to make Dotty nervous. Their daughter Harriett was thirteen years old and seems a pale carbon copy of her mother. I felt badly for her as she tried to squeeze a few words in during the rapid-fire conversation taking place between her parents and the two of us. The Cohen's five-year old twin boys were cherubic versions of their father. They were remarkably quiet and well behaved during the meal as they happily shoveled food into their mouths until their plates were empty.

Earlier in the day, when we met Nelson briefly, he said we would have a "short orientation session" after dinner. The short session turned out to be close to four hours and my head was spinning when we were finished. We blocked out the first week's activity program for the boys' camp, and went through a long list of details that had to be tended to before the start of counselor orientation, followed by a final list of things that had to be covered during orientation, and his expectations of what must be ready by opening day when the campers arrived. By the end of the meeting, I was exhausted, but glad we had come early. There was still so much to do. I would need the time to get ready. Dotty was asleep when I arrived back at our cabin.

The next morning the sound of reveille blasted us out of sleep and into the reality of camp. Dotty woke with a start, and Celia, startled, started crying. It seemed rather bizarre to hear the PA bugle call in an empty camp. I looked at my watch and realized we really did need the wakeup call. We were due at the dining hall for breakfast in twenty minutes. The Cohen family was well into their breakfast by the time we got there. Nelson said "Hi" and was out the door chasing the plumber, whose truck had just driven past the dining hall.

He returned as we were finishing and joined us for a cup of coffee and a few minutes of pleasant chatter. Cindy offered to give Dotty and Celia a tour of camp, and they were off. Then the two of us headed back to my office, where I wound up spending the entire day. Nelson was constantly on the run: chasing carpenters, electricians, and plumbers. He seemed to need to be in a dozen places at the same time. Between runs, he was back with me and never seemed to lose his train of thought. I understood that getting camp ready to open was an annual race against time and that I had come in just as Nelson and the camp were in the final stages of that race. Thinking ahead to the camp I hoped to own someday, I wondered if I would be able to organize things so it would not be quite so hectic just before the start of the camp season.

We spent most of the morning going through the boys' counselor staff. I read their original applications and follow-up evaluations for those who were returnees. Nelson completed their profiles by filling me in on their strengths, weaknesses and idiosyncrasies. He seemed to know them all so well. A high percentage were returnees from last summer while five of the new counselors were boys he had coached in football when they were in high school. He was confident they would all be great. He told me that this would be the best counselor staff he ever had, and that it would be a joy for me to work with them.

In the afternoon I plowed through "camper confidential reports", forms sent to camp by the parents of incoming campers informing us of their children's likes, dislikes, fears, and hobbies. I started making notes of kids who tended to panic during thunderstorms, those whose parents worried they would be homesick, and of the children whose parents expected us to train their kids to be soccer stars, Olympic swimmers, or professional baseball players. They didn't use those terms, but their aspirations for their kids came through loud and clear. As with the counselors, Nelson supplemented the paper records with anecdotal accounts of many of the campers returning from last summer.

I was in danger of overload by the end of the afternoon. My head was so filled with details I didn't really know which kids belonged to which facts and which stories. Happily I had it all down on paper, and for now, that would have to do. Once the campers actually arrived and the names meant something to me, I would re-read all of the paperwork.

We took a break that night. Nelson offered us his daughter's services as babysitter for Celia. We were a little nervous about leaving Celia, but accepted the offer. In fact, their daughter Harriett, who was rather abrasive when communicating with her parents, had a very nice way of interacting with Celia, and we felt reasonably comfortable leaving her. We went to a drive-in movie a few miles from camp. After we stocked up on candy and popcorn, affixed the speaker to the car window, and adjusted our seats just so, the movie started. I sat back, reclined my seat and promptly slept through the entire double feature. Dotty laughingly filled me in on what I missed on the drive back to camp.

After breakfast the next morning Nelson was again off and running. He told me to watch out for Paulette, my female counterpart, who would be returning for her fourth summer at camp. I was looking forward to meeting her since I assumed we would be working closely together through the summer. At about ten o'clock Paulette bombed into camp in a small Green

two-door sedan. I could see it was packed to the roof. A cloud of dust followed as she drove through camp and pulled in next to what was obviously her cabin. She turned the car off, somehow managed to slither out of her packed car, and headed my way, toward the office, clipboard in hand. I watched as she moved with the assurance and lithe efficiency of a gifted athlete. I intercepted her before she got to the office, introduced myself and told her I looked forward to working with her. She smiled, gave me a pat on the back and offered a firm handshake.

"Nice to meet you. I'd love to stop and chat now, but I've got to get my camp keys, unpack my car and get to work. I wasn't able to get here yesterday when Nelson wanted me to come. By now you've probably seen that he considers every minute precious at this time of year. You and I will have lots of time to chat after I make my peace with the boss, and get myself ready to work." Before I had a chance to tell her I understood, she was gone and I heard the outside office door slam. Two minutes later she passed me by with a wave and moved quickly back toward her cabin and car.

Right after lunch, Nelson, Paulette, and I went into conference. The subject was a review of all of the camp policies related to the boys' and girls' camps working together. Theoretically the conference was to weigh and evaluate existing policies, but the reality was there was no intention to change or alter anything. I soon understood this conference was to clue me in on all of the details that went into maintaining the policies and letting me know how vital my role would be. I was astonished by the amount of detail devoted to keeping the boys' and girls' camps separate. I had given little thought to the subject before arriving, assuming a greater physical distance between the camps than actually existed. In fact, there was no distance between them at all. To be sure the girls' cabins were on one side of an imaginary line and the boy's cabins on the other. However, the two camps shared many facilities and used them at different times. There were rules as to where the girls could walk and where the boys could walk when going from one activity area to another. There were detailed rules about how and where counselors from the two camps would and could get together and when they must pass one another by without any social interaction at all. For the first time I could see that the camp layout, beautiful though it was, would present problems. I became convinced that the rules would have to be interpreted liberally or they would be unenforceable. I expressed my doubts and was assured by both of them that it was all completely workable.

Nelson had heard doubts like mine before and he was ready with the answers. "Most of our campers are returnees and many of the counselors as well. They know the rules. There has never been a problem, and, as long as the lines are clearly drawn and everyone knows the rules there never will be. Ours is a Brother-Sister camp rather than a coed camp. It is not so much a matter of distance between camps as it is one of a state of mind. We bear down on the rules at the beginning of each summer and there is no problem at all. We've been at this a long time now. Take my word for it. It works."

I was still skeptical, but decided it would not be fruitful or even wise to get into any further discussion of the problems I foresaw. However, that night I gave Dotty a brief run down on our afternoon session. "Are you kidding? Two counselors aren't allowed to talk to one another if they pass each other on a path?"

"That's right. If the two want to arrange a date for that night after hours, one of them delivers a note to the office and our office girl delivers it to the other counselor during the next meal."

"But what happens when both camps line up together in the assembly area for flag raising and flag lowering? Can they talk then?"

"Simple answer: the boys line up on one side of the flagpole, while the girls line up on the opposite side. Then they go into the dining hall from two different entrances. We had both noticed that the dining hall is L shaped. I didn't realize until this afternoon it was built that way for a reason. They are really distinct dining halls off of one kitchen. Our table is near the entrance to the kitchen and we can see both dining halls, but the campers' tables are situated so they can barely see one another once they are inside. Nelson assures me it works because everyone knows and has agreed to the rules."

Well good luck, I thought. I hope those rules don't wind up giving us grief.

The following day was the first day of Counselor Orientation. They started rolling in around mid-morning, and the influx of new people continued through the day. All day long people were unpacking cars. There were little knots of counselors gathered here and there throughout camp as old friends greeted one another. Early in the afternoon we organized a tour of camp for the newcomers, both for the boy's staff and the larger number of new female counselors. At four that afternoon I drove into town to meet and greet the few counselors who were arriving by bus. They were all new to camp, and I did my best to put them at ease on our short ride back to camp. By dinnertime everyone who was expected that day had checked in. I noted that the dining hall tables were well integrated and our young men and women both seemed happy with that arrangement.

We had our first formal Orientation meeting that night at eight o'clock in the Rec Hall. Nelson gave an enthusiastic welcome to everyone and then went into what I assumed was his traditional talk on the role of the counselor in camp. It was a good talk. Some of the old timers nodded their heads knowingly, as though they had heard it all before, but it was an inspiring enough talk that everyone listened attentively. I was impressed by the sense of urgency he was able to convey about the need to view every single child's welfare and happiness as a singular responsibility and mission for the counselor. "Every child in your cabin or in your activity is part of a group and that group morale is important, but each of them is an individual for whom we, as counselors, as a camp, must do something very special this summer. It is our task to figure out what makes each child special and to give each of them the chance to capitalize on his or her strongest assets." It was a powerful message, delivered well. I could see they were all impressed, even the guys who had been there for years.

There was a pause, and then came introductions of all of the key people in camp. Paulette understandably got top billing as the most important person on the girls' staff. She too gave a lovely welcome speech, neither as long nor as well delivered as Nelson's, but very good nonetheless. She sat down to warm applause. Then I listened as Nelson introduced me to the staff.

"Gentlemen, Ladies, it is my pleasure to introduce and welcome Vico Leone, our boys' Head Counselor. Vico teaches English in Hewlett, New York during the Off Season." He waited for and got an appreciative chuckle from the counselors all of whom appeared to be in a receptive mood. "For the last several years Vico has been Senior Group Leader at Camp Unity in New Hampshire. He and I have had the opportunity to work together on and off since December, and I have gotten to know him very well. We are lucky to have him with us. He has a great store of energy and a lot of good camp know-how. He is a very sensitive human being and I know he is ready and enthusiastic about the prospect of helping all of you on the boys' staff working with your kids. Moreover, he is a fun-loving guy with a lot of creative energy. You're going to like him. I have no doubt about that. But don't let his smiling face deceive you into thinking he will be some sort of easy mark. He knows all the tricks, and is well prepared to make sure you don't forget what your job is here at camp. Right Vico?" I nodded assent. "Would you like to say a few words?"

"I'm not prepared to make a speech, but I do want you all to know how very pleased I am to join you here at Camp Adventure. This is a beautiful camp with everything we need to make a wonderful summer for our campers. We'll work together as a team, and teams that do that always finish in first place. That's our goal for the camp and for every camper here this summer." I sat down to polite applause.

The next to be introduced was waterfront director, Roland Samson. He had joined the Camp Adventure staff in Nelson's first year as Director. Nelson had always played the dual role of Director and boys Head Counselor. Roland had been his second in command. During our meetings, Nelson had impressed upon me that it was important to get him on my side. I couldn't help asking "If he's been with you so long and you rely upon him so much why didn't you just elevate him to Boys' Head Counselor?"

I remembered his words as Roland started to speak.

"Roland is reliable, solid and 100% responsible down there on the waterfront, and he loves this camp. He is very loyal and would do anything for me, but I would not want him as a Head Counselor. I'd be losing a great waterfront director and gaining a potential headache. Roland sees the world in black or white. There are no shades of grey in his view. If a counselor makes one mistake, he is damned forever in Roland's eyes. This is a problem, but not the most important one. Roland does a lot of shouting. Sometimes he loses his temper and shouts. Other times I think he shouts as a matter of habit. He was a sergeant in the Marines during the Korean War, and I think he just got used to shouting orders. Down at the waterfront that is OK because everyone understands that he has the responsibility for the safety of everyone down there. They know he doesn't shout unless he sees something wrong. The problem is shouting is his reaction to big important things and to relatively minor ones. I would worry the counselor staff would be up in arms in no time if he was Head Counselor. I don't think he can control that temper of his. He's never touched a kid or even come close, but he scares the life out of some of them with his booming voice.

That's why I never thought seriously about offering him the Head Counselor job, which I know he wanted, and consequently it is so important that you make every effort to hit it off with him."

Roland was a great big guy, obviously in top physical condition. He seemed diffident and shy, as he got up to speak, not at all the image of him Nelson had planted in my mind. His talk was short, but warm and touching. He spoke of his long association with Nelson and Camp Adventure, and how much he looked forward to the chance to work with wonderful campers and counselors every summer. Toward the end he seemed to feel it necessary to insert a little gruffness, perhaps to protect his reputation. "You guys had better be on the ball and stay alert down there or you'll hear it from me, loud and clear." He sat down to loud applause and foot stamping from the returning male staff.

Next up was Joey Katz. He was returning as the boys' Senior group leader, frequently the most challenging job in camp. I knew Joey was a student at Columbia and, according to Nelson, quite brilliant. He was clearly a representative of the current breed of university students:

long-haired, bearded and dressed sloppily, even by summer camp standards. Though he spoke very briefly, it was long enough for me to be aware of the charisma he exuded. Nelson had him pegged right. He was a born leader and one I would need to cultivate to assure good communication with the staff.

Joanne, the girls' camp Senior group leader, spoke next and she was quite a character. She has been at Camp Adventure forever, starting as a seven-year-old. She had started camp prior to Nelson buying the camp, and seemed to feel a degree of ownership and superiority over everyone, including Nelson, Paulette and anyone else who thought they were in charge of her camp. Nelson told me she was great with the kids, but had to be viewed as unpredictable and had to be handled with extreme care.

A few days later, the campers arrived, and I spent much of my spare time trying to match faces with the information I had read about each of our ninety-eight male campers. The Camp program ran very smoothly. I was in the best position to know. I planned the daily program and it was my job to check on all of the activities each activity period. With four age groups busy during three activity periods in the morning and three more in the afternoon I was constantly on the move. It was hectic, but things were going so well I enjoyed every part of it. I loved watching the kids playing and appreciated even more the excellent counseling I observed. The only disturbing note that week was Nelson's somewhat neurotic fixation on minor details. I had observed this to some extent during the pre-camp period, but it seemed to manifest itself more frequently once the campers arrived. This was only a minor irritant and I refused to let it interfere with my good mood and sense of accomplishment.

During the second week, I noticed a letdown. Everything was happening about the way it was supposed to, just not quite as well. The counselors seemed somewhat less enthusiastic and the campers didn't have the boundless energy they displayed during the first week. A few counselors were testing the rules in subtle ways. However, the most disturbing change was Nelson's attitude toward me. I thought I was imagining it, but as the week wore on, I was convinced there was a distinct change. He appeared to be looking for mistakes so he could pounce on them.

Very early on, I was made aware that he had an obsession with locks and keys. It was a fact that every door and every cabinet had a lock. It was also a fact that no two locks could be opened with the same key. There was no such thing as a master key for multiple locks. I could appreciate the need for many of the locks. Surely it was necessary to lock the rifles in the rifle range and even to have locks on the storage room that contained new athletic equipment. It was even defensible, in my view, to lock the supplies for the mimeograph machine. But I asked myself, "Why was it important that thumb tacks, paper clips, pencils and even old rags be kept under lock and key?" I could never find a satisfactory answer. All of those locks created the need for a great number of keys. As one of the keepers of the kingdom, I was blessed with an enormous ring of keys. That ring started to feel like a lead weight in my pants pocket. It went everywhere with me. My only release from the tyranny of the key ring was when I closed the door of my office and removed the accursed thing from my pocket. I would set the ring on my desk right next to where I was working. If it was a hot day and the windows were open, I would even use the key ring as a paperweight. The first time Nelson came into my office and saw this I thought he would blow a gasket.

"Don't you realize that the key to the bullet cabinet is on that ring? If some kid ever got ahold of that we could have a catastrophe!" He was right in theory, but I found it hard to believe any camper would come into my office and steal the keys sitting right in front of me. I agreed to keep them in my pocket and thereafter I only removed them when it was time for bed. Apparently, even Nelson didn't think a kid would come into our cabin at night to abscond with my key ring.

Another of his little itchy things was the electric bill and the curse of lights left on unnecessarily. God forbid I should leave my desk light on when I left the office, even if it was just to go to the bathroom. I wasn't certain what size the camp electric bill might be, but I couldn't imagine the seventy-five-watt bulb in my office was a significant part of it. The camp did, after all, have refrigeration, freezers, water pumps and hot water heaters that had to be left running twenty-four hours a day. After a few "reminders", I did remember to turn the light off every time I left the office. There were other picayune things too, some so little as to be laughable, but there were also bigger and more important issues.

The biggest of these was making sure all of the counselors who had nights off checked back in on time and were back in their bunks by staff curfew time, which happened to be midnight. At college, these kids had no rules at all. They could stay out all night if they wanted. A few of my guys, who were going into their Senior year in college after camp, would very likely be drafted into the army in the near future. It was ludicrous to think of them having to follow these restrictive hours so literally. Before camp started this was one of the policies I thought would turn out to be unenforceable. I was wrong, the rule was enforceable and enforced, consequently a source of considerable irritation for the staff. I understood it was my job to be at the office by midnight to make certain that every counselor had checked back in. If a counselor who was off duty for the evening was unaccounted for by midnight, I was to wait there for his return and deliver either a warning or a punishment, depending on how egregiously he was off on his timing.

One night, Jeff Saunders, one of our Unit Leaders and a great kid, was about three minutes late getting back for check in. Nelson greeted him before I had a chance. "Where were you? If you can get back three minutes late you could just as easily have come back three minutes early. Make sure this doesn't happen again. Am I understood?" Jeff sheepishly agreed, and headed down to his cabin. Then Nelson turned to me. "Vico, I expect you to make sure these guys get back on time. If someone is even one minute late, I want to know about it."

I never did have the opportunity to tell him a counselor was late. He was there with me every night at check in time. He insisted it was my job, but he kept doing it with me, or perhaps more accurately, *for* me. I assumed this was a manifestation of his lack of trust in me. From my standpoint, I was losing sleep and time with Dotty every night for no purpose. I couldn't continue this surveillance every night and still have the energy I needed to properly do the job I was hired to do. My day job required a lot of energy.

At the end of each meal there was another potential crisis point, a situation in which Nelson was not entirely happy with my job performance. The administrative staff generally ate before the campers. This gave us the opportunity to walk around the dining hall chatting with staff, to observe problem eaters among the campers and at the same time evaluate the popularity of each meal. In addition, Nelson wanted us to go out to the assembly area before the kids completed their meals. The boys and girls often wanted to stop and chat with one another on the way back to their cabin areas. This was as much a constant with the counselors as it was with the oldest campers. Our job, mine and Paulette's, was to be out there and break up any such conversations, sending the kids on their way. Paulette was very good at this. She just moved those girls right along. I think they were a bit afraid of her. It was clear the boys did not have a similar fear of me. I have never used fear as a means of persuasion with my students at school or campers in previous camp situations and I didn't intend to use threats or fear here. Oh, I got them moving all right, just not fast enough to please Nelson. He was particularly upset if he came out and saw male and female counselors talking to one another. I could recite his admonition to me by heart. "If you let one stop, they'll all feel they can stop. Then who will there be to mind the kids as they head back to their bunks?" He was right, of course, but it was all a matter of degree. Perhaps he sensed my ambivalence. Maybe the counselors did as well.

Another point of contention was a matter of geography, where male and female counselors could socialize on their unassigned activity periods. The official camp policy stated "counselors being allowed daytime free periods are restricted during such periods to their own campus." One day while I was in my office working on program for that night, Nelson stormed in, his face livid with rage. "Vico, I want you to get out there and move them right away!" I looked out my office window and could see Tubby Brown with one of the new girl counselors playing tennis on the boys' courts, which were right in the middle of the campus. Tubby was a nice boy, unit leader for our youngest campers, and an agreeable kid who would never intentionally break rules. I hated to have to scold and embarrass him.

"Vico, you know she has no business being there. Can you imagine Paulette looking out her office window, and not rushing out to move Tubby off her courts and away from her campus? Vico, you've just got to be on the ball. That girl Shari is new this year and it's possible she didn't know, but Tubby has been here every summer since he was eight years old and he knows the rules perfectly well. He's testing you, Vico. You'd better get right out there and do something about it."

"Of course. I'll go right out now. I really didn't know they were there. I've been concentrating on plans for tonight's program." I went out the door and down to the courts.

"Guys you've got to move. Tubby, you know the two of you shouldn't be here together." Tubby didn't say anything, but Shari, who probably did know she was breaking a rule, looked and sounded petulant.

"We're not doing any harm. Tubby checked the master program. There were no boys scheduled here this period. Why can't we use the court?"

"You know it's a camp rule, and Nelson is the one who spotted you. He wants you out of here." Tubby didn't say anything, but I could see he was hurt. They went off in opposite directions, and I headed back to the office, where I knew Nelson would still be waiting and fuming.

"Nelson, I did what you asked me to do, and they moved. Tubby didn't say a word, but neither of them was very happy, and, I think they had a point. The courts were free and so were they. I think challenges to this policy issue will come back to haunt us before this summer is over. You might want to reconsider this particular policy."

"I've run the camp my way for a long time, and I'm not about to change it, even if you don't agree. My job is to run a camp where the children are well cared for and happy. If this sometimes interferes with counselor fun, so be it. They have to be mature enough to accept the camp policies. Despite your concern, I don't think this will create any real problem because so many of my guys have been here for years."

I was becoming more and disenchanted with Nelson's policies and had difficulty understanding how and why they had apparently worked well for him in prior years. If counselors are grumbling and unhappy, the campers feel this, and some of them are bound to catch that unhappiness. Still, I understood I was here and committed to live with his theories. By the time ten days of the camp season had gone by I knew for sure I had picked the wrong camp. Nonetheless, unhappy or not, it was still my job to do everything I could to make this a successful camp season for the camp and its campers. It was also my job to placate Nelson, which meant picking the counselors up on every infraction, no matter how small. I attempted to do just that. Nelson almost always managed to get there first. Not a day went by when he didn't point out some counselor dereliction I had missed. I realized that, having been his own Head Counselor in years past, it was hard for him to let go of the reins and allow me or anyone else to do the job.

The one thing that bothered me perhaps more than it should have, was his mania about time. Since I started my brief camp career, I felt one of the most positive intangibles was the relaxation of time pressure both for the staff and campers. It seemed obvious to me that Nelson's insistence that everything must be done by the clock subverted that relaxation. One of his personal practices I found truly disconcerting occurred at General Swim time. He would plunk himself down at the waterfront with his watch in hand and note the exact time each group arrived. He had made a chart which told him exactly when each should arrive depending on where they were in camp the previous activity period. If the Junior

Unit was late coming down, it was my task to talk to Jeff Saunders about it. Jeff was the Group leader for the Junior Unit. If in fact they did arrive late, both Jeff and I were somehow responsible for a serious dereliction of duty. I have to say, I found this maddening.

At the end of each day, I would arrive back at our cabin physically and emotionally exhausted. The physical part didn't really bother me. That was part of the job. I wasn't sure how much longer I could absorb the physical challenges and emotional and mental punishment. Dotty urged me to quit.

"Honey, you've always viewed camp as a kind of vacation for all of us. This summer is certainly not a vacation. I know you wanted to get administrative experience, and you're certainly getting it, but think of the price. You'll need a vacation when this is over. You won't have energy left for your classes at school. Happily, we don't really need the money from this one summer. I know you don't want to leave Nelson once you've made a commitment, but don't you see, he doesn't need you. He doesn't really want you. He wants to keep running the whole show himself as he has in the past. That's why he seems to be picking at you all of the time. He sees himself as the only one who is indispensable. Surely by now you know that."

"I can't argue with anything you've said. In spite of that reality, I just can't get myself to quit. First of all, I signed a contract. I gave my word. I didn't give it lightly, and I'll live up to it no matter what. I do agree Nelson thinks he can run this place without help, but he just doesn't understand times are changing. He doesn't get what's going on in colleges these days.

He doesn't seem to understand the stress these kids are under, worrying about the war and wondering what they'll do if and when they are drafted. I'll bet some of our counselors have spent as much time attending protest meetings as they have classes during the school year. How can they take these rules seriously, rules that seem so petty to them? He doesn't get their mood even when they're away from school. The way he's run camp in the past may have worked well for him for a long time, nevertheless it's not working anymore. I hear the complaints every single day. He may not think he needs my help, but he does. There is trouble brewing. I hate to think what might happen if we leave.

3
Counselor "Demands"

Vico

The camp season was two weeks old when we had our first formal counselor meeting. These meetings are scheduled to take place every Sunday night, generally involving a review of the past week and a preview of the program for the week ahead. We also typically discussed issues as diverse as personality conflicts between campers, particular meals that turned out to be unpopular, maintenance issues that need to be addressed and occasionally remonstrance to the staff for minor misdeeds, typically items that never came up for discussion during Orientation period. Such meetings were one way of establishing communication between administration and the counselor staff. I looked back fondly at the good-humored staff meetings at Camp Unity last summer, with the rather easy give and take between the Director and staff. This is what I had anticipated and hoped for here.

Even before the meeting started it became obvious to me the mood was not one of easy give and take. Counselors were clustered around the dining hall tables in small knots of conspiratorial whispering heads. This did not bode well for the meeting. As soon as Nelson came into the hall there was an instant and rather deathly silence. This was in contrast to the chatter at similar meetings during Orientation only two weeks earlier. Nelson started quietly, and spoke in a matter of fact manner that was belied by his primary message.

"Ladies and gentlemen," he always called them ladies and gentlemen, "I have observed some very good counseling and good athletic instruction this week from some of you, and I thank you for that. On the other hand, I have not been at all happy with what I saw from many others of you. Too many of you have been going through the motions. When a person signs a contract to work here at camp, I assume he is signing it as an adult, ready to take on adult responsibilities. This is the commitment you've made and some of you appear not to want to live up to that commitment. You know as well as I do which ones of you are doing the job."

"I also want you to know that I have noticed a few of you have been casual about adhering to camp rules. You all know the rules. All of our rules have been created in furtherance of carefully considered policies. Some of you seem to think you can choose which rules you approve of and disregard the rest. I'm sure those of you who have chosen to disregard rules have managed to kid yourselves into believing you are living up to your contracts. If you do only those things you like and obey only those rules you approve of, you are not living up to your contract. You are just paying lip service. What would you think if, at the end of the camp season I chose to live up to only part of my agreement? I could rationalize it easily enough. I could tell myself this guy only worked about half the time so I'll only give him half of his agreed salary. I know what your reaction would be to that. You know I would never do such a thing. Conversely you are doing the equivalent every time you knowingly disregard one of our camp rules."

"Your job is to take care of your campers. That is first and foremost, number one. You can't do that properly if you are busy socializing part of the day. You can't do it if you stay out so late at night that you are not able to give peak performance the following day. You certainly are not doing it if you are drinking in camp at any time or out of camp when it will affect your ability to work properly with your campers. You are not doing your job if you fall asleep during rest period, or if you are standing around chatting outside the dining hall while your kids run back to the bunks. And you are most certainly not doing your job if you spend time politicking while you should be with your campers."

"Paulette and Vico are just as disappointed as I am. We're completely fed up with your hanging around after meals. Do you think we enjoy going out there every day saying "move along?" Believe me, it's more than annoying. It's your attitude toward the rules that stinks. We all had a chance to discuss these rules during Orientation. We talked about a lot of things and not one of you voiced any objection to the camp rules. I'm really not going to stand for this kind of nonsense."

"I do want you to know that I think some of you are doing a grand job and I'm sorry your friends have created a situation where you have to hear me speaking harshly like this. If any of you have anything you want to say on the subject, say it now. Let's have it out." Nelson stopped and waited, glancing from table to table around the room. He was just about to end the meeting when Cozy Martin's hand shot up.

Cozy is a twenty-one-year-old college senior. He is an enormous young man and a very strong athlete, strong enough to have been given a full football scholarship to University of New Hampshire. He had recently been honored as Defensive Lineman of the year for New England small colleges. Despite his size and obvious physical ability, he considers himself an intellectual, writing poetry and devoting free time to serious literature. He seems to take pride in being part of the tattered student generation, wearing his torn jeans and sweatshirts as an emblem of belonging. He describes himself as a "Restrained Radical," and with very little encouragement, will rhapsodize on the future fall of capitalism.

"Nelson, it seems to me that some of your rules are simply not realistic. I'm sure we all agree you are absolutely right about the need for us to pay maximum attention to the campers, and I think anybody who has been drinking or is under the influence of anything ought to be booted, no second chances. But when we get to your rules which prohibit us from stopping to talk to girls for a minute, that seems pretty unrealistic."

"Mr. Martin, I'm sorry you think some of our rules are unreasonable, outdated, and unrealistic. If they are so unreasonable and you can't live with them, you are free to go home. We'll miss you if you do, but that is your option. You read the rules before you ever signed a contract, and you certainly understood what you read. I didn't trick you into signing a contract, did I? Did I somehow give you the impression that camp would be a great social whirl?"

"No, of course not. I did read the rules and the rules themselves gave me a misimpression of the camp geography. Reading the rules and never having seen the camp I believed they were entirely reasonable, but I visualized the two camps being much further apart. I couldn't imagine how close the two camps are; that the boys' camp is right on top of the girls." This last brought a few laughs, and even Nelson smiled, but Cozy continued and Nelson's smile disappeared. "Even that silly business of sending notes between the offices instead of trying to talk directly to the girl counselors for a date made a kind of sense assuming the camps were further apart. Now that I know the physical setup, all of the rules related to keeping the two camps separate seem to belong to a different era. I certainly like my job here and don't have any desire to leave, but I think some of the camp rules should be updated to reflect today's reality." With that Cozy sat down.

"Thank you, Cozy. You and I can discuss your concerns privately. Nobody else here wants to change the rules, do they?" He paused and looked around. All hands remained down. "Very good. Meeting adjourned." Nelson got up and left the dining hall. Roland followed close behind. I was the only one in the administration still in the room.

It was a very subdued group that Nelson left behind. Others were more than subdued. I could see they were frustrated and looked angry. Primarily, I think because the meeting had ended so abruptly and with so little actual dialogue. It remained very quiet for a minute or two. I think they were giving me an opportunity to leave before they resumed what I now realized was their own pre-planned meeting, or perhaps they just needed time to gather their thoughts.

Joey Katz got up to speak. "I asked you all to remain after the staff meeting tonight because I was reasonably sure that meeting would go about the way it went." Then he turned to me. "Vico, I don't know how you feel about staying from this point on. I'm sure we are all happy to have you remain. You're a decent guy and we have nothing against you, but you are part of the administration and we certainly have issues to discuss you may prefer not to hear." The ball was clearly in my court, and I knew whichever course I chose there would be repercussions. This was both an ethical and a strategic decision. However, my curiosity about what they had in mind settled the question.

"If it's all the same to you, Joey, I'll stay. This is still a staff meeting and I am a member of the staff." There was a general murmuring of assent, and Joey continued.

"What we saw here tonight is typical of what's been happening this summer. If someone opens his mouth or has an opinion he gets shot down. We have to make Nelson realize we should not be treated this way and won't be treated this way any longer. We have all got to stand behind Cozy. Nelson has to start treating us like human beings rather than robots functioning at his command. I'm sure we all agree that the distancing rules between boys and girls and particularly between the staffs of the two camps are archaic and do not make sense in today's world. And we should take a careful look at some other camp rules that should be revised or perhaps revoked."

It was at that point I understood those were fighting words. Joey spoke well and he was a good strategist. He started with the proposition that they wanted to be treated like human beings. Nobody would disagree with that. This was the rallying point. Then he continued and turned to specific gripes. He didn't call them gripes. He first called them issues and later elevated them to demands. When he used the word "revoked" he had moved beyond suggesting peaceful dialogue.

"The curfew is absurd. All of us in college have managed our lives without a curfew and I'm sure we can do so in the summer as well. Nobody wants to stay out all night or even thinks that would be a good idea. It is our responsibility to take care of the campers and we need a reasonable amount of sleep to do that well. On the other hand, we don't need Nelson to determine exactly how much sleep each of us needs to do our job. We are mature enough to make decisions like that on our own. We shouldn't be required to check-in before midnight. The curfew has got to go." He was on a roll, when Tubby Brown stood up and shouted out.

"That's all well and good, Joey, but what about the poor counselors who are standing on duty waiting for you lovers who have girlfriends to check back in? With no curfew we could be sitting there for hours. We can't abandon our posts and go to sleep. Without a curfew it's the last counselor back in each unit who determines how much sleep the night duty counselor gets." A few of the veteran counselors chuckled because Tubby was well known for his fondness for his pillow and bed. But, chuckles aside, he had made a legitimate point. I waited to see if anyone else would shout agreement. It didn't happen so it was up to me.

"Joey, I don't think Tubby's objection should be brushed aside with a laugh. Assuming for the moment that you get Nelson to abolish a formal curfew, it seems you really would be sentencing the poor guys on duty to possibly additional hours on duty and lots of lost sleep. It might not be important to some of you who don't require a lot of sleep, but there would be many of you who will resent having to wait around for the one guy with a heavy date to return to his cabin after a night out. I haven't noticed any of you are thrilled to have OD assignment now, and everyone does get back by midnight. I think a lot of counselors will wind up getting angry at one another for lack of consideration."

After a lengthy discussion, it was conceded that the issue was not so much the curfew it was the pettiness of the check in and the verbal abuse some of them had taken for being just a few minutes late. I could and did sympathize with them on that score. I sat silent as the discussion continued. It was clear to me. Joey had won the day. A vote was taken, and they voted to "Demand the abolition of Curfew." It was then I learned there was to be a list of demands. Now I was starting to feel more uneasy about my decision to remain.

Demand Number Two was a truly outrageous attempt to usurp the role of administrative policy making. The exact wording of the demand was: "Counselor days off shall commence at the sounding of Taps the evening before the counselor's day off." Days off had always started after breakfast and ended at curfew, not only at Camp Adventure, but at my two prior camps and every other camp I knew. The way Camp Adventure was set up, each cabin or bunk had one counselor who lived in the cabin with the campers. If that counselor left the night before his day off it would effectively mean there was no counselor in the cabin over night to take care of emergencies.

This was clearly untenable. I understood their desire. The time span of the current day off was such that only relatively short trips out of camp could be planned. Starting the night before would allow them to leave camp the night before. Most likely it would allow groups of day off male and female counselors to go off early in the evening, rent motel rooms and spend the night very much together. That was not my concern, but I knew I would oppose such a policy if it was my camp because it would mean inadequate coverage for the campers. I noted my objection, but, since I did not vote, the demand passed unanimously. Joey said they didn't really expect to get this one, but it could be used as a bargaining point, one they would be prepared to surrender to gain other demands.

Demand Number Three was directed at the tight geographic

limitations on meetings between counselors of both staffs. The demand was read aloud by Joey as follows: "Counselors shall be allowed to socialize on the campus of Camp Adventure on their free periods, excepting only the cabin areas and the areas immediately adjacent thereto." This was written very broadly and spoke directly to their freedom of movement. Joey said, "I will go to the mat on this one."

Demand Number Four seemed less controversial to me. "A Room shall be set aside for counselor use during their periods off." There was even a rather polite request added to the demand. "If possible, this room shall be equipped with a television set, and have magazines available for counselor use. Board games would also be appreciated." I was convinced this demand was a throw in, and not a serious issue with the counselors, though clearly such rooms were available at some other camps. I thought Nelson wouldn't even object to this one if he could find a space for it. He already had provided a modified version of that in an off-campus house known as The Green House, which would fit the bill if it was in a more convenient location. Unlike the other demands, it did not really affect camp policies or rules.

Joey Katz was clearly the driving force, and ran the meeting. He led the discussion which was carried out in a rather orderly fashion. When the talk turned to how to present the demands everybody whose attention had lagged came right back to full participation. How to face Nelson Cohen with their demands was no longer abstract, and all sorts of suggestions were thrown into the hopper. They finally agreed there would be a written declaration of rights and demands.

Bob Weinberg, who had always been looked on as a radical by

the other counselors, made a vehement argument for a building take-over. He was quickly hooted down. Someone suggested they just slip the written list under Nelson's door during the night. There was general dismissal of that idea as being too cowardly, an approach he would take as a sign of weakness. Finally, they decided they should invite him to a meeting and they should all be present at such a meeting when the demands would be read to him. Joey agreed he would be the one to read the list. Now they just needed somebody to "invite" Nelson to the proposed meeting. I knew where this might wind up. At that moment I truly wished I was back in my cabin with Dotty and Celia.

"What about you, Vico? He'll listen to you. If any one of us went down to his cabin now he'd probably refuse to even see us." What a predicament! If I said yes it would put me in an impossible situation. The staff had decided I was the perfect one to do it, and if I refused, I would lose respect in their eyes. On the other hand, I was a member of the administration. Nelson would almost certainly be upset that I had remained at this obviously anti-administration meeting. He would see me as being on their side. I really didn't want him to view me as an adversary or as being disloyal to him and the camp. It was an agonizing position, but one I had put myself in by remaining at the meeting after Nelson and Roland had left. With great reluctance, I agreed to invite him. The meeting ended and I was left to contemplate the dirty job ahead.

The counselors left the hall and started back toward their group areas. I slowly made my way toward Nelson's cabin. He had the sport section of *The Sunday Times* open in front of him. I sat down and accepted his offer of coffee. His manner was unusually friendly and cordial. He appeared more relaxed than I had ever seen him. He was pleased with the way the counselor meeting went and was totally unaware of anything that happened after his departure.

"I think I really cleared the air and nipped this summer's griping in the bud tonight. What do you think?" He apparently didn't have a clue how far his message had gone from clearing the air to heightening an already antagonistic and adversarial mood for the staff. I stalled a bit trying to figure out how to diplomatically disabuse him of his self-congratulatory mood. There was no easy way.

"After you left, all of the counselors stayed in the dining hall. Some of them didn't like the way the meeting went at all. They said you didn't give them a chance to tell you the things that were on their minds."

"That's ridiculous. I gave them a chance to speak. I invited them to speak. Only Martin spoke up and I'll talk with him tomorrow. If anyone wants to talk all they have to do is come and talk with me. I'm always open to a reasonable discussion."

"I think it's gone beyond that. They don't want to talk individually. They want to have another full staff meeting with everyone there." He laid his coffee cup and newspaper aside. His good mood had completely evaporated, and I felt responsible.

"Okay, Vico, what's it all about? Don't hedge. Give it to me straight. They had a chance to talk tonight and they didn't. Something's going on, and if you know what I'd like you to tell me right now."

"They didn't have courage to speak up at the meeting, but I think they do now. They asked me to tell you they would like another meeting, another chance to speak up. They asked if we could have that meeting tomorrow night right after Taps."

"You're not telling me everything. Before I agree to go to a meeting tomorrow night or any night, I want to know what it's about. I don't want any surprises. I don't want to be put on the spot that way."

"They want changes in the rules that relate to them and the girls. That's mostly what it's all about. Unfortunately, they have come up with a list of proposed changes."

"Go on. Go on!" He shouted at me. I could see his temper was rising, and I didn't dare use the word "Demands". That would have been like waving a red flag in front of a bull. I was careful to say requests. "Tell me what they want, item by item."

From memory I recited the demands one by one. He leaned back in his big wing chair, hands clasped behind his head, and listened. When I finished, he started making notes, and read them back to me. I assured him he had the essence of everything they wanted.

'What's your position on this, Vico? Are you on the counselor team or are you still a member of the administration? Somewhere along the way everyone has to stand up and be counted. This is your time to be counted. I need to know."

"Nelson, I'm your Head Counselor. They asked me to invite you to the meeting and so I have, but I'm your Head Counselor. There is no question in my mind about that."

"All right, so you were there and you have invited me to the next round, I want to know your position on these requests."

"I think some of them are reasonable and some are unreasonable. I also think if you want a peaceful happy camp season it would be helpful for you to pick one of their requests and agree to it."

"What will happen if I don't agree to any of them, if I don't give in? I want to know about you. I want to know whether I can count on you to carry out camp policy or not. If I can't count on you to carry out camp policy there's really no point to you're staying here at camp. You have ambivalent feelings, which is your right. My feelings are not ambivalent at all. Not on any of them. I think it's all a lot of crap, but I don't mind you having those feelings. I want to know your actions rather than your feelings.".

"I know my position. I'm your Head Counselor. You can count on me. You hired me to carry out camp policy and I will, of course, do that. I don't have to agree. You're the boss and I work for you."

"Good, I like your answer. I feel better about you now than I did a few minutes ago when I wondered whose side you were on."

The next day we went about the business of running a camp. I saw little knots of counselors whispering together here and there around camp. The whispering stopped when I told them to break it up and get back to their kids. Nelson appeared to ignore the whispering groups and kept a smile on his face as he made his circuit of camp activities. You would never suspect there was anything upsetting going on in his mind.

After Taps, Junior Counselors replaced the cabin counselors with more alacrity than usual and the counselors rushed to the dining hall for their meeting. For this gathering it was not just the boys' staff. Apparently, the entire girls' staff had been "invited" by the boys. All together it was very likely the promptest response to a meeting in the history of the camp. It was certainly the promptest response I had ever seen to any meeting. Everybody was there by nine o'clock, that is everybody but Nelson. Nelson came in closer to 9:15. His daytime smile was gone and replaced by a visage reflecting war clouds. There was total silence as he entered.

"Ladies and gentlemen, you have invited me to a meeting. Well, here I am. What is it you have to say?"

Joey Katz stood up and read the list of demands. He also handed a printed copy to Nelson. There was momentary silence as everyone awaited Nelson's response. It was as though we were all collectively holding our breath. Yes, I was holding mine too, having no idea how Nelson planned to handle things.

Nelson's eyes scanned the room, resting briefly on each of us, catching our eyes and making it clear his response was to each and every member of the male staff. He more or less ignored the female contingent.

"What do you expect me to do or say now? How do you expect me to react to your Demands.' His voice pounded the word Demands. "Do you expect me to give in to some of them and reject others? Do you expect me to debate your points with you? Will you be satisfied with anything less than a total abdication of my responsibility to our campers and their parents? Now hear this. I cannot and will not accede to any of these demands. I don't have the right to even consider them. You may think you are still in college and I am like a Dean, who can bend and change rules. In college you can protest and argue for your rights and have sit down strikes and protest for your great and noble causes. That is all fine in college. But this is not college and I am not your Dean. This is camp and the rules were never set up for you. They were set up for the benefit of our kids, the people for whom we are responsible. Parents entrust their children to me, not to any of you. Our campers are my responsibility, and I have to do what I think is right for them. I have to be consistent with my ideals and I have to live with my conscience."

"If a camper drowns at the waterfront because some counselor was not looking where he should be, I'm sure the counselor will feel very bad, but he will not be the one held responsible. I will be, and rightly so. After all I hired you and set the rules that told you to watch the children while they are in the water. It would be my failing. Or suppose a situation where two of your campers get in a fight in the middle of the night and one of them cracks his head against the corner of a cot. Whether the counselor should have been in the cabin when that happened or not, who do you think is responsible? Me, that's who, that's why I can't even consider your demands. I don't have the right to bargain away rules designed with the safety of our campers in mind. I don't have that right at all."

"When you came to camp you knew the score. You knew about curfew. You knew when days off start and when you are expected back on those days. These were not a surprise to any of you. I cannot absolve myself of responsibility for our campers' wellbeing just to placate you. I want you to understand I have ultimate responsibility for everything that happens here. I can delegate authority, but never responsibility. I care for you. I've known some of you since you were young campers. I've known others of you for the past summer or two. I care what happens to you, but my responsibility for you is vastly different than the responsibility I have for our campers. I cannot and will not bargain any of that away."

"As for your *demands*, I shouldn't have even listened after I first heard the word demands. That word makes me ill. You have no right to demand anything. You are here as employees of this camp." His voice rose to a crescendo. "You're being paid to do a job. Do it!" Then he paused a moment, either to gather his thoughts or to reign in his emotions.

"If any of you has a request or a suggestion, I will be happy to discuss it with you at any time and give it the consideration it deserves. I always consider reasonable suggestions, but that is not to be confused with this ill-conceived meeting with your list of demands. That's a cowardly way to approach things. If any of you want to sit down with me to chat about anything just let me know."

With that he picked up his clipboard, turned around, and left the dining hall. The screen door slammed shut behind him. Paulette, Roland and I left right behind him. I wasn't about to allow myself to get caught in another aftermath meeting. I was impressed by Nelson's statement of principles, but was afraid his blanket refusal would have an immediately negative effect on the staff. It did not bode well for the rest of the camp season.

4

Years of Struggle at Risk

Nelson

When I left the dining hall, I was angry, bitter, and frustrated. I had always thought of myself as a problem solver. This was a problem not so easily solved. I view myself as a man who can overcome obstacles, but today's challenges are going to take more than hard work and long hours. I've always thought of myself as a man in charge, a commander, and now these young kids are challenging that. I've always been able to sway group opinions to my way of thinking — now I'm not so sure I know how to sway the opinions of these college kids. I can't understand what is happening. These kids, Joey and Cozy and Jeff, they were on my team. I was their coach. I couldn't even imagine that one day they would be tempted to confront me in this way. I'm sure they still have a reservoir of respect for me. I just have to figure out how to bring it to the surface before they go too much further and the situation becomes irreversible. One thing I'm sure of. I will not allow my camp's fate to be determined by a bunch of spoiled over-educated adolescents, who had been handed everything all of their lives.

I feel betrayed particularly by Joey and Cozy and also by a few others, who I coached when they were in high school. But they are part of this generation, a generation so spoiled by success that they feel they can get away with anything. They have no admiration for the traditional value of honest labor. They don't yet understand that people have to make a living and that someday they will be in that position too. They expect to sit back, college degrees in hand, and glide through life, and somehow the goodies of life will wind up theirs. It doesn't matter to them that we have scrimped and saved and worked for ten years to make this camp the success it is. It doesn't matter to them they can destroy the whole thing just to buy more play time for themselves. I have to figure out a way to reach them without compromising on anything truly important for our campers.

I thought back to conversations I had in the city with friends. I recall with a sense of irony my patronizing attitude toward college Presidents and Deans who had seemed so baffled by their students' protests. "All they have to do is let the students know who the boss is and that they can't get away with their nonsense." I believed it when I said it, but I can appreciate their dilemma with a little more sympathy now. I smiled to myself at the irony of all of our friends believing I'm the expert on teenagers and their behavior. I'm the expert since I've been working successfully as a teacher and coach with them for years. My friends at home think I'm the one who understands them. I can't remember how many times I said "all you have to do is let them know that you're the boss."

I have always been *the boss*. I was forced into that position at a very early age when my Dad died and my mother was out of the house working so many hours every day. I was the boss of the house. I was big for my age and, without having to expend too much effort, was very good at my schoolwork. In my mother's eyes, I could do no wrong. She told me I reminded her of my dad. Things might have been different at home if my mother had remarried a different man, but her pick, Phil, was a disaster. When the two of them had met he was a businessman, wore a suit, and went to work carrying a briefcase. She thought she was gaining security for her child, but it turned out she had just bought another mouth to feed. Shortly after their wedding his business fell apart, he declared bankruptcy, and retired from the working world. My enduring image of old Phil is of him sitting in the rocking chair in our parlor reading or watching TV and falling asleep in that damned rocker. Phil never went anywhere and he ceded household management to me. I was really running the household by the time I was eight.

My mother must have known that it wasn't good for me to be in charge at such an early age, and it was certainly not good for me to see her growing contempt for Phil. She couldn't help herself. He was such a contemptible man, a sponge not even looking for work, while she was working long hours to support us. When she left for work I was in charge of myself, the house, and even Phil.

In spite of my current aggravation, I find myself drifting off, and my mind retreating happily to my school days. In the Frank Ward Elementary School, I was the biggest kid in the class. I remember being the best athlete too, and that didn't hurt. I was the Captain of both the football and baseball teams. Clearly, I was the leader of my class.

By the time I was in high school my physical size was no longer the factor it had been in earlier years. Some of the boys over whom I formerly towered had caught up, some were even taller. But by then my self-confidence gained through the years allowed me to prevail in all sorts of situations. I always got my way on everything that was important. As a student my most important goal was a college scholarship, so I began studying hard to get the grades I needed. That free four-year ride certainly helped.

I began to understand myself in college, to appreciate my strengths, and to recognize my weaknesses. I never kidded myself that I was an intellectual, but I worked hard and attained dean's list grades. I knew I was never going to be a great football player, but I studied the game, worked my tail off and made the starting team. I remember being thrilled when I was elected President of the student government my Senior year. The best thing that happened to me that year was Cindy. I knew I was not the most dashing or best-looking guy in school, still, I set out to win the heart of Cindy Cooper, and, once again, I succeeded. I felt like dancing on air when she agreed to be my girl. We did everything together my last semester.

I was used to achieving and succeeding by sheer force of will. Camp Adventure was the first challenge in which success did not come easily. Now, finally, after ten years, I felt an immense sense of satisfaction. This was the year the mortgage would finally be paid off and we would be able to live a little. In our first few years with the camp it had taken every spare penny from us, eating up our small savings and making us poor, as our friends and contemporaries grew rich. Now we could breathe easier. It was finally going to pay off.

We had bought the camp ten years earlier. It had been an old Christian camp which had fallen on difficult financial times. Its parent organization was low on funds and finally decided to put the camp up for sale. The physical plant had been allowed to deteriorate over the past several years, and there were many areas which would need repairs and upgrading.

Cindy had been opposed to us going into the camp business.

"What do we need it for? Teachers' salaries are going up every year and the extra money you get from coaching is very helpful. In a few years, when Harriett is ready for school, I can go back to work and we'll be fine. What do you want with all of that responsibility? If you just want to work with kids in the summer, it will be a lot less expensive to get a job coaching baseball for an American Legion team."

"Come on, Cindy, this isn't about wanting to coach. You know I've always wanted to own my own business, to build something to grow with and hold onto, and I can't think of a single better business for me than a camp. This is my chance, our chance. The layout of this place is beautiful. Oh, I know it's run down, but all of the basics are here; a good lake, beautiful grounds, hiking trails, and flat areas for ballfields. It won't take long to get it into shape. The only reason we can afford to buy a place like this is precisely because it is run down. We'll never have a chance to buy another camp this good for so little money. When it's all paid off, we'll have a terrific asset. Eventually we'll make a lot of money, and you won't have to get a job to enable our kids to go to college. After a few years I should be able to give up teaching and devote full time year-round to the camp. Then, years from now, when we're really old, maybe our kids will want to take it over and run it. If not, it will be an asset to sell for our retirement. Cindy, this is my chance to do something important with my life. I know we'll have to scrimp for a few years, but that's not so terrible for the big payoff in years to come. There are plenty of camp directors who drive Cadillacs and live in Great Neck and Scarsdale. Don't worry. We'll make it a success."

"Nelson, sometimes you really are a dreamer, and I love that you're a dreamer, but this is not going to be easy. You know kids and you can learn how to run a camp program, but you don't know the first thing about finance or running a kitchen or fixing plumbing. You think you can do everything with your bare hands, but you can't. You know it will be years, maybe many years, before you can give up teaching and coaching. While you're busy teaching, how are you going to find the time to go out and recruit campers and interview counselors and do all of the other things it takes to run a successful camp?"

"I never said it would be easy. I just said we can do it. There are plenty of camp owners and directors who are also teachers and even principals. If they can do it, why can't I?"

"Yes, I know, but how many of them do it alone? They all have partners who share the work. It's too much for you to do alone. We don't have extra money to buy professional help and you do not have the time to do it alone."

"I never thought I could do it alone. I've got my partner all picked out and her name is Cindy. You're right, I can't do it all alone. I'm counting on you to help drum up business. I'm counting on you to do the bookkeeping and probably a dozen other things I haven't thought of yet. I can't go into this without your help! I need you to not only say "Yes", but to buy into this completely for it to work."

After weeks of discussion, argument, and analysis, I won her over. We made our deal. It was going to be a tight financial squeeze no matter what, and it was compounded by the fact that we could not get a mortgage longer than ten years, which meant much higher monthly payments than if we had been able to get a traditional twenty-five-year mortgage like a normal borrower. We soon learned banks were not anxious to lend money to children's summer camps, which they viewed as a very risky business. They had seen too many privately owned camps fail in the past.

I figured that if we were able to run at capacity during the ten year mortgage period, based on the tuition rate I calculated, we would be able to clear about ten thousand dollars a year. That, in combination with my teaching and coaching salaries would give us an adequate income, and hopefully some money to put into the camp. That was how I had calculated. The reality turned out quite different. My assumption that the camp would operate at capacity was a dream. It didn't take long for the awful truth to make itself known. Very few people send their children to a new camp. It didn't matter what kind of a reputation you had as a teacher or how much people liked you. They would not gamble their children's summer in a camp's first year.

So that first year was an artistic success and a financial disaster. Instead of the ten thousand dollars I hoped would be left at the end of the summer, we had to dig into and wipe out our personal savings account to pay the end of season payroll. The seven thousand dollars that disappeared had been our "New House Fund."

"Nelson, sell now! We've only lost the seven thousand. It could get worse before it gets better. Where will we go for money at the end of next summer if we need cash for the final payroll? I could ask my dad, but he and Mom are barely scraping by as it is. They thought they had enough when Dad retired, but inflation has eaten away at their retirement fund. I suppose we could ask your mother too, if we had to. She's not in such great shape either, living on social security and your Dad's small pension."

"I know it's tough and I hate to think of having to make life more difficult for your parents or for my mother. Please Cindy, give me just one more season, one more. We came pretty close this year, and the kids had a wonderful summer. Their parents will spread the word. We've started to build a solid reputation. Next year we'll have more campers, and we won't fall short at the end. You'll see."

The second camp season we did have more campers and so it was better financially, though it still fell far short of my optimistic projection. We probably would have been all right financially had our shallow well not started to run dry in the middle of August. It cost a fortune to get that drilling company in to locate, drill, and install a new artesian well. The new well pumped far more water and from greater depth than the old one and consequently required a more powerful pump. It was all one big fat money package. We had no choice. A dependable drinking water supply was the most essential asset, without which we would have had to abruptly end the camp season, send the campers home, and then refund a lot of money.

That September, I felt so ashamed to have to ask my mother for money — but I did. Mom turned over her savings account book, and said "It's yours. Take what you need."

The third summer we did not lose money. Camper enrollment was now close to capacity which meant a lot more dollars coming in. It was truly a breakeven year. We had some money left to live on, but nothing left to repay my mother, or to think about our own savings. Nor did we have any money to sink back into camp. Now that the camp was in use, the wear and tear was taking a toll on the already crumbling physical plant.

Camp Adventure and I were gaining a reputation in two different directions. On the plus side were many supporters who felt that I was a great guy and was running a wonderful camp that their children loved. Unfortunately, there were plenty of detractors as well.

—"He's not willing to put a dime into that place. Where does he get off charging as much as he does for a facility like that?"

—"That cabin Johnny was in last summer was literally falling apart. I could see daylight through the corners of the building, and Johnny told me they had cups and buckets all over the floor to catch the leaks when it rained."

—"I heard some other kids complaining that the toilets were out of order all the time. My kid's not going back there, and I'm thinking of contacting the Board of Health. I know he's got some sort of license. Maybe that should be looked into."

Fortunately, the supporters outnumbered the detractors over the next few years. And by year eight we had our first cash surplus. None of that surplus ever came out to us. It went back into desperately needed repairs. Cindy referred to camp as our sinking fund. Money went in and sunk out of sight forever.

By the start of the current summer even Cindy was optimistic. We had built a solid staff, had a good reputation, and were operating at capacity. We had just made our final mortgage payment, and, no matter what, there would be money left at the end of the summer.

It was ten years of struggle I reviewed that night, prowling around the darkened campus, trying to decide whether I was too tough, or not tough enough. "God help them if they destroy this place with their lousy attitude." The thought of my staff in turmoil made me feel physically ill; but it would turn my stomach to give in to their demands. "If I give in now it won't be the end. It will just be the beginning. This won't make them happy. It will just make them bolder."

I decided. "I have to make a stand here and now."

It was four in the morning when I finally dropped into bed, emotionally drained and physically exhausted. I fell asleep almost instantly. It seemed only moments later the alarm rang, signaling the start of another day. Wearily I changed out of the clothes I wore yesterday, shaved and left the house. The sky was gray and cloudy, approximately matching my mood. I made my way through the still dark dining hall and into the brightly lit kitchen. Bob the chef and his wife Anna, the dining hall manager, watched as I filled my first cup, leaned against the counter and sipped. The coffee was too strong as always, obviously not affected by the turmoil in camp. I never complained about the coffee. It was made the way Bob liked it, and when all was said and done, Bob, who had been with me from the start, was the single most valuable person in camp after myself.

Bob watched and waited until my first cup was gone and I was refilling before assaulting his boss with a recitation of the perennial kitchen crises. Today it was a problem with the dishwasher. Yesterday it was rotten peaches and a late bakery delivery. I listened through the morning recital, my mind elsewhere, nodding occasionally, and agreeing with all of Bob's suggestions. Thank God for Bob. Bob is a pro, and whatever needs to be done to keep him happy I will always do. I don't know much about the kitchen and I'm delighted to defer to him on everything. He does his job. He always produces acceptable meals and what more can I ask of a chef? He guards the kitchen like an avenging angel against any counselors who have the courage to trespass into his domain. He watches the food budget carefully and cooks with pride and enthusiasm. He doesn't ask for much and is delighted when I remember to give him praise for an especially good meal. I wish the rest of the staff were as professional as Bob.

Three cups of coffee later I left the kitchen, better able to face the day. I made my way through the dining hall and into my office. It was about time for reveille, and the office boy hadn't shown up yet. I cued the record, and was about to turn on the PA when the office boy rushed in to do the job. The trumpet call blared forth its message of morning at Camp Adventure. Vico came in a moment later looking about as tired as I felt. I guess he didn't sleep much last night either. Vico went into the kitchen and came back with his wake-up cup.

"What will today bring, Vico?"

"Your guess is as good as mine."

"It won't be long now."

5

Major Breach of Camp Rules

Vico

Reveille had just sounded when I came into the office. We didn't have long to wait to discover what kind of mayhem this day might bring. Normally as soon as reveille was sounded, we would hear a great deal of loud chatter coming from the cabins of the youngest boys. In many cases, they had been awake for a long time, and reveille was their permission to make noise. Today there was total silence. Nelson and I went out into the assembly area. It was not only quiet but there were no signs of movement anywhere on the campus.

"Nelson, do you want me to go down and see what's going on?"

"No, whatever it is we'll find out soon enough. Let's just wait and see what transpires."

The next scheduled bugle call was for Assembly. That would normally be accompanied by a mad dash by the younger campers to the assembly area followed by their less energetic counselors and finally by older campers and their counselors. On this day assembly call produced neither movement nor sound.

"It looks like a ghost town down there. Where do you think they have all gone?"

"I don't know where they are, but wherever they are hiding out they will hear this." He turned on the Public Address system and picked up the microphone. "Ladies and gentlemen, Assembly call has sounded. We will be raising the flag in two minutes. Breakfast will be served, as it always is, immediately after flag raising. Those who are not able to make it to the Assembly area in time for flag raising will not be admitted to the dining hall for breakfast. It is a long time until lunch. Your choice."

I fully expected Nelson to take out his watch to time their arrival. He disappointed me on that one. Within minutes we heard the unmistakable sounds of a large group on the move. Soon we watched as the entire population of camp marched together from the direction of the boys' Senior area. We heard a whistle blow, and then an enthusiastic rendition of "We shall Overcome."

Nelson muttered under his breath. "Those bastards couldn't resist bringing the kids into it, could they?" Nelson was clearly angry and I was fearful he would blow his top once they were all within earshot. Never had Camp Adventure seen an assembly like this one, and it was unlikely it ever would again. The teenage boys and girls came into the area wrapped as pairs with blankets over their shoulders. The counselors for both Senior groups were similarly entwined as they came into the area. The younger campers came in a less organized gaggle, with their counselors herding them toward their usual lineup areas. When they had all made it into the assembly area, they sang a final rendition of "We shall Overcome" and then stood quietly waiting for announcements and flag raising.

It was Nelson's move. As an observer of this surreal morning scene I could not predict what would happen next. As angry as I knew him to be, Nelson chose to grin and bear it. I admired his unfamiliar restraint. He was obviously angry with the counselors, but did not want to show it and upset the kids. They had been told they were playing a practical joke on the Camp administration and they were enjoying the joke. Few, if any of them realized they were being used as pawns in a dispute. I was not sure if even all of the counselors realized how they were being manipulated. Nelson said nothing about their late arrival or the coed togetherness being flouted in front of him. Instead he pretended to enjoy the whole thing as a wonderful joke. His performance was very convincing. I knew it must have taken a great deal of will power on his part to restrain his temper.

But the problems of the day were not over yet. At breakfast there was an orchestrated slowdown. Counselors chatted with one another; ordered more of everything, dawdled over their coffee and did everything possible to make the meal go slowly. Happily, they at least kept their kids at the table with them.

Paulette and I went to the assembly area prepared to break up groups and move them back toward their bunks, but the joke was on us. We stood in that assembly area alone for a long time. When they finally emerged from the dining hall, we had had more than we could handle. Nobody was moving fast. Group after group stood around talking. With prodding, they grudgingly headed back toward their cabin areas, but it took an inordinate amount of time and effort on our part to accomplish this. The whole thing was maddening, not just to Nelson, but to Paulette and me as well.

We reset the time schedule for the day, allowing an extra half hour to account for the delayed start. That did not account for deliberate foot dragging on the part of the counselors. When it was time for morning cabin inspection, nobody was ready. Cabin after cabin appeared to be in a state bordering on chaos. I told each group of campers I would be back again to inspect and they had better get busy. Then I called each of the counselors outside alone and gave them a message I hoped would have meaning to them. "I don't care what your quarrel is with Nelson and the camp rules, you are not doing right by your campers. This stalling business is depriving them of the activity time to which they're entitled. You're hurting your campers more than you are hurting Nelson." Generally, my little message seemed to get through to them, and the cabin groups started moving out to activities. They had apparently agreed to this slowdown as a way of hitting Nelson's well known obsession with promptness, but they really were being harmful to their campers and eventually they responded as I hoped they would.

When I returned to the office to make a report I found Nelson on the phone. I sat down to wait, and it became clear he was speaking with someone at the counselor placement office at the New England Camping Association.

"Right now, I don't care about their experience. I need ten warm bodies and I need them in a hurry. I know staff are hard to find once everyone is underway, but I'm hoping you can find some good guys for me." He hung up, and before I could say anything, he was back on the phone with the operator, asking her to connect him with the New York Camping Association. After that call he turned to me, listened to my report, and turned the camp over to me.

"Vico, it's all yours for the rest of the day. You can cope with this slowdown anyway you see fit. While you're at it I think it might not be a bad idea to let it slip that I'm on the phone interviewing new counselors."

I decided it *would* be a bad idea, that the reaction would hasten an irreparable breach. I still had hopes we could resolve the situation with our current staff and that the camp season was salvageable with them on board. Nelson got back on the phone, and made call after call through the rest of the day. He was determined to locate ten new counselors.

Somehow, I managed to cajole, coax, and push the camp through the remainder of the activity day. We made it to supper time. Nelson asked me to round up the Unit Leaders for a meeting. We all squeezed into the camp office, the four of them together with Roland, Nelson and me. Of the unit leaders, Joey Katz was the only one we knew was actively involved in the agitation. Tubby Brown is such a pleasant and generally agreeable kid he was hardly likely to promote any kind of uprising. Randy Daniels was the only new Unit Leader, and one of the very few new counselors on the boys' staff. He would not have travelled all the way from his home in California looking for trouble. Jeff Saunders, Unit Leader of the Junior Unit, had played ball under Nelson in high school. He certainly seemed to me to be committed to his job, he was great with his kids, and had many people who looked up to him on the staff. Joey Katz was one of his oldest friends. They had once been teammates and Nelson had been their coach.

Nelson looked at each of the foursome in turn. He took his time in the process, allowing his gaze to be unmistakably directed at the person he faced. He seemed to me to be deciding which of them to keep and which to fire. I hoped I was wrong. He certainly made each of them feel defensive, individually and not just part of a group. This was a technique I was to see repeated several times during the remainder of the camp season. Given all that had happened so far, and particularly with the extreme disruption the camp had gone through that day, I was amazed Nelson remained so cool and collected.

"What is it you guys want? What have you proved today? If you wanted to prove you could louse up a camp day, you succeeded.

Congratulations on a not-great accomplishment. It doesn't take great talent to make trouble. If you want to show how talented you are, come up with something good for the camp, some new creative program. If you continue with this nonsense and these disruptions, you're not going to change me, you're just going to destroy the summer for our campers. I know that is not what you really want. Let's have an end to this nonsense." I bristled when I heard him use the word nonsense. That might well turn out to be a red flag.

"You guys asked for jobs here this summer, and I wanted you to come. All of you, except Randy, have been here before and shown in the past that you are great counselors. As for this summer, Tubby, you're doing a fine job. Randy you're doing a good job particularly for someone new to camp. Jeff, I've been a little disappointed in your performance so far. It's not that you are doing a bad job, but I haven't seen the kind of dynamic leadership we saw from you last summer. Now to you, Joey, I just don't know what to say to you. Between the football team and your last couple of summers here at camp, I've known and worked with you for six years. Have I suddenly become an ogre? I just don't get it. I just don't understand what is motivating you. Surely you know me well enough to know I would never give in to your list of demands. You know me too well and too long to think that."

"I understand you were part of the anti-war protests at school this past year. I certainly get that, but we have no war to rebel against here. We have kids to take care of. Do me and yourselves a favor, and go back to your job of saving the world once the camp season is over and you are back at school. I even sympathize with your anti-war cause. This war has become an abomination, a disgrace. That has nothing to do with what is going on here. While we're here your job is simply to help create a wonderful experience for our kids."

"I want you four fellas to call this thing off. The rest of the guys will take their lead from the four of you. It's all in your hands. I have no defense against this kind of thing. I know none of you really expect me to give in on policies I think are best for camp. I know you all want the campers to have a good summer."

Tubby spoke up first. "The boys were just upset at the way you spoke to us at the meeting last night. You dismissed us as though our concerns weren't worth noticing. They wouldn't have been so upset if you heard us out and said no to the demands. They were upset because you wouldn't listen or discuss at all."

"I said I would talk to any one of you, and I would have before you guys came in with this slowdown just to upset me. I will talk to any one of you at any time."

"Even though you said you would, that's not the way it came across. You said you wouldn't even consider the demands. It sounded like you hated all of us."

"I'm sorry if I gave you that impression. I was upset and I wanted you to know I was upset, and I've got a right to be upset too, haven't I? I certainly wouldn't want any of you to think I hate you. I most certainly do not hate any of you."

"That's good enough for me, Nelson. You can count on my group working full speed ahead tomorrow."

"Very good, Tubby. I knew I could count on you. How about you, Randy?"

"I can swing them all back to work. I had mixed feelings about the whole business today right from the start. I'm glad it's over."

"I should think you would be. This discord and dissent is like a cancer. It eats away at you and makes you feel lousy inside. How about you, Jeff? What can we expect from the Junior Unit tomorrow?"

"We'll get back in action tomorrow. We just joined the others, taking this one day to show you we were unhappy about the way that meeting ended. I think everyone will give everything they've got tomorrow."

"Joey, that leaves you. What's the story with the Senior Unit staff?"

"I'm not so sure everyone can be talked out of this so easily. Cozy and Major and Dick are all hot and bothered about the actual demands and they're pretty upset."

Until this point, I felt the meeting was going extraordinarily well, better than I had thought possible. Nelson had handled the situation. The Unit Leaders, for their part, seemed more agreeable, more willing to listen and compromise than I had anticipated. It was as though they were as sick of what was going on as we were. But now I sensed Joey hedging in his response, and that made me uneasy. It seemed the good feeling of the meeting might be undone. Moods and tempers were fragile and have a way of erupting with very little provocation. It seemed to me that Joey was about to provide that provocation. But once again Nelson surprised me.

"I want to thank you all for coming. It's been a good meeting, and I'm satisfied that camp will be back on track tomorrow. Joey, I wonder if you would mind staying a few minutes. I think a talk just between the two of us might be a healthy way to conclude the evening and look forward to tomorrow." Joey nodded assent and the four of us got up to leave. For me, it was just a question of moving next door to my office. The partition between offices was hardly soundproof so I heard every word of their one-on-one private conference.

"I don't mind telling you, Joey, I've been disappointed in you this summer. The Senior Unit has been kind of lackadaisical almost since day one. Where is the zip and enthusiasm of last summer? You're the unit leader, Joey. I look to you to set the mood. Now you tell me that Cozy and Major and Dick are setting the mood. Are they setting the mood with your concurrence or are they more influential with the rest of the staff than you are? I need to know. I have to know how to evaluate the things I've seen since camp started. That will tell me how to proceed from this point. As for this slow down or sit down or whatever you guys want to call it, that can't continue. I need you to tell me you can take charge of what's going on with your group and set things straight. If you can't assure me of that, I'll have to make a more drastic response. I probably shouldn't tell you, but I will. I want you to know in confidence, that I have interviewed ten potential new counselors on the phone today. Seven of them are all ready to travel here tomorrow if I call them back and tell them they have jobs. I need your assurance that the Seniors and the rest of camp will not be corrupted by one or two or three bad actors in your unit. If you can't give me that assurance, I will make phone calls tonight, and bring in a few replacements."

"Okay, Nelson, have it your way. Camp will be back to normal tomorrow."

"Don't tell me have it my way. I'm not interested in having it my way. I'm interested in whether or not you are planning to fulfill your basic obligation to do the job you were hired to do. That's the issue."

"Nelson, we both want a good camp for the kids, but the reality is you've been picky about everything this summer. That's what has caused the upset and finally today's action. So, when I say "You'll have it your way that's what I mean. We'll do everything we can to run a great camp and to obey every God damn one of your picayune directives. We'll be on time, on the dot for everything. I hope that will satisfy you."

"Joey, I've known you a long time, and I thought we liked one another but your last comment sounded pretty hateful. I'm sure you didn't mean that and I'm going to accept your word that things will go well from now on, but I would appreciate it if you would keep nasty comments out of it."

"Sorry, I didn't mean to sound nasty. It was just hard sitting here listening to you tell me and everyone else what a lousy job I've been doing, like I'm the one responsible for everything that's wrong this summer. I'll see you tomorrow."

Joey pushed back his chair and walked out, ignoring Nelson's outstretched hand. The meeting was over. Nelson had planned to win this round with kid gloves and he had almost succeeded. The kid glove treatment worked with three of the unit leaders, but with Joey the gloves had come off and his iron fist peaked out. The final few comments back and forth did not sound conciliatory on either side. That did not bode well for the future.

The next few days were surprisingly calm. There was occasional grumbling among the counselors, but no more than the usual quantity of gripes. Things were running more or less smoothly. We were able to concentrate on the normal problems that go with running a camp. There were children who were terrified when we had a dramatic thunderstorm, a bed wetter whose problems had to be dealt with diplomatically by us and by his counselor, a child who was afraid of the water whose parents wanted him to become an Olympic swimmer, problems in cabins with children who needed to learn how to relate to others, painful problems of targeted kids getting picked on, a resurgence of homesickness by a boy who thought he should be all over it by now, but was not. These were the kinds of normal challenges we were there to handle, the things camps can do for children better than schools and in many cases better than parents.

Paulette was having more difficulty with these "normal" problems than I was and that was because of the difference in our counselor staffs. The boys' staff was primarily made up of returning counselors, who had experience working well with their campers. Paulette had a lot of new female counselors, many of whom had very little feel for their jobs.

Ironically, it had been the boys' staff where the morale problems had germinated and blossomed, and there was still an uneasy feeling not far below the surface. On the surface, things were so much better than they had been, so I couldn't actually complain. What was going on below the surface was difficult to label or understand. Little signs of discord were still there. Conversations changed abruptly as I drew near. Sometimes I couldn't help hearing suppressed laughter as I departed from an area. Beyond necessary interaction, I seemed to be cut off from normal communication with most of the counselors. I wasn't sure what I had done to lose their trust, but there it was. I had never had a problem communicating, not as a teacher, nor as a counselor — and now I felt a barrier had been erected, one I could neither crack nor surmount. I had nobody to actually chat with until I was back in the cabin with Dotty at the end of the day.

If the counselor staff ignored and overlooked me, things were even more strained by a lack of communication with the rest of the administrative staff. Nelson was keeping his own counsel. Paulette and I communicated on essentials, but never just sat down to talk together. Roland was an enigma to me. He was clearly a man of few words, and those few were reserved for Nelson. I felt isolated and it hurt. I had never had trouble making friends anywhere.

Nelson no longer hounded me about details. In fact, he barely spoke to me at all. He was operating around me as though I was invisible. When there were changes in plans, I frequently got the information second or third hand, never from Nelson. He stopped discussing camper problems with me, an area where my expertise would certainly have been useful to him. It seemed he had given up on me. I couldn't figure it out, and if that was the case, why he didn't just tell me to go home.

My job was to be in charge of the counselors, their assignments and their program, but they kept by-passing me and going directly to Nelson. They still went to Nelson if there was a decision to be made or a problem to discuss, even though they may not have liked him much. They seemed to understand my loss of power and influence before it became clear to *me*. My position in camp had deteriorated to the point where there was really nothing left for me to do. There were still occasions when Nelson wasn't on the spot and a decision was called for. I would make the decision and Nelson might well come along a few minutes later and reverse it. After a few such occasions, my confidence was so shaken I avoided making decisions whenever possible. One night we were watching a movie in the Rec Hall. A kid asked me if he could go back to his cabin to get something. I responded

"Ask your counselor."

"He said I should ask you."

"Well, Nelson's sitting in the back. Go get permission from him and it'll be all right with me." A minute later I realized If I couldn't even make a decision like that, I had hit rock bottom. Later that night, I resolved to confront Nelson. Either I had to reassert my authority or I should just quit and go home.

Nelson's cabin was more like a home than a cabin. I entered through the door into his kitchen and he escorted me into the living room. It was a great pine paneled room with a massive stone fireplace that took up one whole wall. Cindy came in and offered coffee and cake to the two of us, and then left the room.

"Nelson, I've wanted to talk with you for a while. The last time we really talked was when we were dealing with that slowdown. I've put this conversation off as long as possible, but I think the time has come to ask, what am I doing here?"

"Good, I've wanted to talk to you too, Vico. I know exactly what's on your mind. Right now, you feel like a fifth wheel, like you have no function here at camp. You're debating whether or not to leave. Have I got it about right?"

I was taken aback by his understanding of my current feelings. "Yes, that about sums it up. I don't think you really need or want a Head Counselor. The way you're used to operating, a boys' Head Counselor is superfluous. You seem to want to be everywhere and do everything yourself. You want all authority in your hands, and you are perfectly within your rights, but it leaves very little space for someone to function as a Head Counselor."

"Do you want to resign?"

"No. I don't want to resign. I want to be a Head Counselor. If you are going to continue to do the whole job, I am better off resigning. The camp will be better off too. I really can't go along this way any longer. I find it degrading and humiliating, and I see no point in staying."

"Vico, you have a lot of promise, a lot of good qualities, but I've been somewhat disappointed since the day camp started. I kept hoping you would come around, that you would be salvageable as a Head Counselor. You requesting this meeting tonight is a sign to me that you might be. I wondered how long you would be able to stand playing doormat. I've been trying to goad you back into life. At the beginning of the summer I tried to show you every damn thing that had to be done. I showed and showed and showed, but you didn't seem to get the point. Lately I've tried goading you into taking charge. I know I've been doing my job and yours too. I've been waiting for the day when you would come and say to me "Let me run the camp. Finally, you're here."

"But there are still a few lessons you have got to get through your head. Number one, in this job you can't always be loved. You can't always be the good guy. You've got to learn to say no. You've got to learn that every conference can't be sweetness and light; sometimes people have to be yelled at to get the idea you mean what you say. Vico, you've got to toughen up if you want to get the respect of the staff."

"The fact that you don't agree with all of the camp rules isn't so important. You don't have to agree with them to enforce them, and you've told me you're willing to do that. Most of all, you've got to be able to tell people what to do. Sometimes that means nagging and hounding them if necessary. These counselors, even though they're intelligent college students, are really just overgrown, immature kids. In general, they resent being told what to do. They don't resent it as much if they understand you are sincere and clear in what you expect from them. On the other hand, they will resent you to hell if they pick up a vibe that you are more or less apologizing for what you've told them to do. They won't have any respect for you at all if you convey that kind of emotion."

"These kids need and want direction. They feel more secure when they are clear on what is expected of them. If you're there on top of every situation they'll follow your lead. Say you spot a couple of counselors on the tennis courts, when you know and they certainly know they should be back supervising cleanup in their bunks. If you go right down and kick them off they'll respect you for it and maybe even feel a little ashamed of themselves. On the other hand, if in the process of kicking them off, you give them the feeling that you're just enforcing a camp rule, they come away feeling the rule stinks, but they also come away thinking less of you. If you're the guy on the spot when they are challenging a rule, they're really testing you to see whether you are going to enforce it or not. Early this summer they sensed your ambivalence about certain camp policies, and that very lack of decisiveness is what prompted them to break the rules. More and more they placed you in a position where you had to decide to be the good guy or the bad guy. The more often you decided to be the good guy, the harder it made your job. You've got to let them know from the start that you're not going to let them get away with anything. Then and only then will they stop trying."

"That's been the problem from the start. We both know that we can't go on the way we have been the last few days. It's time for you to put yourself back in charge. The staff has been coming to me for everything. That's not an accident. I've been around all of the time because I've been afraid of how you would respond to difficult issues. This is not a good situation. We have to change it unmistakably as far as the staff is concerned. I'll make myself unavailable over the next few days and that will give you a chance to reassert yourself and take over this staff. Paulette's got enough problems with the girls' staff. I'll spend time trying to help her straighten things out there."

"I know I'm being hard on you now, but I want you to know I don't believe anything you've done or not done was in any way responsible for that stupid counselor slowdown earlier this summer. That was just leftover nonsense from their days of protesting in college for the past year. Now, I wish you luck for these next five days. I'm anxious to see you succeed."

"Thanks, Nelson, that's all the chance I'll need."

"Great! A word of warning, if I see things are not working well, I'll have to step back in. There is too much at stake here for me and for our kids to allow the staff situation to deteriorate further. This has already been a tough summer. Visiting Day is five days off. That's how long you have to get the staff back on track. I'll be watching. I can just shrink into the woodwork. You've got to make every one of those five days count."

"I understand what you're saying, Nelson, but I hope you'll let me do things my way. I'll be firm and consistent, and I can assure you there won't be any uncertainty conveyed by me, but I plan to do it without nagging and constant pushing. That's just not my style. Let me show you that I can make it work and you'll see a new spirit around here."

Nelson listened and seemed to accept my conditions, all the

while looking skeptical. "Okay, Vico, try it your way, but it had better start producing positive results as soon as tomorrow. You'll have the five days between now and Visiting Day to prove to me your way will work. I know five days isn't much of a time span to turn around a staff that has fallen into bad habits, but that's the deadline. Visiting Day is a crucial milestone in the camp season. Other than Opening Day, it is probably the most important day of the year. That's the day we are judged, evaluated, and scored by the parents of our campers. They are not unfair judges, they're parents, and extremely tuned in to their children's emotions. They pick up all of the signals and all of the nuances. If there are problems, they will find them."

I wasn't sure I could work magic in just five days, but I was eager to try. When I left Nelson's cabin, I wasn't at all convinced I would have even the five promised days. Nelson said he'd be hands off. Saying it and doing it might turn out to be two different things. He was not the kind of man used to staying in the background. Nelson sounded positive, but looked skeptical.

I called a quick meeting with the boys' staff right after breakfast the next morning. We sat on the lawn in the middle of the campus, and I kept the meeting to five minutes because I wanted them to get down to supervise cabin cleanup time. My meeting was short and to the point. "Boys, If you guys will do your job, Nelson has told me he will stay out of the way and let me run the camp. He said he's going to shrink into the woodwork." That got a laugh because none of us could imagine Nelson ever being that far out of the center of things. "I don't intend to nag you or push you. I just expect you to do your jobs enthusiastically. This is a chance for all of us to start the season over again, start it on the right track this time. We can make this the kind of camp I know we all want. If this effort fails, I have no doubt Nelson will jump back in feet first. He's given me his word he'll stay out of active management on the boys' side for the next few days. For me, and for all of you, these few days will be the most important days of the whole camp season. I'm counting on you."

I was confident my message got through. I knew they doubted Nelson would let me do what he said, but they were willing to be shown. There were a lot of smiles and even a few congratulations offered my way after the meeting. They genuinely seemed to want to pull together and do the job.

The following two days were the very best days of the summer so far, for me and, I thought for the camp. As promised, Nelson stayed on the girls' side. Our counselors moved from activity to activity with smiles on their faces. The activities ran well and the campers looked happy. For the first time, I began to detect the emergence of camp spirit. Our staff was experienced and potentially excellent. It was great to see everyone performing up to their potential.

Friday morning, the fourth of my five promised days, my bubble burst. When I saw Nelson waiting for me, sitting in my office with his hand wrapped around his coffee cup I knew it was trouble. His face was drawn and pinched. Clearly something was wrong, but I couldn't for the life of me guess what it could be. The camp had been quiet and apparently happy when I went to bed last night.

"Get yourself a cup of coffee and come back. I have something to show you."

I reviewed the events of the last few days as I went to and from the kitchen on my essential caffeine errand. I returned to the office feeling like a condemned man waiting for the chopping blade to fall.

It fell all right!

"Sorry to say it Vico, but the Grand Experiment is over for now." I looked at him questioningly.

"Can you guess why?" I drew a blank. Nothing that happened in the past few days would seem to account for such a statement.

"No, I really can't. Camp has really run well these past few days. I can't imagine what has you so upset."

"It looked pretty good to me too, until last night. I was beginning to think perhaps your velvet glove technique might be working, and it *was*, on the surface. But underneath, bad things were happening. While you have been reasonable in dealing with them, some of these bastards have been thumbing their noses at you behind your back."

"I don't see how that can be. Everyplace I've looked the past few days I haven't seen anything but excellent counseling. They've been great."

"Oh Vico, you said it! You said "every place you've looked" and that's the problem. There were places you failed to look. How did the counselors look when they checked in last night?"

"They all checked in before curfew and none of them looked drunk or impaired in any way."

"It's nice to know I hired such good actors. I'm not saying that they were *all* hiding something, but some of them definitely were. Some of them fooled you when they checked in. Did you happen to stop by the Green House on your rounds last night?"

I didn't have to think. I knew I hadn't. I shook my head from side to side, trying to imagine what might have happened there. The Green House was just far enough off the campus to be inconvenient for regular counselor use and was certainly off the beaten track for me on my nightly rounds. I had to admit to myself that I almost never dropped in on the Green House, both because it required a long detour from the rest of my nightly rounds around camp, and because it was intended as a counselor hang out. I felt like that was no place for me, a member of the administration. Counselors were entitled to some privacy on their time off. For some reason, in that moment of distress, I recalled that one of the demands early in the summer was to create something just like what the Green House was supposed to be, but in a far more accessible location for counselors to drop in when they had a little spare time.

"If you had stopped by the Green House you would have found it very educational, unfortunately in more ways than one. I said I wouldn't interfere with the way you were running camp as long as things were going well, and I think I kept my word. However, I never promised to close my eyes, and it's a damn good thing I didn't. You may not be aware of it, but it has always been part of my daily routine to check every building in camp at least once a day. I check many of those where nobody lives on my nightly rounds. I sometimes make some interesting discoveries, as I did last night. When I walked into the Green House last night, I immediately smelled marijuana residue so I went searching and I found these."

He pulled out a manila envelope and shook out the very small bits of three different cigarette wrappers. There were still small bits of weed stuck to the paper. "You can guess what was in these papers. Sniff them yourself, if you have any doubt."

"No, I know what it is."

"It seems our boys are getting careless. The wrappers were in a rough clay bowl from our pottery shop right in plain sight. After I stumbled on these, I went looking around. I found eight crushed beer cans sitting in a waste basket, partially hidden by the old corner cupboard. In that same basket there were two recently used condoms. Someone obviously smuggled some girls into camp and spent time with them there. I can assure you it was none of our girls' counselors. We had a long meeting last night, Paulette and I, with all of her cabin counselors and specialists, leaving only a few Junior Counselors who were on duty in the bunks. It's pretty clear some of our boys had a party there last night. They were pretty brazen about it, assuming I was out of their hair for a while and they clearly weren't worried about you. They were so cocky or so drunk they didn't make much of an effort to destroy the evidence."

I felt my ears redden. I was embarrassed, chagrined, and felt devastated by Nelson's disclosures. I knew I should have checked the Green House. If not every day, at least often enough so the counselors would know I might walk in on them. While I was busy respecting their privacy, they were taking advantage. That was inexcusable of them, but I had to admit to Nelson and to myself that I had blown it. "I'm so sorry, Nelson."

"Well it's happened and we can't do anything to change that fact. The question is what to do now. What are your thoughts?"

"We can't let them just get away with it, but Visiting Day is the day after tomorrow, and this would be a very bad time to start an investigation. If we do start one now, the word would spread all over camp, and the campers' parents would hear about it pretty much as soon as they arrive at camp. We'd wind up talking about nothing else with them the whole day. We should keep our eyes and ears open and plan to start a serious investigation on Monday."

"Wait till Monday!" He fairly exploded. "We have at least two or three counselors in camp who don't give a damn about camp or their kids!. They've broken the most important rules in camp, and you want to wait until Monday? We've got to find out who these guys are. And they are gone as far as I'm concerned. There are no possible extenuating circumstances. I won't have them here one minute more than I have to. I'll take our chances with the parents on Visiting Day. They'll appreciate that we can't have guys in camp taking care of their children who have so little regard for the difference between right and wrong. I know there'll be a stink if and when word gets to them, but that's a risk we'll have to take."

I was sure that would be a tactical error. A major scandal was almost certain if we followed his path; but, he's willing to risk it to maintain his principles. I had to admire his integrity. I can't help thinking a scandal like this, exploding on Visiting Day, could kill the camp. The combination of Pot smoking, beer drinking, and sex would be hard for parents of campers to excuse with the tired phrase that "Boys will be Boys." This was not easily justified or excusable.

They'd be furious to think that their kid's counselor might be smoking pot, getting drunk, and having sex when he should always be in condition to take care of their children. The more I thought about it, the more I was convinced we were looking at a disaster.

If we start an investigation this morning it's going to get out. How could it not? I can ask them to keep it to themselves, but you can bet they will just have to tell someone. It will be all over camp in no time at all. By the time the parents come forty-eight hours from now, the facts could be distorted and exaggerated. By tomorrow, those two or three guys who were actually cheating in the Green House last night could be brazen enough to throw a big staff party, maybe even involving Senior Campers! Given half a chance, something like this will have a life of its own. The actual facts will no longer matter to the outside world.

"I need to find out who it was, and I want them out of here fast, if possible before Visiting Day. I'm going to discuss it with Roland and probably Sammy and Randy. Either Sammy or Randy may have an idea who was there, and both of them are guys I can trust to keep their mouths shut. I want you to figure out who you can talk to as well, a couple of counselors you feel close to, guys who you think will understand how important it is not to have this spread. Does anyone come to mind?"

I quickly reviewed them one by one. I wanted to believe they could all be trusted. For that matter, I found it hard to believe that any of them could have been so irresponsible, but it was clear that at least a couple of them had been. I thought of the Senior Unit guys first. I had to pick one of the counselors to speak with privately. It had to be one who had not been leading the negative business earlier in the summer, so that would seem to let out Joey, Cozy and Major. Although the more I thought about it, maybe Major. It was hard for me to think of him as any kind of troublemaker. He seemed like such a straight shooter. He was not a Rich Kid. He had gotten into college on an athletic scholarship, and had to maintain not only his average but also good behavior to keep that scholarship. Every time I saw him around camp, he looked good. He was clearly one of our strongest athletic counselors, and I recall seeing him walking to the dining hall more than once with his arms over a boy's shoulders. He wouldn't have been drinking or smoking pot. I know he wouldn't. The only drawback was his relationship with Cozy. They were old friends, and, Joey had indicated earlier that Major was one of the leaders of their slowdown. I didn't believe it.

"I think I should talk to Major. And Jeff Saunders. Nelson, do you think those are good choices?"

"If I thought I could trust Jeff I would talk to him. I've known him a lot longer than you have. Unfortunately, he's one of my prime suspects. I was shocked last Fall when I saw his name in the local newspaper. He was one of a bunch of kids arrested in a drinking party that got out of hand. It made a big stir in our town. I discussed that party with him when I rehired him for this season. He swore to me it would never happen here. Now I wonder."

"Well what do you think about Major?"

"Vico, do you feel close enough to him to confide in him?"

"He's always been friendly to me, even when nobody else seemed to be talking to me. I feel like we have a relationship."

"Well I suppose that is a good sign. Sure, talk to Major. Anyone else you can ask?"

"How about Tubby Brown?"

"If you think you have a relationship with him, go right ahead. "

"Tubby and I have had some long talks. I know about his troubles when he really was a fat little kid and was picked on all the time. I think he trusts me, and I feel that way about him too. "

"Good, I'm glad you feel close to him and I agree he's a good bet. I'm not sure we can trust anyone's silence in a situation like this. When you talk to your two "helpful informants" tell them as little as possible while you're trying to find out what they know. Here's what we have to find out from each of our four guys: we want to find out what they did last night and who they did it with. Unless we are very unlucky in our picks, each of them did something with at least one other counselor. When we're through, we'll take our four lists, add the guys who were on duty last night, and narrow it down to just a few counselors unaccounted for. Of the guys whose whereabouts are unaccounted for, we'll find our culprits."

After breakfast Nelson and I started off on our information-gathering missions. I gave Major what I'm sure he viewed as a swearing in ceremony and then started my not-too-subtle questioning. He seemed puzzled with my thinly-veiled preliminaries, and grew progressively more so as the questioning went on. "What did you guys do last night after things quieted down in the Senior area?"

"I was hungry after that dinner last night. Richie and I rowed across the lake and had a snack at Don's."

"I suppose you had your usual cantaloupe sundae."

"As a matter of fact, after last night's dinner I was ready for a whole meal. I had a bacon and egg sandwich, and then the cantaloupe sundae. I felt slightly bloated when we rowed back."

"Did the two of you go back to Senior Camp or did you stop off anywhere?"

"Vico, this is crazy. What are all of these questions about? We both checked in, came back to our cabins, and I went right to sleep. I think Richie went to keep Jim company by the fireplace. I have no idea how long he sat there. I fell asleep very fast. Any more questions? What's going on? Did someone find a dead body here last night?"

I could tell he was peeved even though he tried to make a joke of it. I couldn't tell him the truth and I didn't want to lie to him. I hoped he would be satisfied with what I could say. "I can't tell you now, but I promise you'll find out very soon."

My next conversation was with Tubby. It seemed he and Evan Spielberg had dates last night with girls at Camp Northwoods. They met at the Gray House, had brownie nut sundaes, chatted for a while, and then headed back to their respective camps. I was quickly satisfied with his answers, and I thanked him. But he was not satisfied.

"What's this all about? What's the score? You've never showed any interest about where I went or what I did after Taps. You planning to write a book or something?"

I decided to level with him, up to a point, but without details. "Someone was smoking pot last night here in camp. We're trying to eliminate as many people as possible before we start questioning those we suspect are the most likely."

"You mean you suspected me?"

He completely missed the point. "No, just the opposite! We are questioning people we're reasonably sure would never have deliberately broken such an important rule."

"Well, if you're just looking for pot smokers, pretty much everyone on the staff smokes pot at least on occasion."

"You too?"

He nodded yes. "That's what I'm telling you. It could have been anyone."

"Do you mean to tell me counselors have been smoking pot here on campus?"

"No of course not. As far as I know, nobody has smoked on campus. I wouldn't think anyone would. We all know the rule, and it's not important enough for anyone to risk getting fired in the middle of the season." He promised to let me know if he heard anything.

It was late in the morning when Nelson and I met back in the office. We excused Karen, the office girl, and closed both doors. She was happy to get an hour off in the middle of a beautiful day. Nelson had just interviewed Sam Samuels and Randy. Together we made up a list of all the counselors whose whereabouts we could account for. When we were through, our list included all but four: Joey Katz, Cozy Martin, Jeff Saunders and Harry Enfield. Two of our suspects, Joey and Cozy, left camp right after breakfast this morning on their day off. That left us with only two on hand to question.

Harry Enfield was our Nature Counselor. He was an undistinguished person and had been an uninspiring nature counselor. In fact, by this point, four weeks into the camp season, there was very little nature study left in the program. Group after group had expressed their lack of interest after a very few of his classes. He also was counselor for a cabin of Sophomore boys and, while not a dynamite cabin counselor, he seemed to be interested in his campers and treated them nicely. Clearly, he was not a bad person or even a terrible counselor. He was the kind of guy who should make it through the summer, but was unlikely to be offered a job for the next camp season. My relationship with him had been cordial, perfunctory. He didn't seem to have any close friends among the other counselors, and he was easy to overlook. To me, he was highly unlikely to be a rule breaker. He didn't have the chutzpah to smuggle a girl onto camp property, never mind smoking pot or drinking beer. But Nelson didn't want to pass him up as a suspect. That meant an interview.

Harry hadn't a clue why he had been paged to the office. His face betrayed nothing but puzzlement. We invited him to make himself comfortable and Nelson started the inquisition. "Harry, do you have any idea why we asked you to come here?"

"No, I can't say that I do."

"Search your mind. Is there anything you can think of that might have prompted our invitation?"

"No, nothing." He thought for a few second and went on "unless you're planning to fire me."

"Why would I want to fire you Harry?"

"I know my nature program was pretty much a bust. I think I'm doing a decent job with my kids, but maybe you think I'm getting paid too much now that I'm really only a cabin counselor. There's a rumor that you've never gone through a camp season without firing somebody. Maybe I'm the one for this year. I hope not. I like it here, and I think my kids are great. I think they like me too."

"For your information, I've never fired a cabin counselor because he's not great at activities. Cabin counselors are the most important people in camp. You can relax on that score. We have no thought of firing you because of the Nature program."

"That's the only thing I could think of, and I'm glad I was wrong. You're just going to have to tell me. I haven't got any idea."

It was clear to me this guy didn't have a guilty conscience about anything he had done and so I eliminated him in my mind, but Nelson started questioning. "Harry, what did you do after Taps last night?"

"I went to bed."

"Did you really go to bed that early, when Taps sounded?"

"No, first I took a shower. Then I read for a while in the dining hall. Then I went to bed. It must have been about 10:30 when I hit the sack."

Nelson had an interesting technique. First, he would ask a question with a harsh tone and then he would moderate both his tone and his facial expression, so that the next question was somehow asking for the sharing of a confidence. He kept trying to get Harry to change his story, to trip him up. I found myself silently rooting for Harry. I believed him completely when he told us it was about ten thirty when he went to bed and all of his campers were asleep when he came in. As far as he knew, nobody had seen him, but we could check with the area OD. He might have seen him go into the cabin. It was all totally believable to me.

"Why do you care what time I go to bed? I go to bed early just about every night."

Nelson finally seemed convinced.

"It's nothing, Harry, nothing at all. Something a little mysterious happened in camp last night. If you had been awake you might've seen or heard something that would help us figure it out. Since you were asleep, I don't have any more questions for you. You can get back with your kids now. They must be wondering what happened to you." Harry didn't waste an unnecessary second. He got up and left that office looking just as perplexed as when he came, but perhaps slightly relieved as well.

Jeff came into the office, with a slightly annoyed demeanor. Nelson waved him toward the empty chair in the corner of the office, where we would both be facing him, and Nelson started out on the attack. He immediately adopted an accusatory attitude and tone. "Jeff, you've been letting me down this summer, but I never believed you would stoop this low." Jeff's face reddened with irritation.

"I have no idea what you're talking about, Nelson. You've been on my back all summer long. I try to do my job, and I think I'm doing a good job. What is it you think I've done?"

"Where were you last night, Jeff?"

"Not that it's any of your business, but I was right here in camp."

"Don't take that tone with me, young man. Just answer my questions. Where were you in camp, and was anyone with you?"

"Cozy and I were playing ping pong at the Green House."

"Is that all you were doing there?"

"Yes, we played ping pong from about 9:30 and probably finished about eleven o'clock. I came back to my cabin, took a shower and went to bed."

"What time did you actually go to bed, the truth this time?" I could see Jeff was getting more and more agitated. Nelson had just flatly accused him of lying. That was obviously more than disconcerting to him assuming he was as innocent as he claimed. But his apparent exasperation could also be because Nelson was honing in on the truth.

"Don't call me a liar. I told you the truth. I went to bed about eleven o'clock, possibly a few minutes after. What's this all about? What difference does it make what time I went to bed?"

"Never mind what it's all about. You know what it's all about if you were at the Green House. You want to stick to your story? that you and Cozy were alone there just playing ping pong? Was anyone else there?"

"No!"

"Jeff, there was a girl or maybe more than one girl at the Green House last night. Was she there with you or with Cozy or with both of you?"

Jeff looked startled at the accusation, but his response remained adamant. "I told you there was nobody else there. I don't know where you got the idea there was a girl. There were just the two of us, Cozy and me."

"Jeff, let me show you what I found there when I checked through shortly after one o'clock." He reached into his desk drawer and pulled out the three remnants of pot papers and a crushed beer can. "I also found two recently discarded condoms, not very carefully disposed of. Do any of these help your memory?"

"No. I don't smoke pot, and yes I've had an occasional can of beer, but not last night. Believe me, I don't know anything about any of that stuff."

"How about the girl? You must agree there's pretty strong evidence there was at least one girl."

"There may have been a girl and there may have been pot smoking, but not while Cozy and I were there. Everything you're talking about could all have been there all day. We would not necessarily have noticed them. Your assumption seems to be that it happened that night. I have no idea who was there or when, but you can bet on one thing. It would not have been Cozy or me or anyone else who plays college ball. We have to stay in shape for the Fall. We can't jeopardize our scholarships by messing around with that stuff in the summer."

"Jeff, I want to believe you. I hope you wouldn't smoke pot or mess around in any way that would affect your play or your responsibility as a counselor. But tell me this; do you know anyone on the staff who does smoke pot?"

"It would be easier to tell you who doesn't."

"You're telling me just about everyone does?"

"Just about everyone except you, Vico, and Roland." He paused and then went on. "You can add Cozy, Major and me."

"Okay, so the whole staff smokes pot, but how about this summer and in camp? Do you know anyone who's been smoking in camp this summer?"

"Actually, not specifically, no, they'd hardly advertise it if they did. Everybody knows that the surest way to get fired is pot smoking or drinking on campus. So, they wouldn't be bragging about it. I could guess, but my guess wouldn't really be any better than yours. There are just too many possibilities."

"There may be a lot of possibilities, but last night we've eliminated all but four, you, Harry, Cozy and Joey. Assuming we believe your story that leaves only three of you, and we just got through talking to Harry. His denials were very convincing. If we believe you and Harry that leaves only Joey. It seems highly implausible to imagine Joey arriving alone at the Green House just after you and Cozy left at about eleven o'clock; sitting there, smoking pot, drinking eight cans of beer and having sex with some unknown young woman all before I came in to check some time before 1:30."

"You're right, the whole thing sounds implausible, but I told you the truth. I know you're very upset about whatever happened there, and I can't say I blame you, but that isn't the worst thing you have to worry about around here."

"What do you mean by that? What's worse?" Nelson had a horrified look on his face, and I shared that same feeling of dismay. What could be going on right under our noses that we both missed?

"I have no idea who might be involved. If you take a look through rubbish barrels at the end of the day, I'd be willing to bet you will find some syringes. That's why I say whatever happened at the Green House isn't your biggest potential problem in camp this summer. I can tell you something else too, but I'd better not because it's only a rumor. What I told you about syringes, that's real."

We were both stunned. Nelson seemed almost in shock. It was as though Jeff had slapped him across the face. For the first time since I met him, Nelson was genuinely surprised. He seemed to sag in his seat. The one thing that had always seemed to mark his outlook on camp life was his readiness to imagine and prepare himself for the worst possible behavior from people, particularly his employees. He had appeared angry about the pot smoking and the beer drinking, but not truly surprised. Even the evidence of illicit sex just before he walked in was not such a shock to him. The possibility of a heroin user in camp was wickedness beyond his worst imaginings. For a while he just rocked in his swivel chair, hands locked behind his head in a familiar thinking pose, absorbing the information and its implications for his camp.

Reluctantly he turned back toward Jeff, at this point convinced that everything Jeff had told us was the truth. Jeff was transformed in his mind from number one suspect to a trusted source of damaging confidential information.

"Jeff, I appreciate what you've told me, and I believe everything you've said. You can't just drop that bomb and not tell me more. Marijuana is one thing, heroin quite another. If we have a heroin user in camp, he is almost certainly an addict and a potential pusher. This isn't kid stuff. I'm sure you know we have a duty to rout this guy out for the sake of every camper and counselor in camp."

"Nelson, I disagree with you about a lot of things, but I completely agree with you about this, and if I had any reliable information on his identity, I would blow the whistle on him this minute. In fact, I would have blown the whistle the minute I found out. The word has been out and circulating through camp all summer that there is heroin in camp. Nobody has ever attached a name to it."

"That's all you've got, Jeff, a rumor, nothing concrete, no clues at all?"

"That's all I have, but I would bet on it. Nobody seems to know where the rumor started, but I've never heard a rumor in camp that didn't wind up having some basis in fact. In college, I've seen so many guys hooked on so many stupid things I do believe it. There's so much stuff floating around the dorms and fraternity houses that anyone can get started."

"Thanks, Jeff. I appreciate the information, and I'm sorry I put you through the wringer earlier. I'll ask you to keep your eyes and ears open and your mouth shut. We're trying to figure out what happened at the Green House last night, and I'm sure there will be rumors about it. I'd rather not have anything else blow up right now."

I was not surprised when the rumors started to spread and grow. In a matter of a few hours, news of the Green House investigation had spread though camp. Paulette told me the speculation and chatter among the counselors on the girls' side was on the identity of the girl. They all agreed it must have been someone on the girls' staff. I knew that on the boys' side the speculation was on the identity of the guys involved. Some of that speculation had a humorous vein to it involving the time span and how quickly the guilty party had been able to accomplish so much. But much of it was just mystification and speculation as to the ultimate punishment. I overheard lots of theories."

"—Whoever they are, they'll be gone by morning. Nelson is

furious."

—"No, it won't be tomorrow. The firing will have to wait until Monday. He wouldn't dare fire anyone just as the parents are arriving."

Someone speculated that nothing at all had happened, that Nelson had planted the evidence as a way to get rid of a counselor he wanted to fire. The talk went on and on and became less discreet as the hours passed.

After the fact I learned that some Senior boys heard the story, quickly improved upon it and happily shared it with their parents the following day, by which time it had indeed grown to involve much of the camp staff.

While all of these rumors were circulating, I went back to my regular job of trying to make the camp run smoothly. Nelson stayed out of sight. I think he was rather shell-shocked and he also had to prepare for our counselor meeting that night. I put the Green House out of my mind as much as possible since, with Joey and Cozy out on their day off, there was nobody else left to question and nothing more to do until the counselor meeting that night. Joey, Cozy and a few other counselors would be back from their days off in time for the pre-Visiting Day meeting tonight.

6
Joey Katz: History of a Rebel

Joey

My family lived in Great Neck, the Estates section, where the winding little streets meander here and there; sometimes going in circles; other times coming to an end for no apparent reason. This was a neighborhood well beyond comfortable, but not quite rich. My father, Abe Katz, described his living condition as "very confortable." Dad's rather successful business was selling adult diapers, rubber sheets, and other related supplies to hospitals and nursing homes. "Tank Got ve can be of service to da sick." And thank God he did — every morning and every evening in his bedroom, and in the breakfast nook, and the dining room before every meal. And on Saturday, the Shabbos, he spent every morning thanking God in the Shul he and his friends had founded shortly after they moved into Great Neck. To my father, Judaism was more than just a religion. It was a way of life. Jewish life had a rhythm. Prayers must be said in the morning and they must be said in the evening. The Commandments must be kept, and, most important, Shabbos must be observed and honored.

He would never have said it out loud, but I know when I was a little boy I was a disappointment to him. I was small, timid, and plagued by asthma. "How is this boy ever going to do honor to the Katz name?" As though God wanted to play a little trick on Abe, his wife Rose had given birth to twin girls, beautiful, healthy and strong, and just two years behind me. But, to his credit, my father was determined to make a mensch of me.

Looking back on it now, I'm sure we made a pretty picture as we all marched off to Temple together on Saturday mornings: Abe, little Joey, and his two pretty red-headed sisters. I hated those mornings in Temple. Every minute seemed agony, every hour torture. Why couldn't I just stay home with Mommy, listen to the radio, and help her set the table for our big Shabbos lunch? Why must I go with my big fat father, sitting in that stuffy Temple as the prayers droned on around me hour after hour? Sometimes I tried to listen and understand what they were saying, but I would soon give up. It was hopeless; almost as hopeless as arithmetic classes at North Elementary School. At least in Temple the Rabbi never asked questions during the service. Nothing much was really required of me except to sit quietly, stand when everyone else stood, and not fall asleep. My mind was allowed to wander at will.

There was only one other boy from my class at school who also had to be at services on Shabbos. That was Ezra, the Cantor's son, who didn't count as a regular kid. It was easy to understand why Ezra had to be there, but why me? School I understood. School had to be endured by everybody. Temple, on the other hand, seemed to be a torture my Father had designed especially for me. I wasn't sure what I had done to deserve such punishment, but I accepted it as such, with misery and loathing.

Our walk home from Temple invariably took us past groups of kids playing in their yards or on the streets. I envied their baseball gloves, their footballs, their sleds and their skates. I envied them most of all in the Spring and Fall when the days were warm and sunny and perfect for playing. If only I could play on Saturdays, I could get good at some of these games. I'd get better and better if I had all day Saturday to play. I could become the best baseball player in Great Neck, the star of the team. I dreamed myself into the pinstripe uniform of the New York Yankees. These same boys and girls I passed by on Saturday mornings, years later, would be lined up outside the gate at the ballpark waiting to get my autograph. They'll like me then, all right. My face lit with a smile as I watched myself race around the bases with yet another home run in my quest to break Babe Ruth's record.

"Vatch out, dumcup." My father brought me back to reality just in time to avoid walking into a lamppost or perhaps stepping too far out into the street. The walk home continued, my happy dreams held in abeyance until arithmetic class on Monday, when I would again achieve greatness and fame while the teacher droned on about long division.

My hours of greatest contentment occurred when I was sick in bed with one of my frequent asthma attacks. My sisters were at school, my father was away doing his good deeds in the business world, and I had Mommy all to myself. I savored the warmth of the bed, the radio soap operas playing on my night table, picture puzzles I spent hours assembling, hot chicken soup and mummy's musical voice always close at hand. But there was a price to be paid for these pleasurable hours. I had to endure wracking coughs so strong I thought I might never stop. At night, the phlegm and mucus accumulating in my nose and throat would not allow me to sleep. Worst of all, there was always the day I was well enough and would have to return to school.

School was always unpleasant, but it was bearable day after day. Mondays were normally the days of most difficulty, but the days I came back after an illness were the most difficult of all. I was never convinced I was well enough to return, even though Dr. Glassman assured me that I was. I was certain I would have an attack of wheezing as soon as I entered school, and frequently I did. But the most painful part of returning to school after illness was that long lonely walk to school; the horrible sinking feeling as I approached the schoolyard and was observed walking alone by all of the other kids. They would be playing stickball or tag or hide and seek. Most of them ignored me as I got close, but there were always a few who snickered and taunted.

Once the actual school day started, I was on my own private island. None of the boys had anything to do with me. Some of the girls were nice enough in a casual and distant way. Nobody wanted to sit at my table, stand next to me in line or work with me on a project. At recess, nobody made a place for me in any of their games. If there were games organized by the teachers where they had to let me play, I was always last picked and it always hurt. Worst of all was standing during the picking as the other eligible kids were all chosen and I was finally standing all alone and was assigned by the teacher to one of the teams.

Arithmetic was my particular dread. I never could understand what was going on so I learned to look as busy as possible, with my head close to the desk and my pencil in motion. Occasionally I would be called upon to answer a question and would give a stumbling frequently unresponsive answer to the amusement of the class. Momentarily disgraced and happily buried back in my seat I resumed my dream world which had been so rudely interrupted. There I was again in Yankee Stadium. The game was on the line and I was at bat. The third pitch was just where I liked it, and it exploded into the right field grandstands. The roar of the crowd was music to my ears. Mercifully, without further incident, the class ended with the clang of the blessed school bell. Other times I awakened from my dream to find the teacher standing next to my desk, asking her question for the third time.

As the school day came to an end I would hastily gather my books and walk swiftly out of the schoolyard as though I had an important appointment somewhere. Once I had outdistanced my classmates, my pace slackened and I rather enjoyed my solitary walk home. Those first few minutes at home were always the best. I always arrived home before the girls and I enjoyed sitting alone in the kitchen with Mommy, munching on Hydrox cookies and gulping a big glass of chocolate milk. What could be better?

When I started Junior High School, a whole new world opened up for me. There were a lot of important changes in my life, all of which were to have a profound effect on who I am. First, my years of resentment and anger toward my father gave way to a thinly veiled mutual hostility, manifested on both sides by silence. I continued to attend Services with my father on Saturday mornings and I now also went to Hebrew School three afternoons a week. Surprisingly, I found I rather liked Hebrew and had little difficulty mastering the eccentric looking Hebrew alphabet. I found I never wheezed or coughed in Hebrew School and I always knew the answers. Success was a new experience. I was actually the best in my class, and it was an exhilarating reality for me. At the end of the term, I won the award as top Hebrew scholar. I was proud of myself, and I could see that my father was impressed with his son the scholar.

Probably the most important change in my life that year was that

I made a friend, a real friend. It all happened because of a lucky bit of geography. My Elementary school class was split into two districts for Junior High. As it happened my street was a dividing line between districts, and only Johnny Greene and I were on one side and would attend North Junior High, while all the rest of our class went to South. That first day of school, I was walking along toward school and I could see Johnny walking on the other side of the street. Johnny was just a little ahead of me on the other side when I saw him cross over and stop to wait. We walked on together, two new boys coming together to a new school. The next few days I rushed out to be sure I was on the corner when Johnny walked by. After a few days that tactic became unnecessary. Whoever arrived at the corner first waited for the other. Now I looked forward to school. Walking alone had been always been half of the battle.

Johnny was a true extrovert, and in short order he had made a whole raft of new friends in the new school. Happily, for me, Johnny always included me in. He was actually my admission ticket to this group of new friends who seemed to accept me as part of the group. Johnny had a lot of friends, and I knew I wasn't his best friend, but that didn't matter. From Monday to Friday I knew I would never have to walk alone. This Monday to Friday friendship seemed to work well for both of us. It gave us both someone to walk and talk with, but to me it was more important than that. When I arrived at school with my friend, I knew I belonged.

One day, it was a Thursday, when we were walking home from school together Johnny asked if I wanted to go to a movie with him on Saturday. What an exciting thought. I wanted to say yes right away, but I didn't dare. Going to a movie on Shabbos was unheard of.

"I'll let you know tomorrow. I have to check with my parents in case they made a doctor's appointment or something for me."

"Mom, I have to go. He's my best friend and I really want to go."

"I'll speak to Daddy about it."

I was happy to leave it to her. I was determined to go to the movies somehow, but wanted to avoid an explosion with my father. That night I eavesdropped while my mother pleaded my case.

"He'll still go to services with you in the morning. I'll buy his ticket on Friday so he won't have to handle money on Shabbos. They don't have to ride. They can walk to the theater from here, and I'll send along candy for both of them so they won't buy anything at the refreshment stand. Abe, he's a boy and he needs to have fun. He's got a friend now. It's important. Let him do this with his friend." I heard my father say "Let him go" and I was so happy I almost gave away my listening post by a shout of joy, but caught myself just in time.

I did my best to make a joke of all of the conditions as I outlined them to Johnny. Saturday I was so excited when I rushed home from Temple I was too excited to eat my lunch. I met Johnny and went off to the most wonderful afternoon of my life. I'll never forget that day. It was a great double bill, *The Legend of Tarzan* and *Abbott & Costello Meet Frankenstein*.

It was a strange and wonderful winter for me. I had always been the smallest boy in my class, but suddenly I was growing. All that year I kept outgrowing my clothes. They seemed to be shrinking around me as I added inches and muscle to my once puny physique. Best of all, I went through months without a single asthma attack. Never before had I felt healthy for months at a time. My schoolwork improved too. For reasons not clear to me, I was no longer sitting in a fog during class. I paid attention, I understood, and then at the end of the semester I brought home my first positive report card ever.

In the Spring, Johnny asked if I wanted to go to the playground to play ball. I went but showed my lack of experience that day. I had never played anything those six years of Elementary school. I kept at it on my own day after day. Every day after school I pitched to our garage doors with a tennis ball, having drawn a strike zone on the doors. I threw high fly balls to myself in my own backyard. I timed myself running a neighborhood course I laid out for myself and my time kept improving. I worked at it because I knew it was important. If I could play ball I would be accepted by any group of boys. I discovered, much to my surprise, I was actually pretty well-coordinated. The only part of the game I couldn't improve alone was hitting. A couple of afternoons a week, after school, Johnny came home with me and pitched batting practice to help me with my hitting. I never did get to be a good hitter, but I was confident enough to go out and play ball with the other kids. I never got really good, but I was good enough to be an acceptable player in the neighborhood games.

The following fall I turned my attention to football. In baseball, I had started from too far back to ever become that World Series pitcher I used to dream about, actually too far back to ever make the school team. But with football it was different. Very few of the boys from our neighborhood played football in elementary school and most had not advanced very far in their skills by eighth grade I tried out for the Jr. High team. I did this without the accompaniment of Johnny. I really worked hard at practices, and caught the coach's attention, but two afternoons a week I had to go to Hebrew School and had to miss practice. The coach told me I would have made the team, but it wouldn't be fair to other boys who had been there for every practice to have to leave one of them off the team for me to be on. I told the coach "I'll be back next fall, and I won't have to miss any practices for Hebrew School. Once I have my Bar Mitzvah and graduate from Hebrew School that will be that."

After I was cut from the team, I figured out ways to keep practicing. I rigged an old tire from a tree in our backyard so I could practice passing. I timed myself running around the block, and was pleased to see my time get faster and faster as winter approached. During the winter months, I read books on football strategy, concentrating on books about and by quarterbacks. All that fall and winter I continued to grow and to fill out.

As I entered ninth grade, my world was so different from that of a couple of years earlier, it was hard to believe. Physically I was now one of the big kids, strong and healthy, asthma a distant memory. I now had a good sized circle of friends. Hebrew School was no longer part of my life. The previous spring, I had performed and celebrated my Bar Mitzvah with distinction, and was number one in my Hebrew School class. I could tell even my father was proud of me, and we had achieved a kind of uneasy truce and a compromise on what was acceptable on Shabbos. I still went to Temple with him in the morning, but it was understood that Saturday afternoon belonged to me.

I wasn't at all sure that I loved football, but I went out for my school team and made it. I was first substitute quarterback. For the first three games, I mostly sat on the bench, inserted into the lineup only when the final outcome was no longer in doubt. In the classic tradition, the star becomes disabled and a new star is born. It actually happened that way for me. It was game four on our schedule when Jimmy O'Reilly, the quarterback, went down in a heap, and didn't get up without help. He couldn't walk without assistance. It turned out he had a broken ankle. I got my chance that day. I had a really big day. I ran for one touchdown and passed for two others. I was finally the real athletic hero of my childhood daydreams. That night in bed, as I replayed the day, I allowed those dreams back in, and I reveled in the adoration of the crowd.

My family came to the final game of the season. I was astonished when I learned my father was going to take the afternoon off from work. Nobody in the family could ever remember this happening before. I experienced more than my usual pre-game jitters knowing my family would be in the stands. Things started badly as I fumbled the first pass back from the center, but that was my last mistake. After the first bruising contact, I forgot all about my father in the stands and played like a demon. It was my best game of the season, two running touchdowns and two passing. After the game, I was mobbed by my teammates and congratulated by several of the parents who had come to the game. I could see my family standing and cheering in the grandstand. I was thrilled to see them all smiling and cheering and looking very happy.

Abe and the whole family were thrilled to realize what his son and their brother had done, and that all those people mobbing him were cheering for their Joey. After the game, the phone didn't stop ringing for days. My dad got calls from old friends who read about his son's exploits in the sports pages. He swelled with pride.

By the end of the season and through my ninth-grade year, there was a good deal of speculation about me playing quarterback for Great Neck High the following year. As one consequence of my newfound fame, I was constantly invited to parties. I found myself much in demand. It was all so unbelievable, and I was flattered by it, but I was still not entirely at ease with such an expanded circle of friends, many of whom I didn't really know. I wasn't sure whether they all actually liked me or they if they suddenly wanted to be friends because I was a star. The only one I felt truly comfortable with was Johnny. I knew he was a real friend.

I approached the start of tenth grade and entry into the high school with enthusiasm and confidence. When Johnny and I got on the school bus we found ourselves surrounded by our former elementary school classmates, from whom we had been separated for three years. I knew Johnny had maintained friendships with a few of them through those years, but I hadn't seen any of them since sixth grade. A few of them had actually seen me playing football against their Junior High team, but several of the boys I remembered ignoring me in the old day asked me if I was really the same Joey Katz they remembered. Though it was gratifying that people were so impressed, it also made me uncomfortable.

By the time of that first bus ride to school I had already taken part in the team's pre-season practice and was established as a member of the team. Based on my enthusiastic play and success in those workouts during the sweltering hot August weather, Coach Nelson Cohen let me know I was the likely starting quarterback.

With the start of the football season and Abe Katz's new interest in the sports pages, a crisis erupted in our household. My father discovered that the high school football games were played on Saturdays. When I was in Jr. High the games had been on weekday afternoons. When this realization came to my father, this was just a step too far as far as he was concerned. I knew at once it would be a battle.

"I'm sorry Joey, I know football has been important to you, but Saturday is Shabbos, a day for prayer and rest. You can play with your team the rest of the week and I vouldn't interfere, but on Shabbos they'll be no football."

"Dad, I'm playing. I've got it all worked out. I'll do everything possible to follow our religion, but my team plays on Saturday afternoons and I intend to play with them. When we have a home game, I'll go with you to Temple in the morning like always. After Temple, instead of coming home with you, I'll walk right to the field. Half the games are at home. When we have a game in another town Mom can drive me over on Friday. I'll stay in a motel overnight and go to the local temple in that town in the morning before I walk over to their high school field in time for the game."

"Joey, Shabbos means rest. I've seen your football. It is not rest. You cannot follow God's commandment by resting half of Shabbos. I cannot allow it."

It was a quiet dinner table that night. I waited for the explosion I was sure was coming. I warned my mother to expect fireworks. Dad was angry, but hadn't had a chance to talk to her about it yet. My sisters were somewhat oblivious to what was going on, but even they felt the tension in the room. My mother recited the prayer over the Challah and my father recited the blessing for the wine. My mother and the girls brought in the platters of brisket, roast potatoes, asparagus and a bowl of extra sauce, one of the favorite family meals. Very few words were said after that. We sat and picked at the wonderful dinner. We ate in silence. Finally, my father stood up, and held his wine glass aloft.

"To our football hero." He took a sip of wine and set his glass down. "So, Joey, you want to play football on Saturday so you'll play on Saturday. I can forgive you, but you will have to make your own peace with Adonai. If football is more important to you than your father's wishes; if it is more important to you than offending our heavenly father; if it is more important to you than your very soul, by all means go and play football. I cannot give you my blessing, but, my son; I do vish you good luck. Play well and do not get hurt. L'Chaim!" He took a sip, put down his glass and retreated to the den.

My father never let me forget my sin. On the weeks I was not with him in Temple he found it hard to concentrate on his prayers. His mind wandered, he said, from his proper prayers to images of me lying battered and bruised on a football field. "I pray for you to stay healthy and play well. Most of all, don't get hurt. This is what's on my mind when my mind should be giving itself to the rest of Shabbos."

On weeks when there were home games, Abe could almost forget. The two of us walked together and sat next to one another in Shul, reciting the traditional prayers. But as soon as the service ended, instead of staying for the Kiddish "as a proper young Jewish man should" I grabbed my satchel from the coatroom and ran off toward the high school. As I headed toward the field, I too regretted the loss of our leisurely walk home together which had been part of the tradition and that part was gone.

My father allowed it to happen, allowed me to play on Shabbos, but I knew he never came to peace with his decision or with his son disobeying the commandment to keep the Sabbath. As time went on, I became aware my father was getting more and more upset at himself for allowing it and at me for doing it. A wall of silence grew between us, and it was breached only when strictly necessary. Everything had soured between us except for those few hours we were together in temple on Saturday mornings. The pride he had felt at his son's accomplishments the year before had soured. It didn't matter that the phone kept ringing with people congratulating him; with colleges interested in recruiting me and that I was written up one day in *The New York Times*. None of it mattered to Abe. The only thing that mattered was that "his son had cut himself off from the traditions of his people."

My father's bitterness rubbed off on me. It diminished the joy I should normally have felt at the tremendous success I was achieving weekly on the football field. Coach Cohen let me know he was thrilled at my play and at my attitude. He called me aside one day and offered me a summer job working for him at a camp he owned in Maine. He explained I was too young to be a counselor, but I could be a counselor in training. The idea was appealing to me, but not to my father, and I decided not to fight about it.

At the end of the season, I was named to the Greater NY All Scholastic Team, the only Sophomore to make the team. When I attended the award dinner it was bittersweet. I was the only player receiving an award who didn't have a family member in the wildly appreciative audience. My father had refused to come and insisted my mother not go. I overheard them arguing about it, and my mother wound up in tears. The girls wanted to come, but Dad said they were too young to travel to New York City alone by train, even though he knew perfectly well they would be going and returning with their big brother for whatever guidance and protection they might require. I went alone and returned home with a hollow feeling, a sense of abandonment. I was bitter and felt alienated from my whole family. I forgave my mother and sisters because I understood the pressure they faced, but still I felt they should have come. I was the only boy there, all alone. There was nobody there to cheer for me when I went up to get my award. After that I stopped speaking to my father at all unless forced by circumstances to respond. If he felt bad about it, he never showed it. He never apologized for not being there. He never said anything that would make me feel kindly toward him.

I did nothing he could complain about, and there were no arguments, just silence between us. I know how it affected my mother. One day we had a long tearful talk. By the end she was not the only one crying. She told me how the bitterness in the house was a heartache to her. She felt torn between the two of us, and didn't think the breach could ever be mended. She felt she was losing me, her baby, how I always needed her protection when I was little; how I was the one she had loved most because I most needed her love. She felt her baby didn't need her anymore. I had sprouted emotional wings and flown from her protective nest. Now, to preserve her marriage, she had to side with her husband. We would never have another talk like that as long as my father was alive.

If my life was silent and bitter at home, it was just the opposite away from home. I had left the old Joey behind in many ways. I became involved in virtually every activity at school. I was a member of multiple clubs, went to all of the school shows, the concerts, the games, and the dances. I was everywhere. My circle of friends included every social grouping in school. It turned out I was becoming an adept political animal, able to compartmentalize my life between groups without alienating any. The group of friends I had met with and through Johnny was the one with which I most closely identified. They were boys, like Johnny and me who had grown up in solidly Jewish neighborhoods, Jewish but not particularly religious, we all adhered to the basic values of hard work in school, good marks, college, Buick sedans, and success. I shared a love for sports with my football teammates. Together we rooted for all of the school teams along with the Knicks and Yankees in season. Several of them played on multiple teams, and they all loyally rooted for every school team. Another group I characterized as the Party group, revolved around Sally Owens. Sally was very pretty, the head cheerleader, admired and desired by every boy in school. Our relationship began during football season and grew to girlfriend-boyfriend status by late fall. The most incongruous of my social groups were those I thought of as the intellectuals, boys and girls with long hair and torn jeans, who read underground newspapers, discussed philosophy and professed to be embarrassed they lived in handsome homes in Great Neck. They despised their parent's materialism.

When I took stock and recognized I successfully juggled all of these disparate groups I began to look on myself as a politician. For reasons I never fully understood, these people all seemed to respect and like me, even the intellectuals, with whom I never felt entirely at ease. I didn't buy many of their ideas and they knew it, but still they listened to mine, which was puzzling but gratifying.

That spring, I decided to run for President of the Student Government. All of my friends were behind me and they all said they wanted to help in my campaign. I had never actually paid attention to a school election before, but I thought it would be a mistake to have a single campaign manager because whoever I picked it would identify me too closely with that one group, alienating other groups. I immediately learned one of the eternal truths in politics. It is not possible to run for elective office without offending someone.

As soon as he learned my intention to run for office, Johnny came to offer his service as campaign manager. I explained my thinking, how it was politically important for me not to be too closely identified with any one group, and that naming anyone as my campaign manager would label me. I could see he was hurt and I felt terrible about it. After all, Johnny was my best and most loyal friend, but I didn't feel badly enough to change my plans. I thought I'd find a way to make it up to Johnny somehow, but the opportunity never came along. Johnny was still ostensibly my best friend, and he backed me up enthusiastically at rallies, but the relationship had changed, and I knew my selfish decision had caused the change. I was right about the campaign strategy. I won.

My Senior year was a year of trauma and transition. The confluence of two major events altered the course of my life. The first was simply an accident, an injury. I broke my leg in the fifth game of the season. The doctor assured me it would heal, but he said if I went back to football when it healed, I would run the risk of becoming seriously crippled or at the very least require long-term physical rehab. I accepted the doctor's verdict with good grace and less distress than I expected to feel. I realized I was more bothered by the discomfort of the cast and crutches than by the thought of giving up football. It had played a very important role in my life the past few years, but I no longer needed it. I'm an adult now and I no longer have to hold on to a kid's dream.

That was what I told myself, but my dreams were cluttered now with political campaigns and elections. They brought me landslide elections; successful years as governor of New York; a United States Senator, and inexorably led me to the White House as the leader of the Free World.

It was a time of political upheaval in the country, with massive protests against the ongoing war in Vietnam. I seized on this issue. It became my political rally point.

An even more profound loss struck a month later when my father suddenly, and with no warning, had a fatal heart attack. I was numbed by the speed and suddenness of the loss. I tried to feel the sorrow I knew a son was supposed to feel at the loss of a parent, but it simply was not there. But I did feel. I felt an emptiness. My father's death was the disappearance of one of the immutable facts of life. It was as though I came home one day and the house was missing. I came to understand my father had been my signpost, always telling me which way he and God wanted me to go. True, I had often chosen to reject it, but it had been comforting to know the signpost was always there where it belonged. How could so much power and life have simply disappeared in an instant?

The hatred I had long nursed was gone, but it was not replaced by any longing or love for the departed. I recognized I was my own man now. I would no longer have to keep fighting and proving myself. I was free to do whatever I wanted. I could eat a ham sandwich if I wanted, or dance a jig in front of the Temple on Saturday morning. I was also a little frightened by all my newfound freedom. Somehow each Saturday morning I found myself dressing for Temple. I don't know what drove me there. I tried to explain it myself, but there was no rational explanation. Somehow Saturday meant Temple and there I was, at first with my mother and sisters and months later all alone, but still there. Bacon and ham, two forbidden delicacies I sometimes enjoyed at friends' homes, now stuck in my throat. The thought of eating them made me feel ill. I also decided I had more responsibility for my family now. After all, I was now the man of the house. One day I sat my two sisters down and subjected them to a lecture on the importance of working hard in school, dating Jewish boys, and keeping the Sabbath. Sometimes I worried I was turning into my father.

The next fall, I was off to Columbia University. Colleges that fall and winter were overshadowed by the injustice of the war in Vietnam, fears of being drafted, and the dynamic protest movement. I agreed with the protestors and jumped wholeheartedly into the fray. In September, I attended rallies. By October, I was helping to organize and advertise protest meetings, and two days before Thanksgiving, I found myself, megaphone in hand, on the steps of the college library exhorting hundreds of fellow students to prepare for a strike as soon as they returned from their holiday. All I could think about was the war.

While I was at school, I so busy with the protest movement I had no time to check in with my high school friends. I did manage to carve out a sacred half hour every Friday night to call home to speak with my mother and check up on my sisters, but it wasn't until Christmas break that I attempted to make any contact with Johnny, who also was home for the holidays from his school in upstate New York. We spent a few hours together one day, recalling and trying to recapture our long-term friendship. We enjoyed recalling the wonderfully heady days of high school. But I was disappointed that Johnny didn't share my passionate opposition to the war. It was clear he didn't even want to discuss it. Once we finished our reminiscences, all Johnny wanted to talk about was the girls at

Cornell, and one particular girl. During the nearly three weeks remaining of our vacation, we failed to find another time to visit with one another. Nor did I seek out any of my many other high school friends. They were all part of my childhood, and I didn't feel I had time or emotional energy to waste that way when every day of the war brought a new horror. I saw it as my job to help bring it to an end.

My decision to accept Nelson Cohen's invitation to return to Camp Adventure that summer was a retreat, a retreat from the turmoil in which I found myself embroiled night and day through the Spring. I needed a break. I was physically and mentally tired from the rallies, the picketing and the sit-ins. They all took their toll. I was sick of listening to theories and arguments. For that matter I was tired of giving my own speeches, repeated over and over again to hordes of eager students who wanted to be part of the new religion of dissent. I was tired of studying too, and listening to our tiresome middle-aged liberal professors, who talked a good game, but did nothing when it came to meaningful action. I was exhausted from all of it, and, I admitted to myself I was even bored by Kerri, my girlfriend and constant companion over the past several months.

I had been lucky to spot Kerri in that crowded rally early in the fall. She was beautiful, and our relationship was beautiful too, at first. I liked her while she liked and admired me. We appeared to have many of the same interests. She agreed with and adopted many of my theories. Our relationship was uncomplicated from my standpoint. She demanded nothing and gave everything. She helped build up my sense of being right in all of my opinions.

Looking back now, I couldn't pinpoint when the relationship

had started to change, but surely it had. She seemed to dominate all of my time. I found myself having to account to her as though she was my mother...or my wife. And, worst of all, she had recently mentioned getting married, a thought I considered patently ridiculous. I countered with the proposal that we share an apartment in the fall, that we be roommates. When she kept returning to the subject of marriage, which was plainly absurd, it poisoned our relationship. Why couldn't she just be content to just live with me? Why couldn't we just go on enjoying one another? I knew I wasn't ready for a lifetime commitment as a college freshman, with Kerri or with any girl.

I was honest with myself. I knew I was calling Nelson Cohen as a way of running away from college strife and away from Kerri. I needed time to rest and recharge my batteries, a simple summer of games and relaxation. I loved the out-of-doors and I loved sports. I had been happy at Camp Adventure the previous summer. Coach Cohen was an honest, straight shooter, and tended to see things in a straightforward manner, from coaching a winning football team to making kids happy at camp. I was offered the job of Senior Unit Leader, a perfect fit for me. I said yes, and felt like I had made a good decision. I felt great about it. I would give my mind a rest and enjoy doing things I enjoy. It didn't hurt that I would also be earning some money to help defray some college expenses.

It was May when I broke the news to Kerri that I would be going to camp for the summer. What a May it was! The Viet Cong and North Vietnamese forces were making major gains. The US was bombing Hanoi and the Ho Chi Minh Trail and there were endless discussions about the futility of the war and questions about its ultimate resolution. There were student strikes all over the country, and I had been in the middle of all the meetings, phone calls and conferences. I was happy to put it all behind me for the summer and go to camp. I tried to break the news gently to Kerri, but I hadn't counted on her hysterics and recriminations. Eventually she stopped crying and resigned herself to my decision. In the process she had made a decision of her own. "Joey, I'll go with you. Call your coach and ask him if he has a job for me too."

That thought had never occurred to me. I marshaled every argument I could think of to try to dissuade her, but all to no avail. I pointed out that she had never been at a camp before as a camper or a counselor; that she didn't play or like sports; that she really wasn't a fan of any outdoor rugged activities; and also, with this job, we wouldn't be able to spend much time together. But she had made up her mind and she was determined. "I'll be close to you, Joey. That will be enough." She insisted that I make that phone call. She clung to my arm as I dialed Nelson's number.

"Nelson, I know a girl who will make a great counselor ... No, she has no camp experience ... No, she's not an athlete ... but she has done a lot of babysitting and the kids love her ... Yes, we'll come over Saturday ... Yes early afternoon will be fine."

She hugged and kissed me and cried in her thankfulness. And I was happy too. What could I have been thinking, planning to leave her for months? I really did love her and I would miss her terribly if we were apart for eight weeks. It wasn't Kerri I had needed a break from. It was the turmoil of the world in which we lived.

7

Joey Becomes the Spokesman

Joey

Almost from the moment we arrived in camp, I realized Kerri was wrong for camp and camp was wrong for her. By the end of the first week, she hated everything about it. She just wasn't cut out for the world of sports and little girls. She had no interest in leading cheers and fight songs. And she was constantly frustrated by the fact that the two of us had very little time together. She wanted us both to quit. "We should go back where we belong, where we were happy."

I wouldn't even consider that. "I signed a contract and the kids need me. If you want to go back to New York maybe you should. I'll miss you, but it may be for the best."

It was wrong, all wrong. You can't run away from the world. It has a way of catching up with you. I recognized I had exchanged the day-to-day political battles about the indefensible war and the pettiness of college politics for the less important but personally irritating pettiness of camp policies. Truly, when viewed against the backdrop of the impossible war that went on and on, the camp rules and policies were narrow-minded, old fashioned and abrasive. Even though they weren't truly important, they were an abomination for college men who were considered old enough and responsible enough to fight and die for their country. I didn't remember Nelson Cohen being so narrow minded and rigid the previous summer. But the new Head Counselor, Vico, was worse than

Nelson. He turned out to be a sanctimonious bastard with no backbone at all. You never knew where he stood on anything. He seemed to have one attitude about camp rules when Nelson was around, and a different one when he wasn't. How can you trust or work with a guy like that?

I knew from my experience in college that I had become a natural leader. It didn't take long for me to become the focus for the many unhappy counselors in camp. As much as I was upset at the rules, I was nonetheless puzzled at the widespread discontent I found around me. A high percentage of the guys had been at Camp Adventure the previous summer, and they all seemed happy enough and agreed to return this year. Maybe it was the few new counselors, mixed in with the returnees, who had changed the temper and mood of the group. Or perhaps all of them were changed in their attitudes by the increasing hostility they were witness to in the outside world. Or maybe Nelson Cohen had changed since last year, or perhaps it was the insertion of Vico, an additional personality between Nelson and the counselor staff. No matter what the cause, there was, without doubt, a great deal of grumbling and most of those doing the grumbling managed to find their way to me.

Cozy Martin was the first to approach me with his agenda of complaints. We had played together a couple of years earlier on Nelson's high school team. I had always thought of him as a happy-go-lucky jock who delighted in the sheer physical pleasure of matching his brute strength against the heft and power of opposing lineman. Off the field, Cozy was known to guzzle a lot of beer, chase girls, and get into physical brawls. That Cozy had disappeared during his college years. The Cozy who appeared at camp this summer was quiet, so soft-spoken you had to pay close attention to hear what he had to say. He spoke a lot about the poetry he was writing. He read some of his work to me. I found it impressive but totally incomprehensible. His attitude toward camp was one of contempt for the camp, for his old coach, and even for himself for "wasting my summer here." I didn't really like the new version of Cozy any better than I had the blockbuster I remembered from high school, but when Cozy proposed we take days off together I didn't want to alienate my old teammate, so I agreed we would at least go on our first day off together.

We had been in camp ten days when our first day off came. Kerri and I, Cozy and his girlfriend, Rachel, went to a local beach to soak up the sun. Lying on our blankets with my arm around Kerri, the sun beating down on us and a gentle breeze stirring the sand softly over our backs, I was totally at peace and happier than I had been in ages.

Kerri was happy too. The whole day was ours to enjoy together. The frustration of her counselor days melted away with the warm breeze and the gentle rhythm of the surf. When our bodies had absorbed enough sun, we took a quick dip in the icy water. This was followed by a hamburger at the lunch stand and a game of bridge on the beach. It was a day of delightful relaxation for all four of us.

It was late afternoon when Cozy started in. I had heard it all before, and agreed with much of what Cozy had to say, but was annoyed the wonderful relaxed mood of the day was being derailed. I listened as Cozy recited a list of woes: the curfew was number one, followed by the fact they couldn't ever get to see their girlfriends except on days off and nights out, there's no place to go at night, and on and on he went. There was nothing I hadn't heard from him and others. Cozy was waxing eloquent in his bitterness. His quiet well-modulated voice was rising in a crescendo which I feared might eventually reach the thunderous bombast of his high school days. Despite my wish to bring the discussion to a close and get back on a more relaxed track, I found myself defending Nelson and giving the reasons for the hated rules. Round and round we went. The girls joined in on Cozy's side, and finally, wanting to end the discussion, I said "OK, You're right."

"So, you're right. If I were running the camp, I would do things differently. But why are you beating your brains out. You can talk until you're blue in the face and it won't change Nelson or any of the rules. He sees things his way. He pays the bills, and I guess he has the right to run the camp the way he likes. He's not leading a country or a college. He's just a private guy running his own little business. You may think he's wrong from now till doomsday and I can agree, but it's really not your business or mine. Cozy, if you hate it so much you can always leave. Nobody is forcing any of us to stay."

"Thanks, Joey. *Nobody is forcing us to stay.* You've given me the answer to how to get the rules changed. I don't know why I didn't think of it."

"If you're talking about having the whole staff threaten to quit unless changes are made, you've got a case."

"Why not? There are plenty of guys who don't like some of the rules. We can just tell Cohen the things we want to have changed, and let him know if he doesn't change some of them, we're going to quit. Don't worry. He'll give in. He won't want to risk losing the whole staff.

Cozy wasn't angry now. In fact, there was a smile on his face, the first I had seen since Cozy arrived for the summer. This was the real Cozy I remembered from school. The mild soft-spoken guy who showed up at the start of the camp season was a phony. Cozy relished the prospect of the fight. Now I understood what all the talk had been about. Cozy was looking for a fight and needed my support. He was waiting for me to give my blessing to the prospect of a confrontation with Nelson. I remained annoyed at the argumentative intrusion into what had been a lovely relaxing day, but I now understood why.

"Cozy, it won't work. You think the counselors are going to say 'put up or shut up' to Nelson, and take a chance he'll tell them to go home. Some of these guys really count on their summer earnings to help defray the expense of college. They're not as likely to gamble as you think. Just because they're grumbling doesn't mean they want to quit. Don't kid yourself." I was pleased to see the smile disappear from Cozy's face and be replaced by a questioning doubting look. I realized I could actually sway Cozy's emotions and turn him this way or that at will. "It just won't work. Nelson's got the trump cards. However, your thought does have some possibilities. It'll just take some refinement and a little effort." The happy gleam was back on Cozy's face.

"Right now, the guys may be unhappy with some of the rules, but they don't hate them. Before they'll put their jobs on the line, they are going to have to hate the rules, or at least think they do. What really has to happen for your plan to work is for the whole staff to wind up seriously angry with Nelson. Currently they are just irritated with and by him. For your plan to have a chance we have to create a situation where they wind up really angry at the man."

As I said this, I knew I was now conspiring to betray my old coach, a man who had been good to me and fair with me. I knew perfectly well Nelson Cohen was not a bad man, and probably did not deserve what we were about to do to him. I was not proud of myself, but I had to acknowledge that after a few weeks away from the turmoil of the school year, the habit of protest reasserted itself, and I allowed excitement to take over.

My mind started churning once again. Gone completely were my arguments for the camp and along with them went the last of my resolution to enjoy a peaceful two months of sunshine and sports. The chase was on. I am the hunter and Nelson Cohen is the prey. After the four of us returned to camp from our day off, I found it impossible to sleep. I spent most of the night weighing different situations in which Nelson could be made to appear totally unreasonable. By morning my plan was formulated and I was ready to begin short meetings with a few select counselors to evaluate their degree of upset.

My closest friend on the staff was Jeff Saunders. He, like Cozy, had also played for Coach Cohen at Great Neck High School. We were teammates and Jeff had been my most frequent pass receiver. We had achieved a true friendship during our shared experiences. Since we were both enrolled at Columbia, our friendship deepened and matured in our two years of college. This was Jeff's second summer at Camp Adventure where he was Junior Unit Leader. Jeff was a clean-living guy and a true athlete. He was the only one of the three who was still playing first string varsity ball. He worked hard at conditioning, and took every opportunity he could to throw a football around. Football became one of the popular activities in Jeff's Junior Unit. I truly liked Jeff and admired both his integrity and his work ethic. I viewed Jeff's reaction as crucial since if there was one guy on that counselor staff who was looked up to and whose opinion mattered almost as much as mine, it was Jeff.

I knew I couldn't manipulate Jeff as I could Cozy, but I hoped to persuade Jeff of the justice of the cause, and get his informal pledge not to stand in my way. I felt reasonably sure I could accomplish this because Jeff was in love. He had fallen madly in love with Gloria, one of the more attractive girls on the Camp Adventure staff. I knew Jeff wanted to spend every spare minute with her if he could. My goal with Jeff was not to enlist him, simply to neutralize him.

Jeff agreed that some of the rules were a nuisance, but he understood the reasoning behind all of them. Jeff made it clear to me that he liked Camp Adventure and considered Nelson Cohen a friend. He wouldn't want to do anything to harm the camp or the coach. The way I presented the case to him we would be requesting minor changes in some of the rules and a rethinking of some policies. Jeff didn't think it would upset Nelson much if it was done in a nice way, and agreed he wouldn't talk against the suggestions when they were brought up at the next counselor meeting. I had accomplished my goal. I suspected there was a good chance the whole thing would have collapsed had Jeff spoken against it at the meeting.

The next conversation I had was with Bob Weinberg. There isn't much I liked about him, but he could be a valuable ally. He was the kind of guy who seemed to stir up trouble just for the excitement it would provide. In introspective moments, I sometimes accused myself of sharing that trait, but Bob was flagrant in his taunts and frequently unwise in his tactics. I knew that he had once been featured on the six o'clock news for spitting in a police officer's face, got clubbed on the head as a result, and was thrown in jail. Subsequently he sued the city for the use of excessive force. That civil suit was still pending. Thus far this summer, Bob had radiated gloom, spreading it liberally wherever he went. From the day he arrived in camp he had challenged authority in a variety of small ways, as though he was begging to be fired. One night he arrived barefoot for dinner, clearly against the rules, and angrily showed contempt for Vico after he was sent back to put on shoes. I had heard about an incident earlier in the summer when Bob lit a cigarette in the Rec Hall while his kids were rehearsing for a play. Nelson happened by and told him to put it out, gave him a lecture about the smoking rules and that was it. After the fact, Bob had laughed about the mildness of Nelson's reproach. There was clearly no pleasing this guy and, apparently, he had no real sense of responsibility, either. He habitually wandered away from his campers and activities to which he was assigned, anticipating the frequent reprimands he received. Each time he received a mild reprimand, it confirmed his contempt for the camp administration.

I didn't have to look for Bob. He came to me. "Joey, we're having a little party tonight up on the ledge. Would you and Kerri like to join us? I've got a couple of new songs you'll like and I've got plenty of good quality stuff for everyone."

I didn't want to think about attending one of Bob's parties, which I was sure would include pot and probably more. I may have had issues with camp this summer, but I knew that taking care of kids and taking drugs did not go together. I had sworn off for the summer, and certainly didn't want to get mixed up with it in an illegal party. I was convinced Bob's party would attract every misfit in camp, all the oddballs I despised.

"I hope you'll come. Cozy is coming and he says you have a plan to get the camp rules liberalized. I'm all for that, and the others want to hear about it too."

"If Cozy's going to be there you won't need me. He certainly knows my views and he is a pretty persuasive guy. I promised Kerri we could spend some time alone together tonight, and I don't want to disappoint her. We haven't had that much time alone this summer."

I was glad I avoided having to go to Bob's gathering, but I had left him with the understanding that Cozy would tell them all my ideas. Cozy would also let them know I had agreed to go along with trying to change some of the camp policies. Best of all, I wouldn't have to spend my free time that night at Bob's party with people I didn't like. This was really all Cozy's idea. Let him be the leader and take whatever flack will come from it. I'd stay out of it, at least for the time being. I would be interested in hearing Cozy's version of what happens tonight.

The following morning, the day of the first big counselor meeting, I had brief talks with Tim Brownstein and Dick Reback. Both had heard something was brewing and they stopped by to tell me they were with me. After that, I met with Cozy, and together we went over the plans for the meeting. I coached him on how he should be the one to question the rules in a quiet and polite manner. I counted on Nelson's angry reaction, and Nelson proved me right. When he showed his anger by walking out on them, he exceeded my expectations.

That night, the only thing that didn't go according to my script was Vico's surprise insistence in staying on with us after Nelson's meeting. As an official representative of the brass, Vico's presence put limits on what could be safely said and in what tone the post-meeting might take. Also, his being there insured that we would eventually have to water down our demands to Nelson to some extent. I didn't want it to be obvious that our goal was to get any angry reaction. But, even watered down I was reasonably sure the use of the word "demands" would be a red flag for Nelson. No matter how politely or carefully they were presented to him, Nelson would never agree to "Demands." *He* might make demands, but he would never listen or agree to demands made of him.

Of course, I was right. Nelson rejected the demands without discussion. I came up with the idea of the slowdown, which was designed to irritate him even further. Nelson really surprised me! I admitted to myself that I had underestimated his determination and shrewdness. His apparent readiness to replace us with new counselors if necessary was a powerful counter thrust. With two of the Unit Leaders on Nelson's side, and Jeff unwilling to join in the battle, I saw that we would have to bide our time.

It was the day before Parents' Visiting Day when I had my next day off with Cozy, Rachel, and Kerri. As soon as we returned to camp that night for the pre-Visiting Day counselor meeting, we heard about the "big investigation" into the Green House pot-smoking beer-drinking sex party. It was on everyone's minds, and was the conversation discussed by all the staff. As soon as I heard about it, I figured that Cozy and I would be cross-examined before the night was over. Talk around camp was that Cozy had been one of the culprits, but everyone was wrong, and I told them they were wrong. My guess was that it was probably Bob Weinberg, and a couple from his crowd who were spreading that rumor. I waited for my summons into the office. It never came that night. The camp's ancient water pump was clogged and the current camp water supply was limited to the two five-hundred-gallon tanks under the dining hall. Nelson's full attention was focused on the installation of a replacement pump, current water pressure readings, and the team of plumbers working to restore their vital lifeline before morning. Nor did a summons come the next morning, Parents' Visiting Day, a day when the Camp Director's primary job is meeting with campers' parents and attempting to solve problems, some of which we never knew existed until the kids complained to their parents that very day.

After the last parent said goodbye, I started waiting for the call I knew was coming. That night, there was an all-camp movie in the Rec Hall. Nelson got the camp into the Rec Hall and headed back toward the office. He motioned Cozy and me to come with him, leaving Roland in charge in the Rec Hall. I hadn't seen any sign of Vico until he greeted us at the door to the office.

8

Are Joey and Cozy Guilty?

Vico

My big moment was at hand. I knew this would be a test of my tact and diplomacy, my ability to question the two culprits. It was important to prove to Nelson, and to myself that I have the ability to pull this conference off right. Nelson handed it to me as though it was a present. If that's his idea of a gift, I won't mind if I am not on his Christmas list.

Nelson said "This is your job, Vico. I could question them myself, but I think it may be more effective if you do it. If I do it and decide they are lying to me, I'm not sure whether I'll be able to control myself. I'll go over to the Rec Hall and send them back over here to you. I'll wait for your report down at my house. It's all yours."

I waited, nervously, for them to come over from the Rec Hall. This conversation could wind up being a turning point in the camp season. Nelson was convinced that Joey and Cozy were the culprits. My job was to get them to admit it. Anything less than an actual admission would be unsatisfactory. If we wind up firing them without getting an admission from them they were guilty, it won't sit well with the rest of the staff. There would be a whole new uproar, which we could live nicely without. While waiting, I suspected I was more nervous than they were. After all, they knew full well when they smoked pot and drank beer on campus they had broken the cardinal rules. The sex was a different story and obviously involved at least one other party. Neither Nelson nor Paulette had a clue who the girl or girls might be. It might even be a relief for Cozy and Joey to know they had been found out. Then they'd only have to worry about what kind of punishment Nelson would decide on. Of course, the worst we could do was fire them, and, in a sense, they seem to have been asking for that almost since camp started.

My eyes were trained on the Rec Hall door waiting for them to emerge. Finally, Nelson came out with them. The three of them stood together talking for a couple of minutes, and Nelson motioned toward the office. He watched them as they came my way, and then he walked away, headed down toward his house.

They stormed into the office, plunked themselves down, and we stared at one another for a few seconds. Joey was obviously furious.

"I'm not confessing to something I didn't even do! If he wants you to fire us, fire us; but don't expect Cozy and me to confess to this bullshit charge. Someone may have been smoking and drinking at the Green House but it wasn't us." He paused for a minute, as though a new thought had just occurred to him. "Say, Vico, how come you got left with the dirty work? Nelson usually likes to nail people himself." Before I could decide on an answer, a new thought occurred to him. "I just figured it out. He planted those things there himself. It actually never happened! Nelson just wanted an excuse to get rid of us, and with a story like this he could nail us and not upset the staff. That's the only reasonable explanation for him not doing the hatchet job himself. He's actually feeling a little guilty. The whole investigation was a phony from the word go."

It was incredible. I was supposed to be running this meeting!

Joey had somehow taken it over, and now he even came up with that hare-brained plot. I had to cut him off right now and take over the meeting. "Joey, you should consider going into fiction writing. You know what you just said is just plain absurd. You know Nelson better than that. He may be stubborn at times, and even harsh, but he's completely honest and he would never do anything stupid like that. And you know it."

"Yeah, you're right. Probably someone was over there doing things they shouldn't, but it wasn't either one of us. I just was trying to come up with a reason why *you* were the one questioning us. You're right, we know Nelson, and that's not his style."

I decided to lead off by questioning Cozy. "I know you were at the Green House earlier in the evening, playing ping pong. You said you left at about eleven o'clock, give or take a couple of minutes. Is that still your story?"

" Not a story. It's the truth."

"Fine, I'm not questioning that. Where did you go after you left the Green House at about eleven o'clock?"

"I told you before. I went back to my bunk and went to bed."

"No stops along the way? No conversations with anyone? You just went directly back to the cabin and went to bed? Is there anyone who might've seen or spoken with you after eleven thirty? If so, that'll end all the questions. Why are you being so stubborn about this, both of you? You did it or you didn't, and if you didn't and can tell us where you were for any part of the time between eleven thirty and twelve thirty and if anyone else can vouch for what you say, that will be the end of it. We'll know you couldn't have been in two places at once."

"If Nelson has decided to get rid of us, like Joey said, one way or another he's just going to get rid of us. What difference does it make what we say? Just fire us and get it over with."

"Nobody said Nelson wants to fire either of you. Quite the opposite I think."

Joey gave me one of his sour looks. "I don't see any point in us sitting here wasting your time and ours. Let's get out of here, Cozy. Vico, you can tell Nelson we'll be packing. He can get our final checks ready, and we'll need a little travel cash too. Tell him we'll be out of here in two hours." With that, the two of them got up and left the office. I watched as they headed toward the Senior Camp area. I had a sinking feeling inside. Nelson is not going to be happy. If they leave camp without having admitted to anything, there'll be trouble with some of the staff, particularly in Senior Camp. And he'd be out a Unit Leader! I rang Nelson's house on the intercom.

"They're packing now."

"What! I'll be up in a minute. I want to hear all of the details. This is not good news! You'll have to get people in to cover their bunks immediately." He slammed the receiver down before I could say anything more. Two minutes later, he was in the office looking grim. I replayed the whole scene to him as accurately as possible, and he listened for every word and every nuance. He was clearly angry. This was apparently not how he thought my interview with them would come out.

"Well, it's too damn bad. They've been two of our best counselors with the kids and activities. Now we have to replace them. I don't think they would have just quit and walked out like that if they weren't involved the other night. Vico, don't worry. No injustice has been done. If they were innocent, they would have been happy to give you proof of their innocence and throw it in your face. They didn't do that at all. What they did was plant the seeds of doubt in your mind. They wanted to deny us both the satisfaction that comes with certainty. We can't worry about that now. The night is young and we have a lot of work to do. First, we've got to make sure they really do pack and get out of here in two hours. If they stick around here long enough there will be lots of teary goodbyes. There will be trouble for sure."

"You may never have experienced this before, but I have, more times than I like to admit. When you fire a counselor, they instantly become heroes who've been unfairly dealt with. It doesn't matter that they deserved it. It doesn't even matter that everyone in camp would, if asked, agree they should be fired. If the counselors who I've let go stay around too long saying their goodbyes, it always winds up badly for the camp."

"Usually when I fire someone, I arrange to do it on a trip day, when the whole camp will be going out for the day. Just as the trip is about to leave, I call aside the guy or girl who I'm planning to let go, and say I want to talk with him or her. The trip leader has been tipped off and has already assigned someone to cover their campers. That way the departing counselor doesn't have a chance to poison the mood of other counselors or of campers. When they come back from the trip, he's gone. It may sound heartless, and there will be grumbling from his friends on the staff for a few days, but the deed is done. The break is clean and there are rarely serious repercussions."

"Right now, the best we can hope for is a speedy send off after the movie. If the two of them are all packed and ready to go it won't be too bad. I'll start their payroll work now. You should go up to Sr. area and make sure they actually are packing. You might even want to give them a hand."

"Nelson, this is different than the situation you described. We didn't fire them. They chose to quit. They said they were going, and walked out of the office in the middle of a talk. They can't possibly claim an unjust firing."

"That may be the way it happened, but you can bet that's not the way they'll tell it. They'll have no trouble convincing the staff they were fired, and nothing we say will change everyone's minds. No matter what, the important thing now is to get them out of here before their lingering presence becomes a festering sore. I'd like you to go up and move this along as best you can."

I ran up to the Senior Camp. There was nobody there. Their trunks were out, and each one contained a very few items. I called out and there was no answer. I tried the shower house. It was empty. I checked the other Senior cabins, knowing full well they wouldn't be there. There was no doubt in my mind. They were already up in the Rec Hall, spreading the word and saying their goodbyes. I came back to the office to give Nelson the bad news.

"Too bad! It's too late to do anything about it now. If we were bad guys who fired them, we would look like even worse guys if we prevented them from saying goodbye to their friends. This is exactly why I try to say goodbye to counselors when their group or the whole camp is going out on a trip. There's probably no way we'll get them out of here tonight. The best we can hope for is first thing in the morning."

Just then Roland came bursting into the office. "There's trouble brewing in the Rec Hall! Joey and Cozy came in a few minutes ago, and a big group of counselors gathered around them in the back. I went back there and told the counselors to get back with their kids.

They didn't say no, but they didn't exactly rush back either. A few of the older Senior campers were with the counselors in that huddle around Joey and Cozy. I don't like the looks of it. Nelson, you'd better get over there and do something fast." Roland's face was red with anger and frustration. I marveled that he'd been able to control himself during the confrontation in the Rec Hall. It must have been a real struggle for him.

"It's okay, Roland. How long would you say they've been at it?"

"I'd guess about twenty minutes. At first there were only one or two counselors with them on the back bench, but then they gathered more and more counselors over. They had practically the whole staff there at one point. I'm not sure what they were saying. They shut up fast when I got back there with them."

"Okay, Roland, you and Vico go back to the Rec Hall. Vico will fill you in on what's been happening tonight on this end. Vico, even if they are surrounded by other counselors, tell the two of them I want to see them, now!"

By the time we got to the Rec Hall, the gathering Roland described was over. Everything looked entirely normal. Almost all of the counselors were sitting with their campers. On the back bench were just Cozy, Joey, and the other two Unit Leaders talking. I went over and asked them to come out on the porch for a minute so we could talk. They started out with me, and Roland went back to the front of the Rec Hall and took his usual seat with our youngest boys. Once we were out on the porch, I said "Nelson wants to see the two of you in the office."

"I assume that means he has our checks ready, and that's good of him. Tell him we'll be over for the checks as soon as the movie ends. Then we'll finish our packing and get out."

"He said he wants to see the two of you now."

"Is that an order?" Joey asked.

"Yes, I think you should consider it an order."

"Sorry, Vico, if you asked us, we might have gone over now, but we don't work here anymore so we don't take orders from you or Nelson."

I felt the heat rising in the back of my neck. Throughout the summer there had been times I'd been ignored, or avoided or circumvented, but this was the first time I had been met with a straight refusal. There was no doubt in my mind that had Nelson come over and given an order, they would never have challenged his authority this way. I knew they had too much respect for him, apparently, not enough for me. I didn't have much respect for myself at that point.

"Look, boys, why don't you just cooperate. I know you don't give a damn about watching the movie. You're just looking for a fight."

"I don't know about Cozy, but I think this is the best flick we've had this summer, and I intend to see it through to the end, right Cozy?"

"Right."

I don't often get truly angry, but I didn't deserve the kind of flippant treatment they were giving me right now, and I was angry. "Okay! If that's the way you want to play the game you can get out of here right now. You say you don't work here anymore. This is a movie for campers and counselors and you guys are neither. You're just here as troublemakers and trespassers, and you have no right to stay. Go now, get out!"

"Vico, you surprise me. I never thought I'd see you lose your temper. I didn't know you had it in you. Why don't you just relax and watch the movie with us instead of running errands for that bastard. He gives you all the dirty jobs. First you had to fire us and now he sends you over here to boot us out. Think about it. Why isn't he here?"

I did think about it, and did wonder why Nelson sent me over to do the job. The answer is, it really didn't matter. I was here now and I had to deal with the situation.

"I *didn't* fire you. Neither did he. That's exactly what he wants to discuss with you."

"That's right, I forgot. You didn't really fire us, did you? You just said we drank and smoked pot on campus, the one rule in camp that calls for automatic firing. What do you think you were doing there in the office if you weren't firing us?"

Was he right? I didn't think so when I was doing it, but from their eyes I could see his point. I turned away from them without another word. This conversation was not going to lead to anything. Unless Nelson wanted to come over we'd just have to wait for the movie to end. I walked back to the office.

"We won't have long to wait. The movie was about half way through the last reel when I left." Nelson nodded and we waited together, tight-lipped and anxious. We could hear the movie's dialogue from the office porch.

When the movie ended, I expected to see the usual helter-skelter dash back to the bunks that immediately followed most camp movies. Instead, there was an unnatural quiet for a few minutes. Nobody was coming out. After a few breathless minutes of silence, I watched as they emerged quietly from the Rec Hall. Rather than heading toward their cabins they were marching our way, the Senior boys in the lead. Then they started to chant.

"We're all in this together, together, together. We're all in this together, together, together." They repeated it over and over again even as they came to a halt just below the office porch. The little boys, who were in the rear of the procession, looked bewildered. They clearly had no idea what it was all about, but they were happy to be in on it. It was exciting for them, certainly more exciting than going to their cabins to bed. When Nelson stepped out onto the porch the chant petered out. He waited for complete silence, and achieved it in short order.

"Counselors, take your campers back to your bunks. It's late and they should be getting to bed." There was a little laughter and then some semiserious booing from the oldest boys. Nelson waited for quiet. "If any of you counselors want to meet with me after your campers are in bed and the ODs have taken over your cabins, I'll be happy to meet with any or all of you, but you know what your responsibility is now." The counselors with the youngest boys started to count heads and gather their troops together, and headed off. Jeff and his group of Junior Unit campers and counselors followed suit. That still left the Seniors and all of their counselors. Our Senior boys are teenagers, most of whom have been coming to Camp Adventure every summer since they were very little kids. I guessed many of them were starting to feel a conflict of loyalty between the camp they loved and two of their favorite counselors, realizing they had been placed in the middle of a fight they knew little about.

Nelson spoke directly to the campers now, ignoring the counselors for the moment. "You boys should head back to your cabins now. Roland will go up with you and stay with you until your counselors come up. I want lights out in fifteen minutes and no nonsense about it. Your counselors can stay here and talk with us if they like, but the nature of the conversation is private business, and frankly it's not your business."

"It's our business when you fire two of the best counselors in camp! We don't want them fired. We want them to stay."

"I know you want them to stay in camp, Paul, and maybe they will. But there's no way we can hold the conversation that has to be held with you guys here. The conversation between me and Cozy and Joey is private. If they choose to have some of the other counselors stay for the discussion that is their choice, but we won't even start talking until you guys head back up to your area."

Roland took over and the campers went with him toward the Senior area. The counselors, pleased with the compromise that allowed them to stay, encouraged their kids to go along with Roland. I watched as the boys headed toward Senior camp. I admired the response Nelson was able to achieve, but understood that the real challenge was ahead.

"Okay, Cozy, it's your choice now. Do you want the other counselors here while we discuss this or not?" I wasn't sure it was a good idea leaving it up to the two of them. I wasn't sure which way they would decide and I wasn't even sure which would be best for the camp. But I was freshly impressed by Nelson's ability to react calmly under terribly stressful circumstances. The implications of this night and the conversation that was about to take place were potentially devastating for his camp. No matter what resolution was achieved, the campers' letters home tomorrow were bound to cause heartache for Nelson and damage to his camp.

Joey and Cozy elected to have the whole Senior counselor staff as witnesses to the ensuing conference. Nelson looked as though he was glad they made that decision. I couldn't tell if he really was, or was just play acting. I was relieved that the responsibility for running the meeting would be his and not mine. The office wasn't large enough to hold us all comfortably, so we moved into the dining hall. Most of us were sitting in chairs, but Nelson was perched on the corner of one of the dining hall tables, looking out at a ring of grim set faces.

"Joey, you've proved the kids like you and Cozy. I knew that without this display. What else were you trying to accomplish with this high drama you staged?"

"It's really very simple, Nelson. We don't want to be fired. We don't want to leave. We were accused of serious rule-breaking and fired without any chance to defend ourselves against the accusation. Frankly, I figured you'd back down on the firing if you saw the whole camp was with us. That's what I wanted to accomplish and I hope I have."

"That's a pretty blunt statement, Joey, and I'm sure you succeeded in getting the camp on your side. There's only one thing wrong with this scenario. I don't recall firing either one of you and Vico tells me he didn't fire you either. He said you were talking together and that you upped and quit and walked out on him. Now you have me confused. Vico says you quit and now you tell me you don't want to leave. You can't have it both ways, Joey. Which way is it?"

Joey looked first at me and then at Nelson, an exaggerated look of incredulity on his face. His tone was calculated to match his new mask. It was as though I was watching two master actors in a staged confrontation. "You don't call that a firing, what Vico did to us?"

"No, I don't call that a firing" Nelson replied calmly. "You refused to answer his questions and then you quit. Look, Vico's here. If you want to call him a liar here's your chance." Nelson had tossed the ball right back at Joey again. It felt more like I was watching a tennis or ping pong match, the ball being slammed back and forth, with occasional slices and cuts. I kept waiting for one of the combatants to tire of the game and finish off his opponent.

"No, I won't call Vico a liar, but those couple of statements you repeated are far from the whole truth. When we walked into that office, Vico's attitude was that we were guilty. He told us every other counselor had already been questioned and checked out, and he thought none of them did it. He said it had to be us and asked us to admit it. He didn't want an explanation and he certainly didn't expect a denial. He would have been satisfied only with a confession. An admission by us would be a ticket home. I don't admit to things I didn't do. As far as I was concerned, we had no option at all. If that's not a firing I don't know what is. Just for the record Coach, Cozy and I were not smoking or drinking or having sex at the Green House. I have never broken a rule like that in this camp and I never would." The ball was back in Nelson's court. Would he volley it back or slam it down Joey's throat?

"I'll accept that. Just tell me what you were doing during the time period in question and that will be the end of it."

"Why won't you simply trust our word? You hired us to take care of kids. You've known both of us for a long time. Have you ever known us to lie to you? If you can't trust our word that we didn't do it, why should it matter the details of where we were and specifically what we were doing? If we would lie about one thing we would lie about the other. If you don't' believe us, you don't and there is nothing we can do about it. Somebody is lying to you, but it isn't the two of us. You said you've questioned everyone and they all denied involvement. Why should you believe all of them and not believe us?"

"Joey, I don't want to believe you or Cozy would lie to me. That's why you were not fired. If and when I want to fire you or anyone else you can be sure I will do it myself. It sounds to me that when you were questioned by Vico you were just looking for trouble. You didn't give him a chance to believe you when you refused to answer his questions. You got into a huff, walked out on him and said you'd be packing to leave. The truth is you had no intention of just packing and leaving. If you had, you wouldn't have gone to the Rec Hall, generating support. If you really believed you'd been fired, I could forgive your rabble-rousing techniques, but you're too smart for that. You knew perfectly well Vico didn't fire you. You walked out simply to make an issue. Now I have to decide whether or not to fire you. It's something I have to consider carefully, and it won't be as a result of a democratic vote. This is not a democracy. This is a business, my business, and I make the final decisions. The only thing we really have to decide now is whether you and Cozy were serious when you said you were quitting or whether you meant it a few minutes ago when you told us you want to stay in camp."

Nelson was a keen strategist. It was no longer a question of Joey and Cozy being wronged. That wasn't the issue. The only issue was for them to make up their minds whether or not they wanted to stay at camp. I watched the other Senior Camp counselors as their eyes went back and forth, following the serious verbal thrust and parry game.

"If it's really up to us, we'll stay" said Joey. Cozy nodded assent. I knew the instant crisis was over, but the ending was certainly not entirely satisfactory because the big mystery of what happened in the Green House that night remained unsolved. Cozy and Joey were still members of the staff, but who won? The rest of the counselor staff would be the jury and the jury is out. If Joey's motive was a big confrontation with Nelson to prompt a big angry explosion, he had to be disappointed. If, on the other hand, he and Cozy had been the ones in the Green House that night they had succeeded in getting off scot-free, and could congratulate themselves on a successful conclusion.

9

Looking for Solutions for an Unhappy Season

Roland

This is the unhappiest summer I have ever spent in camp. I admit my unhappiness started way back in November. I knew Nelson had decided he needed to have a Head Counselor for the boys instead of doing both jobs himself. Until November I thought I'd have the job. That's when he broke the news that he was planning to hire someone from outside. I had to sit there quietly in his living room while he outlined his reasons for not promoting me to the top spot. He was worried that college students were in turmoil during the school year and it could well boil over into camp this summer. He thought I might not be able to handle the many confrontations which might occur, and besides, he told me he would never find another Waterfront Director as good as me. At least he was right on that score. I agreed to return as Waterfront Director. I tried not to show my hurt, but it was there. I should be the Head Counselor. I have the experience and I'm qualified in every way.

During Christmas vacation, I got a call offering me the job as Head Counselor at Camp Beaverbrook. It sounded mighty tempting, but I had given my word, and I wasn't about to break it after nine summers with Nelson and Camp Adventure. Margie wanted me to take the Beaverbrook job. She was sure Nelson would release me from my contract. "You're ready to take on more responsibility. You're ready for a bigger challenge." She didn't understand. It wasn't a matter of a contract. I had given my word and I would not go back on it now.

Very early in the summer, I began questioning my decision, asking myself whether my unhappiness was because I still resented not being given the Head Counselor job or if it was truly because of what I observed going on. This is my camp as much as Nelson's, and I want it to run the best it can, and I can see and feel this is not happening. The summer ahead seems fraught with peril for Camp Adventure.

I can't figure out how Nelson could ever have picked this guy. It's not that Vico is a bad guy. It's that he doesn't seem to have any strength or backbone. I know he means well and seems to be trying hard. He's not nasty or unpleasant. He just doesn't seem to be entirely with it. I suppose it might have helped him if I was a little more welcoming when he came down and seemed to be trying to make friends. But he didn't seem to realize what a lousy time he picked to socialize. I was breaking my back trying to get the docks set right, and he wanted to make small talk. I'm not quite sure how to put it. The man just seems to lack substance. He can watch things going wrong and they don't seem to register with him. Either he doesn't see it when things are wrong or doesn't realize they *are* wrong. Possibly he sees it, but just doesn't have the guts to do anything about it. Either way, he's no Head Counselor, and we're all going to pay before this camp season is over. I tried to step in a couple of times to correct situations, but the counselors resented it. After all, I wasn't the Head Counselor. Who was I to tell them they weren't doing their jobs right?

But it's not just Vico. The counselors this year are all acting like spoiled brats. They don't realize how good they have it. When I was their age I was in Korea, being shot at day after day. These guys think life is tough if people don't tell them how wonderful they are. My frame of mind isn't helped by those two clods Nelson gave me as assistants this year. Neither one of them is worth a damn at the waterfront. Evan means well. He's just incompetent. I can trust him to watch the kids as they're practicing their strokes, but I can't ever put him in charge of a group or count on him in a key lifeguard post during general swim. They'd run all over him. The most helpful thing he does is bail out the boats in the morning. He's pretty good at raking the beach too.

Bob Weinberg is another story. He's a smart-ass kid who needs a kick in the ass. He's strong enough, so I understand how he could get his lifeguard badge, but I can't figure out how he ever earned his Water Safety Instructor certificate. He apparently got it as part of his phys ed requirement in college. Now he thinks he's an expert and knows everything there is to know about running a waterfront. You can't tell this guy anything! One day Nelson came down to watch while Bob was teaching his class how to do the Dolphin kick. After the class, Nelson showed him how it should have been demonstrated. As soon as Nelson went back on campus Bob returned to teaching it just the way he had been.

I knew big trouble was brewing. I could smell it in the air. I kept seeing little groups of counselors huddled together whispering. They shut up when I walked by. It didn't take long for it to emerge as a brewing rebellion. I warned Nelson it was coming, and that very night there was that awful meeting with their ridiculous demands. Nelson was right to refuse to listen, but when he decided to walk out and indicated he wanted us to follow, I don't think that helped the situation. Neither did it help that Vico stayed there with the counselors when we left the dining hall.

It's never been like this before. The staff is undirected, rebellious, and sloppy. You can see it all over camp. It's obvious when the counselors come down to the waterfront for General Swim and half of them haven't even bothered to change into bathing suits. It drives me a little crazy to watch them huddling in clusters, whispering together, particularly during Free Play when they should be playing and having fun with their campers. If it's obvious to me, I'm sure Nelson sees what I see. I can't figure out why he doesn't do anything about it. The first thing he should do is get rid of Vico. He could take over as Head Counselor again and things would go back to normal pretty fast.

It was a pleasure seeing Nelson finally tear into the staff that first meeting, and letting them know he was unhappy. I guess he did see everything I saw. He was just holding back waiting for Vico to do his job. I'm sure Nelson realizes by now he made a mistake, and that he should have hired me as Head Counselor. Most of the nonsense that's been going on this summer just wouldn't have happened. I'm guessing he's about ready to take over himself and just keep Vico on as window dressing, but I can't figure out why he wants to do that. It's so much harder to work around someone than it is just to do it yourself. Maybe he doesn't want to admit his mistake, even to himself.

No, it has not been a happy summer. That second meeting with the list of demands and then the foolish slowdown were so aggravating. If we have this much turmoil after a little more than a week of camp it's hard to imagine how far it may deteriorate by the fifth or sixth week when even the very best staffs start to gripe. I worry that something truly terrible may happen. I finally went up to Nelson and told him what I thought.

"Nelson, you can't know just how disgruntled the counselors are." He looked at me and gave me that knowing smile.

"I can't know? I can't know how disgruntled they are? The question is whether they have any idea just how unhappy and disgruntled I am. I like that word disgruntled. It fits the situation perfectly. I don't want to sound melodramatic, but we're fighting a little war here. Unfortunately, they seem to have the ammunition, and we're in a holding operation, hoping to get through the rest of the summer without a catastrophe. It would be a mistake to actually let this become an open battle. The camp and the kids will wind up the losers if that happens. I can't afford that. I know you think I should confront them or get rid of Vico or do something dramatic, but I disagree. If it comes to any kind of open hostility this could turn out to be the final summer for Camp Adventure. Just think what the reaction would be among the campers, never mind their parents, if I were to fire ten counselors and replace them with newcomers who haven't got a clue how this camp runs. First of all, I would be hiring them over the phone. That's like a blind date. Who knows what you get? But, even if I got lucky and a few of them were good counselors, there would be one hell of an uproar. I have to think of a way to right this ship without sacrificing the kids' summer."

"I hear what you're saying, and I agree we don't want a major confrontation, but I still don't understand why you don't just fire Vico and take over the job you know so well. I remember you being the one who told me it is easier to do it yourself than to have to patch up the damage being done in your name by someone else.

This seems like that exact situation. The way he plays the game he's always the good guy and you come off as the bastard. Of course, the counselors see right through that. I've heard what they call him. Truly, I think the guy is blind. He just doesn't seem to see what's going on. Yesterday is a good example of what I mean. He was standing at the top of the landing above the waterfront. Just in front of him I saw a counselor punching one of his ten-year-old campers. I saw it from my post on the dock, and somehow he couldn't see it three feet in front of him."

"You're telling me this happened yesterday?"

"Yes, but it would have been worse if I hadn't seen what was going on and shouted for him to stop."

"Why didn't you tell me about it?"

"I'm telling you now. I didn't want to run up to tell you at that moment. I'm not even happy telling you about it now. You might think I'm exaggerating."

"What's to exaggerate? If a counselor is hitting a camper there is no grey area. Either something happened or it didn't, and if you told me it did of course I would believe you. But, confirming your suspicion, Vico didn't tell me about it either and you say it was happening right in front of him. Tell me now who the counselor was and who was the camper? I need to know what went on in case his parents call."

"It was Dick Reback. He was giving Ricky Kramer a bunch of noogies. I saw his arm later. It was all black and blue."

"Jesus, Roland, I wish I'd known about this as soon as it happened! I would have called Reback in here immediately. And I will call him in right after we're through. Has he done this with any other campers?"

"I haven't seen it, but a lot of the kids in his bunk have bruises up near their left shoulders. I did talk to him. I talked to him last night. I told him next time I saw him touch a kid, any kid, I would make sure he was fired. But don't you see, a decent Head Counselor wouldn't have let this happen at all, certainly not right in front of him. They have no respect for him. They figure they can do anything they please if he's in charge. You should get him out of here fast."

"You may be right, and I may have to do just that, but I'm going to try my damndest to avoid it. A lot of what you said was true, and I'm sure most of the counselors consider him inept, but if I fire him, he'll suddenly have people sympathizing with him, and we certainly can do without more negative emotional reactions, for any reason."

"I'm not going to beat a dead horse, and it looks as though you've made up your mind, one final thought and then I'll shut up. The thought is this. If you let him go it will only take a very few days for you to rebuild staff morale and have camp running smoothly again."

"It's too late, Roland. I can't turn the clock back and start the summer all over again. Things have gone too far downhill for that. There are just two things I can do now, and I'm planning on both. First, I plan to hold the lid down on any explosions, avoiding those is the number one priority. Hopefully, we can make it through the rest of the camp season with a minimum of conflict. Second, I want to make a dramatic change in the program for the rest of the summer. You know how I've spoken about the meat and potatoes of camp program versus the lollipops and ice cream approach. I have always favored solid meat and potato programming where we emphasize multiple sports, crafts, swimming, boating, hikes, drama, etc. I've looked down on camps that fill their programs with the lollipops: lots of trips out of camp to fancy beaches, waterslides, amusement parks, shopping malls, and the like — and when their kids are in camp, making every day a party of sorts with novelty events, guest performers, and big food treats. There's no question which is the best long-term kind of program for our kids, but right now I want to dazzle them and keep them so busy with treats there is little time to reflect, discuss or worry about anything that has happened thus far. So, you'll be seeing a lot of lollipops from now on. The counselors will have so few routine days and routine activities they won't have time for complaints. That's my prescription for our sick camp."

10

A Deluge, a Plague, and a Hospital Run

Nelson

We managed to get through Visiting Day, and I think both Joey and Cozy will be with us for the rest of the summer. I am still frustrated we never found out who was so flagrantly breaking rules at the Green House that night, but I think it is best to let it remain a mystery rather than pursue it further. I keep telling myself that, knowing full well it will nag at me all summer.

When I got out of bed in the morning the first thing I did was peek out the window. A light rain was falling and it looked like a dismal day. "Damn it! We haven't had a day of rain all summer, and today, with trips planned for every group in camp, today it has to rain. I quickly reviewed the schedule, and confirmed trips to the White Mountains and Echo Lake for the Senior boys and girls, a trip to Ogunquit for the Juniors, Clark's Bears for the Sophomores, and Storyville for the Freshmen. None of them will be much fun if it keeps raining. I would hate to have to cancel them but if this rain is serious I may not have a choice. That would be a hell of a start to my new lollipop program.

I felt a little better after I shaved and dressed. I headed up to the kitchen. The kitchen lights were on and I could smell the coffee before I went through the swinging doors. I felt better still after my first cup. A call to the weather bureau lightened my mood considerably. The early morning drizzle and fog were to lift, the sky was to clear, and it would turn out to be a beautiful day. The only negative on the horizon were scattered showers here and there. There was a widespread storm headed our way, but it wouldn't reach our area today.

It was still raining as I saw the buses off. I reassured the trip leaders that the skies were due to clear where they were going and the sun would be shining by the time they got to their destinations. I wished I felt as confident as I sounded to them. The whole camp really needs this day out, and I can use a day to relax, maybe even sleep a little, and maybe I'll have time to sort through plans for the final three weeks of the season. The empty camp will give me a chance to recharge my batteries.

By nine-thirty they were gone. Camp was a ghost town. A few kitchen workers, the office girl, my wife Cindy and I are the only ones in camp. Even the Doctor and nurse went out on their own for the day since the infirmary was empty and there was nobody left in camp to get sick. I went down to the house; flopped down in bed and fell asleep. My mind and body both needed it.

Way off in the distance I thought I heard the phone ringing. It rang and rang again. Then it stopped. I felt Cindy come into the room. She sat down on the side of the bed and shook me gently. I was groggy and resisted opening my eyes and lifting my head. She shook me again, not so gently this time. "Nelson you have to get up." I heard her. I forced my eyes open. It took a minute or so before the room came into focus. Cindy handed me a cup of coffee, and propped pillows behind my back. I looked at the clock and couldn't believe it was almost four o'clock. I'd been asleep since ten in the morning. Now I was aware of the beat of hard rain pounding against our bedroom windows.

"That doesn't sound like sunshine out there. Have any of them called in? Do you know the status of all of the trips right now?"

"Roland just called. He's on his way back with a busload of sick kids. He said at least half of them have thrown up and the other half look as though they are about to. He thinks it must be food poisoning."

"Oh my God!" We certainly didn't need this. Are Daisy and Bob back in camp? Have you told them and are they ready?" Without waiting for her answers, I jumped out of bed, ran into the bathroom, splashed cold water on my face, put on my raincoat and was out the door. "So much for the weather forecast."

Rain was cascading from the cabin roofs like a concert of waterfalls. It was a cold and miserable rain. I wished I had put a sweatshirt on under my slicker. Enormous puddles had already formed in the usual low spots. I made my way around the growing puddles and into the infirmary. When I went in, I noted the roof was leaking in the boys' ward just as it had last summer. Too bad we never got to that in the spring. I made a quick count of the beds. Between the ward rooms and the private rooms there were twenty-four cots set up. I wondered if that would be enough. I called George, our reliable handyman, and asked him if we had more cots in storage. He said there were ten, and started bringing them over two at a time. It didn't take him long. The space between the cots was very tight now, but hopefully we had left enough space for Bob and Daisy to get around to check on the kids. I heard the sound of buses laboring up the hill through the muddy road and on their way into camp. The rain was still torrential as I made my way down to greet the first two buses. They were Roland's buses. As the bus doors opened the stench of vomit preceded the first campers and counselors to emerge. Looking at the faces it was hard to tell the sick from the well. They all looked ghastly. Even Roland looked much the worse for the wear.

"Tell me which kids should get to the Infirmary first."

"Just about all of them."

"We can't take sixty kids in the Infirmary, only the sickest." Dr. Bob, Daisy and Cindy had all joined me down by the buses. Together we sorted through the miserably sick boys. Some of them couldn't even stand. We loaded them into cars to take them up the hill to the Infirmary. The others were sent back to their cabins. Surprisingly, none of the counselors appeared to be truly ill, just feeling slightly sick from what was going on in the bus.

The two days that followed were bad, but they could have been a lot worse. The counselor staff, male and female, responded well to the emergency. They really helped with the sick campers. Three of the boys' cabins and two of the girls had been converted into auxiliary ward rooms. These were staffed almost full time by counselors who volunteered. The sickness pattern became clear. Kids got violently ill and stayed that way for about twenty-four hours. Then they were weak and washed out for another twenty-four, and on the third day they were ready to resume regular camp program. Of course, the letters they sent home were descriptive and frightening to the parents. Cindy and I had a nonstop influx of parent phone calls to field. Dr. Bob had assured me it could not have been food poisoning, and that it was some sort of virus that was floating through camp. That was why those infirmary beds kept being refilled, as the virus moved through camp. First it had hit the younger campers and then progressed from group to group. As it went up through the various age groups the percentage of kids becoming very ill became progressively smaller with each new batch. This proved the doctor's contention. The exposure in camp was there early and some of the older campers had built up antibodies sufficient to fight it off. The best guess was that Visiting Day was the guilty party. The virus had come in with the parents of one or more of our youngest campers, probably the parents of a boy and a girl since both camps were affected by it. On doctor's orders, and on my own inclination, I stayed away from the infirmary. I simply could not afford to be sick.

While the viral plague was cutting its swath through camp, nature was doing its best to capture our attention. The storm scene reminded me of a movie I saw years ago which took place during the monsoon season in Southeast Asia. The wind and rain were heavy and steady. Every so often there would be a brief respite and I was encouraged to think maybe it was going to end. Then it would sweep back in with a vengeance. Not only was the weather curtailing anything resembling normal activities, but it was also creating a variety of serious physical problems to add to our health issues in camp.

The water level in the lake rose higher than I had ever seen it, even during the Spring thaw when the runoff of melting snow from the hills refilled the lake every year. The first concern was that if the water rose sufficiently, our wooden swim docks would float off their iron piers and drift all over the lake. Our initial effort to solve this problem was to pile cement blocks on the docks themselves to weigh them down. This helped for a day or so, but it was not a solution. The water kept rising, and the docks started floating off the iron posts which held them in place. All we could do then was tie inflated balls with plenty of rope to the tops of the supporting poles on which the docks would have to be resettled when the water went down. The second day of heavy rain, we also had to remove all of our row boats and canoes from the beach area to higher ground. Roland and his staff did yeoman work, with the willing help of lots of counselors from both the boys' and girls' side. As difficult as the situation was, it was a relief to me to see them all working together like that. It seemed so good for morale that it might just save our season.

By the third day of our incredible deluge, the bridge that was our primary link to the outside world was threatened. The water had risen so high it was lapping at the bottom of the wooden planks. The water level seemed to be rising by the hour, and I realized that even if the rain stopped this minute the bridge might still be inundated, cutting us off from potential supplies. In fact, food supplies were fast becoming another major concern. I spent hours on the phone with our regular suppliers pleading for them to send our food deliveries while it was still possible for them to get through. I listened to the news reports on the radio and learned that transportation was disrupted by the weather throughout the Northeast. Trucks were broken down along the highways, and motorists were urged to stay off the roads altogether. There were reports of cars abandoned here and there, each one creating a further obstacle for the trucks we needed to get to camp.

Meanwhile, we had our epidemic to deal with. Those who had been ill initially had all recovered, when a second wave of illness hit, and then a third. The medical staff was exhausted. Never before had I seen Daisy lose her usual composure. I sat with her for an hour, early in the morning of the fourth day while she lamented the constant stench in the infirmary, the mopping, the sheet washing and the constant sounds of retching from both wards. As the virus traveled from group to group, a few counselors were now also in the infirmary lying next to their campers. It was becoming more and more difficult to clean up. The camp supply of disinfectant had run out. Mops were being used by counselors who had never held a mop before. The mops themselves stunk from not being cleaned sufficiently between usages. The tale of woe went on and on. The battle looked to her like it would never end. There was nothing new I could suggest to Daisy, but I think she felt better just being able to talk about it.

Against the horrendous backdrop of the Infirmary, throughout the rest of camp I could sense an air of expectancy and excitement. The physical forces of nature were presenting all of us with a sense of challenge and the reality of risk. For a good many of our campers, and counselors too, the notion that we might be cut off from civilization held a certain romantic appeal. Without exception, our campers and almost all of our counselors have grown up in affluent suburban neighborhoods and had only ever known the benefits of the age of plenty. This fight against the forces of nature had a certain quixotic appeal. Balanced against the romantic view was the reality and discomfort of being constantly wet and cold. Water was getting into the cabins through leaking roofs and walls and even under doorways. Beds that remained completely dry were rare and everyone's clothes were soggy.

I was aware, as none of the campers and few of the staff were, that if the rain continued unabated, the major threats still lay ahead. I had consulted with Bob, the chef, and he assured me the threat of running out of food was very real, but we could survive for a few days. He reported our supplies of meat and dairy were completely depleted. The cache of fresh fruits and vegetables was pathetically low. Even the emergency, ready-to-heat and serve meals, had already been tapped. We still had an adequate supply of canned fruits and selected vegetables and sauces. Fortunately, we also still had a reasonable hoard of pasta, but that's our only surplus item. Bob assured me that with careful husbanding we wouldn't be in serious danger of starvation for quite a while, and well before then supplies should be rolling in. But concepts like good nutrition and well-balanced meals were already memories. Satisfying meals were unlikely until new goods were able to get through.

Despite the warnings of danger on the roads, as long as the bridge was still traversable, I decided to send George out in our pickup truck to scour the countryside and buy out the stock of every general store he found still open. Two of our healthy counselors would do the same in their own cars. I truly hoped they would all return safely and laden down with food. When they returned late in the day, the results were sadly predictable. The local stores had small supplies left, and were saving most of their scarce goods for their regular customers. Our guys bought whatever they could, and returned to camp. One of the counselor cars broke down, just on the far side of the bridge. A team of counselors and Senior boys waded through a foot of water which now covered the bridge, and carried the food from his car up to the kitchen.

When the electricity went out, it created multiple potential problems for us, but I was spared the concern that I would normally have had for all of the food that might spoil in or refrigerators and freezers. Now there is nothing in them to protect. In our current plight, I worried most about the plumbing, our most vital utility. Our antique plumbing system is vulnerable in two ways. First, is the threat to our critical drinking water supply. Unfortunately, our wells, even the artesian one, were ultimately dependent on distribution of water through camp. The distribution relies upon two pumps of indeterminate age. The newer of the two, the electric one, was put out of business as soon as the camp electricity failed. Our gas pump is in a pump house, set about eight or ten feet above the normal water level of our lake. If the water level reaches the pumps we'll be in serious trouble. Thank God for the two big water storage tanks under the dining hall. We'd have to ration it, but hopefully it wouldn't run out in a hurry.

The second threat caused by the loss of electricity was to our plumbing system. Without water being pumped to supply the toilets, we will have to start filling waste baskets with lake water, and using that to flush toilets rather than using precious drinking water.

Our sewage is also threatened by the sheer volume of water falling from the sky. Under normal conditions our sewage is well handled by a system of septic tanks and dry wells scattered through camp. We have forty-three installations all together. The very diversity and dispersion of the system offers some protection, so it seems unlikely that they'd all fail, no matter what. But if the rain continues beyond any reasonable expectation, the ground can become so saturated as to be incapable of accepting any wastes. If that ever happens, the whole system will back up and every toilet in camp will be permanently blocked.

I knew there was still time before I had to worry about worst case scenarios, but I couldn't stop my mind from working. Happily, the camp's main buildings are situated on the highest point in camp. If worse came to worst we could temporarily house everyone in camp in the Rec Hall to survive a short-term crisis. The toilets in the rec hall and dining hall, both situated on the highest point in camp, would function long after the ones in lower parts of the camp quit. The gas ranges in the kitchen weren't in danger, since they are supplied with bottled gas from our enormous propane tanks behind the dining hall. The tanks were three-quarters full. We had enough gas to heat and serve our limited cooking needs. Nobody was in danger of starving anytime soon. Our first obligation was to keep our kids safe, healthy, and fed.

I was exhausted from working long hours planning for every possible contingency, but I felt exhilarated by the challenges. We were now in a situation where everyone had to work together Instead of being at odds. Very early in our storm, I worked with Roland and the counselors to secure the docks as best we could, and to carry boats up to higher ground. I was no longer a Camp Director. I felt like a General of a besieged small country, working to stave off the advancing enemy! The hours we must have been at it went unnoticed, as did the fact that we were working in terrible conditions out of doors. Physical labor left me weary, but somehow content. Solving physical problems as they emerged from hour to hour gave me a sense of accomplishment and satisfaction. These were clean uncomplicated challenges, totally unlike the nastiness of the staff problems that had been grinding me down since the start of the season.

Everybody was pitching in. We all seemed to relish not only meeting the challenges, but doing it together. Vico was hauling and lugging with the best of them. There was no hesitation on his part. He just tackled whatever needed to be done. Roland, more than anyone, delighted in the challenging physical labor. The enormous physical strength of the man was amazing to me, and to everyone else who saw him at work. I saw my Unit Leaders, each assuming command in their areas and doing vital jobs, keeping their heads and leading in every sense of the word.

Sitting in my office late that night, I found myself chuckling, and realized that with everything that was so wrong I was feeling relatively content. I laughed at myself, noting how ironic it was that these terrible days were the happiest of my summer. Things were going to be all right after all. The rain would stop sometime, and when it did, our staff would be welded together by the brotherhood of shared labor. We would have looked danger in the face and beaten it back. Yes, sir, this storm was going to save our summer. This was an experience every one of us will remember for the rest of our lives. They'd never betray me after this.

I was startled when the phone rang, waking me from my happy ruminations. Earlier in the day we had been flooded with calls from anxious parents, looking for assurance that their children were safe and sound. And then the phone stopped ringing for hours and I assumed it was no longer functioning.

"Yes, Mrs. Greenstein, Phillip is fine...His stomach is better. He's due out of the infirmary today. He's probably back in his own cabin by now, sound asleep....yes, it is still raining here, hard as ever...no, no...we're fine....yes, we have plenty of food. We can hold out for another four days and longer if we have to...I'll check on him myself and I'll tell him you called.....No, I don't think I should get him to the phone now. He's probably fast sleep....yes, I know it was out of order earlier...I'm surprised you got through now. Don't worry if it goes out again. Phillip will be fine. There's nothing to worry about. Be assured, I'll get back to you if anything is wrong with Phillip." I set the receiver down gently, sat back and propped my feet up, happy to indulge myself in pleasant thoughts.

The buzz of the intercom put a speedy end to my reverie. It was Daisy on the other end. "Nelson, we have an emergency! It's Liz Aronson. She's coughing non-stop and has trouble breathing between coughs. Dr. Bob says we have to get her to the hospital! We have nothing here that can help her."

I dialed the hospital's emergency number. I had dial tone on my end, but nothing happened after I dialed. I tried again. Their line was dead. We'd have to get Liz there no matter what. Daisy sounded frightened, and that alone was incredible to me. Daisy had been with us right from the start and I'd never seen or heard her lose her composure. Her crisp English voice, which always sounded so proper and well-modulated, had a clear note of panic. Liz's condition must be very serious. I grabbed my raincoat and ran to the Infirmary. When I got there, I immediately saw Liz on the front bench, Daisy and Dr. Bob hovered on either side of her. The sounds of her rasping, hacking cough reached me as soon as I opened the door. She had a deathly pallor, which was worrisome and frightening to see on a nine-year-old child. Dr. Bob was preparing to cover Liz's head with a big paper bag from the market.

"She's hyperventilating, this should help some. Daisy tells me she's been coughing like this for at least a half hour. I first thought she might have something lodged in her throat, but that's not it. We've tried antihistamines, but they don't seem to have an effect. If we get her to the hospital, they'll spray her throat with codeine and that should control it. Can you get a car started?" He put the bag slowly over her head, and it seemed to slow the cough down a little, or was I imagining that it did?

"My car is running now, down in the lot. I would have driven right up here but I was afraid I might get stuck in the mud on the way. Help me get her down to the car, and I'll drive her in. Bob, you'd better stay here, another emergency might come up here."

"No, I'm coming with you. You'll have trouble enough just driving in this weather. And Liz might need help along the way." Visions of an emergency tracheotomy came to mind, and that was the end of the discussion. The two of us would go with her. I hated doing this, leaving camp; with so much going on. And taking the doctor too. Bob knows the score as well as I do. He wouldn't have insisted on coming if he didn't think it was essential. Liz was gasping, but it sounded weaker. Bob had the paper bag in his hands now, ready to put it over her head again if her cough got worse. Between her gasps her face showed terror. I recalled one time I couldn't catch my breath and how scary that was, and this poor girl had been at this for more than half an hour.

Visibility was terrible as the car slogged its way laboriously through the muddy trenches in the camp road. My God, what if we can't even get out of here and to the highway?" I hadn't left camp since the start of the storm, but the reports of the roads and driving conditions I had heard hours earlier were far from reassuring. Whatever they were, we had to get through.

As we were battling the road, I could hear Bob talking quietly to Liz in the back seat. He was very matter of fact, asking about her bunk, her activities, and about things at home, anything to turn her mind away from terror. She couldn't answer his questions. She was too busy coughing and gasping, but she heard them and they seemed to distract her. When we made it to the bridge, water was already coming up over the top, but it was still low enough to drive. I could still see the wooden planks below the water, and just hoped that we could cross safely. Though the water was up to the rocker panels, the planks on the bridge felt amazingly solid after the squishy muddy camp road. I wondered how high the water would be on the way back, whether we'd be able to use the bridge at all. If not, we would have to swim back to camp!

The ride to the hospital normally takes about fifteen minutes. The road is a good one, wide, newly resurfaced and usually with very light traffic. On this night I couldn't guess how long it would take. The ride was nightmarish. The rain came down in blinding sheets and there was no external lighting anywhere to help keep the road visible. There were occasional widely spaced farmhouses along the way, but I couldn't see any of them. Not a light was showing anywhere. My only navigation asset was the white line in the middle of the road. I rode that white line all the way! It was our lifeline and my compass, as well as being the only visible contact with reality in an otherwise surreal ride. Very quickly I became aware of a whole new set of obstacles I had never even noticed before. There were a number of long, very steep hills between our camp road and the town. I came to dread every hill. Climbing up the steep incline was fine, but every time we went down, I could never tell until we reached bottom how deep the water would be. Each time we hit the standing water, my only option was to splash through and hope. Since we were the only car on the road, if we stalled we couldn't count on help coming along any time soon. Another unexpected hazard were the several cars which had been abandoned along the side of the road. I had to swerve at the last minute a few times to avoid crashing into the darkened hulks.

Somewhere along the way I entertained the illusion I was the Captain of a small boat sailing through a storm in unchartered seas.

Perhaps that illusion helped me keep my mind off the distressing sounds coming from the back seat. Although the sounds were distressing, it was reassuring to hear any kind of sound coming from Liz. My constant worry through the ride was that we might not make it in time, that Liz might die before I could get us there! As long those terrible sounds continued, we had hope. I thank God that Dr. Bob insisted on coming along with me. Just concentrating on the road was challenge enough. I was happy to leave Liz in Bob's care in the back seat. I admired his coolness under fire. He was back there gabbing away as though they were on the way to a movie or a ballgame. He never mentioned her coughing and gasping for breath, and kept asking her mundane questions. He didn't actually anticipate answers, her cough was too constant for that. He kept a monologue going and she seemed somewhat calmer, lulled by his steady voice. I think I was too. I was impressed by how well he was handling such a potentially disastrous situation. He might not be the most diplomatic doctor we ever had at camp, or the one with the best bedside manner in the infirmary. He was often gruff and impatient with kids who had minor complaints. But today, he became a giant in my eyes.

The car was straining. We had been climbing uphill for some time, and we had to be close to the town. The town was built along the top ridge of a small mountain and there is a long uphill stretch just before you get there. There it is I can see it! Thank God we made it in time! The hospital was like a beacon of light. All around us the town was dark, everything except the hospital. Their emergency generator was doing its job. Things looked remarkably normal as we pulled into the Emergency Room lot.

Wow, they are good. As soon as they heard our bell, the door opened, they had her on a gurney and slapped an oxygen mask on her face. She was hooked up to an IV and rolled into an examining room. Bob was talking to Dr. Clarke, filling him in on Liz's condition. Dr. Clarke looked rumpled and tired. He had obviously been in the hospital for days without a break. Liz was lying more peacefully now on an examination table. I stood next to her and she clutched my hand, looking up at me with trusting eyes. I've known Liz and she's known me almost all of her life. Her dad, Harry, and I were childhood friends, and we had maintained that friendship through the years. Obviously, I care about all of our campers, but Liz was not just another camper to me. She was the child of one of my closest lifelong friends, and the thought of possibly losing her was devastating to me.

After about a half hour, they removed the oxygen mask. Her breathing was uneven, and still coming in gasps. She' was still coughing but with lengthening time in between each new cough. She was very brave as Dr. Clarke gave her a shot. She had been brave all night. She gagged a little and was on the verge of tears as he sprayed what I later learned was codeine, into her throat. That spray was like a miracle. Almost at once the coughing ended and she seemed to be breathing normally. The crisis had passed.

"Liz, I have to call your parents and let them know you're here. I don't know if I'll get through on the phone, but I need to try. They need to know what happened and what a brave girl you are. I'll be back in a few minutes. Dr. Bob will stay here with you." She reluctantly let go of my hand, and Bob started talking to her in that easy way of his.

I started out of the exam room. My legs felt weak and I was a little dizzy. I don't know how much later it was when I woke up lying on a gurney just outside the exam room where I had left Liz. Dr. Bob was holding smelling salts under my nose, and suddenly I was very much awake.

"I'm all right. It must have been the smell in there. Hospitals do that to me sometimes." I felt a little foolish. Suddenly I had gone from protector to patient.

"It wasn't the smell, Nelson. It was the relief from the terrible tension of that ride. I don't know how you did it. I looked out the window while you were driving and couldn't see a thing."

"Where's Doctor Clarke now? I want to hear the official diagnosis so I can call her parents and report accurately." He appeared at that moment, as though on signal.

"Well, good to see you're awake now. How do you feel?"

"I feel fine. I guess I must have fainted. I'm OK. Can you tell us what caused Liz's problem? She had no hint of anything wrong until today and then suddenly she appeared in misery. I want to call her parents."

"It's a mystery to me. I don't know what to tell you. There is no reasonable explanation for some things. A healthy young girl like her, it doesn't make sense. Maybe it was all psychological. The Demerol quieted the cough and the codeine knocked it out completely. If I saw her right now for the first time I would never know anything was wrong. She looks that good; but, she had better stay here at least for a day or two. There might be a recurrence and we want to be in a position to do whatever needs to be done."

"Do you think she's in any real danger now?"

"No. If the same symptoms recur, we will knock it right out the same way. I hope you can reach her parents. With this storm she may be here for more than a day or two. Her parents should know about it. Of course, the phone system has been erratic, and you might not be able to get through. If you can't reach them tonight, I'll keep trying. Try not to worry. You can leave her to us."

Doctor Clarke smiled. "You must have plenty to worry about back at camp. I don't imagine you or her counselor or anyone from camp will be able to get back through this storm for a visit in the next few days. We have full staff on and some wonderful young nurses who will help comfort her."

As I picked up the phone, I pondered what I should tell Harry or his wife Sarah about Liz's condition. It made the most sense to just give the facts, including that it would be crazy for them to try to drive from New York to visit her until the storm abates. The issue became moot when I discovered that, at least for the moment, there was no viable phone service. It might be hours or even days before it is restored. I decided I could try just as well from camp. Maybe I'd get lucky and get a call through.

I felt terrible leaving that frightened little girl alone in the hospital without a familiar face, but I just had to get back to camp. God knows what's happening there. I looked in on her. She seemed to be breathing easily and was sound asleep. I didn't wake her just to say goodbye. That might have made me feel better, but it wouldn't do anything for her. No matter what, I knew she'd be frightened and feel deserted when she finally woke up. There was nothing I could do about that.

"Okay, Bob, let's go." We climbed into the car, both dreading the ride back to camp. Surprisingly, with the uncertainty about Liz removed from the equation, much of the nightmare aspect of the previous ride was mitigated. In addition, I had the reassurance of extra help now that Bob was available. He sat in the front seat next to me, and provided a lookout for hazards on the side of the road, while I continued riding the white line. The biggest hurdle we faced was at the bottom of the very long steep hill that led down from the town. I had already determined that when we reached the water accumulated at the bottom of the hill I would just gun my engine and plow through, and that's what I did. We got through, and I knew that was the deepest puddle we would have to face on the way home. I was confident now that we would make it back.

As we entered the dirt road leading into camp, we quickly discovered that the road had become a quagmire, and we wouldn't get far before we got bogged down completely. As soon as possible, I pulled off the road onto a field on the right side that we had always referred to as the hay field, no matter what was being grown there. When we climbed out of the car, we stayed on the field and off the road as long as possible to avoid having to walk in the mire the road had become. Fortunately, we were able to stay on relatively solid ground until a few yards shy of the bridge. As soon as we stepped off the hay field and back onto the road, we were wallowing up to our knees in water. A few struggling yards later, the water had risen up to our chests just as I felt the first wooden planks beneath my feet. The water was icy cold and chilled me to the bone. We had to tread very carefully step by step to avoid walking right off the side of the bridge. The water, which was now chest high, was a swirling, raging torrent threatening to sweep us away. My clothes felt like icy sponges, soaking up water and freezing my limbs. Somehow, I don't know how, we made it across the bridge.

As we stepped off the bridge and back onto the road which sloped uphill toward camp, I could feel the muddy ooze underfoot. For a minute, I felt like Moses crossing the Red Sea. While the water hadn't exactly parted for us, we had made it across and were thankful to be on the other side. I could feel the water retreating from around us as we plodded along. And then we were no longer walking in water! and my legs felt a renewed surge of strength even as we continued upward through the muck.

Bob and I looked toward one another and burst into a brief nervous laugh when we looked down and realized we had been holding hands for dear life as we made it across the perilous bridge.

We were now out of the water, but now the cold wind hit us with a frontal assault. Ahead, all I could see was the all-encompassing blackness of night. I wondered if that meant we had lost electricity or hopefully that the entire camp was asleep and the night lights were too dim to reach us. Probably wishful thinking. I pressed the stem on my watch, which showed twenty past two. Sooner or later we would lose our electricity. It now looked as though we had.

I heard a car door slam. The beam of a flashlight was pointed our way from further up the hill. I called out but whoever it was couldn't hear me yet. Happily, someone had enough concern for us to have positioned someone to welcome us back to camp. "Lord knows," I whispered, "we are tired enough to need an escort, and better yet, a ride back onto the campus."

As we got closer, I heard Tubby Brown's voice. "Nelson is that you?"

"Yes, Tubby, it's Dr. Bob and me, back from the hospital."

The car felt warm after the water and cold. In the dim overhead light, I could see Bob's clothes were caked in mud and slime — and mine too.

"Thank you, Tubby. You don't know how good this feels. Was

this your idea? or did Vico or Roland ask you to do it?" I didn't give him a chance to respond. It really didn't matter whose idea it was. What mattered was that someone cared. Tubby quickly dispelled that illusion.

"There's a big problem, and I was told to bring you to the dining hall as soon as you got back. "Are you serious? What's up, Tubby? It's very late and we're both exhausted. I don't want to play guessing games. Tell me what's happening. Whatever it is it can't be worse than what I can imagine."

"I'm really sorry, but I was told to just bring you up there and not to answer questions. I'm not even sure what it is, just some emergency."

11

The Takeover

Nelson

As the car churned slowly up the hill toward the dining hall, my mind filled with a variety of possible disasters. It would have to be something truly extreme to account for Tubby's reluctance to talk. The worst would, of course be news of a death. Could Liz's acute spell actually be a symptom of something running through camp? But if it was that, why the dining hall rather than the Infirmary? Maybe that was the only place unlikely to have anybody walking in before dawn.

Whatever I imagined; whatever horrible visions had gone through my mind I was completely dumbfounded by the scene that awaited me as we entered the dining hall. Light from candles flickered here and there. I saw a sea of faces. I knew all those faces so well. The entire boys' staff was sitting at tables near the entrance. My eyes scanned the dimly lit room looking for missing faces. The only one obviously missing was Roland. They all sat very quiet and looked uniformly grim. Cozy was the only one standing. Though it seemed astonishingly unlikely at such a time, I instinctively knew what it was about. My first inclination was to laugh, I was so relieved. This was followed by incredulity, and then by both anger and despair. Oh, no! Not more of this. The unreality, the craziness of the picture, was simply astonishing to me. It seemed unbelievable after all we have been through together the past few days, after the teamwork that had been demonstrated, that here they were, obviously politicking again. After I fully absorbed the scene, I recognized that my anger was actually a relief after the hours of tension and fatigue I had just been through. It was almost a pleasure to allow myself a few moments of unadulterated rage. There's no question in my mind who was the guiding light behind this current abomination.

"Say your piece Cozy, and let's go to bed. It's been a very long day and a very difficult night."

"I'll say my piece, but it will probably be quite a while before any of us get to bed. How long it takes will depend more on you than on any of us." He stopped, apparently waiting for a reaction from me. Instead of saying anything I just gave my weary body a bit of relief by plopping down on the edge of the nearest table and waiting. I could feel my body slowly defrosting, as the mud and slime dripped from my clothes onto the floor, forming a small lake under my chair. I could sense a smile on my face. I'm not sure why. Maybe it was relief from tension or maybe just at the unreality of the current situation. The scene had elements of a farce, but I knew it was no farce to the counselors and that I would have to respond. I hesitated, concerned that in my current mood I might say something I would later regret.

"Nelson," Cozy began, "I'm sure you know this has not been a happy staff this summer. Some of us have known you for a long time, and we're not sure what has happened this summer. But we're convinced you're not yourself. You're not the guy we know who has always been fair and reasonable and always ready to help and to do anything for anybody who needs help. That hasn't been you this summer. We think something has made you a different person this summer, someone who is at times unreasonable, irascible, and totally unpredictable. This isn't good for any of us and it is definitely not good for the campers. Even a lot of the older boys have spoken to us about it. For the good of the camp, we propose that you retire for the next few weeks, and let Vico take charge. Let him run the program. Roland can help him and we'll help. We're all here for the camp and the campers, and we'll do everything in our power to help Vico run this camp the way it should be run, the way you have always run it in the past.

It took a while for me to grasp what he was saying. It seemed inconceivable. Was he saying that I had lost it? That I was crazy? Incompetent? The nerve of him! It had to be Joey. Cozy would never come up with anything like that on his own. So, they're going to replace me as director, are they? We'll see about that.

"Thanks for your opinion, Cozy." I chuckled which wasn't easy in my current physical condition. "I'm not sure when and where you got your psychiatric degree, but I appreciate your professional advice. I'll take it under advisement, but for now I'm very tired and I'm going to bed."

It wasn't easy, but I lifted myself off the table, nearly slipping on the icy pool on the floor below me, righted myself without falling, and started toward the door. It was a calculated bluff, of course. What can they do if I just walk out? Obviously, I'd caught my audience by surprise. They expected me to rant and rave or at least start arguing with Cozy. I'd thrown off their script.

I looked back and saw Vico, sitting at a table in the rear, smiling and nodding his head up and down. He was in my corner. He could see I had just thrown the conspirators for a loss. Cozy was momentarily speechless. Surprisingly, Joey Katz was also sitting in the back, next to Vico. His face showed no emotion, but I could see he was not thrown for a loss by my tactic. He recognized it as a performance. Joey was the smartest quarterback I ever had on my team because his mind was so agile and so quick to come up with alternative courses of action. I was not sure what the original plan had been, but I could see Joey was about to step up and take charge. He stepped forward.

"It's no joke, Nelson! This is serious business. Cozy was pretty kind in his little speech. What he didn't say is that the whole staff is worn out from your badgering and tired of your constant anger. We appreciate how difficult this weather emergency is for the camp, but even though all of us have been trying our best to work with you for the sake of the camp and the kids, we have all been feeling harassed by you. The fact is, Nelson, we feel we can't ever satisfy you and we're simply not going to try any longer. We really can't work for you any longer. If you don't resign or agree to a leave of absence before this meeting is over, if you just walk out the door, you may find you are all alone here tomorrow morning when you come back in that door. We are all together on this. If you don't agree, it is our intention to drive out of here tonight. Bad as the weather is, we won't even wait for daylight. If you and the Doc managed to drive to and from town it means we can get out of here too. You have our promise. If you leave here now with no satisfactory resolution of this issue, you'll be all alone here in the morning."

Joey's harangue acted like a shot of adrenalin for me. Suddenly the fatigue and strain of the past hours fell away. I recognized I would have to answer and answer powerfully. This was not a time for kid gloves. This was a time to bring them back to reality.

"Joey, you're a smart kid, but maybe not as smart as you think. You've got your mind made up; and you've got a lot of people thinking your way, but just listen to me now. Listen and think about what I'm saying. Don't close your minds. You and everybody else here saw Dr. Bob and me come in. You saw us half frozen, dripping wet, covered in mud and slush. Common decency would have prompted someone to ask if we were all right, or if there was anything you could do for us to warm us up or make us more comfortable. But common decency seems to be absent here tonight. We left here last night at about ten thirty and it's now close to three in the morning. I'm sure you've all heard where we went and why. When we left here five hours ago, we had Liz Aronson with us in the car, not sure whether she would live long enough for us to get her to the hospital! Again, I am astonished that nobody has had the decency or at least the curiosity to ask if she is all right. Nobody asked how she is. Can this hatred you have expressed tonight have overridden the sense of decency I know you all have? I never would have believed it of any of you. I thought each and every one of you was truly a decent human being."

"Let me tell you about Liz Aronson. The roads were treacherous tonight and the ride was scary. Logic might have dictated that we avoid those terrible roads, that we not attempt to get to the hospital, that we treat her in the Infirmary, doing everything we can for her there, hoping it would be enough. But I couldn't do that. Dr. Bob told me she needed to get to the hospital. She was my child and she was my responsibility. I had to get her there. I suffered with her and worried with her, we both did. I held her hand while they worked on her. She held my hand and felt safe when she knew I was by her side. Thank God the treatments they used allowed her to breathe freely and her crisis appears to be over, at least for now. She has to stay at the hospital just in case, but I had to get back to camp because the camp is filled with my children, children I am responsible for. I had to get back in case there was some emergency with one of our campers or with one of *you*. You're all my children when you're in danger, even you guys. I remember trips to the hospital with some of you. Tubby, you remember, and you, Sam. I remember an emergency trip with you. Neither of your medical crises was life and death; nothing dramatic like tonight, but I was worried enough that one of my kids was hurt and I had to be there for you. I was the one you trusted, the one your parents trusted when they turned you over to me for the summer. Remember, I'm the one our current campers' parents entrusted with their children, not any of you. When Tubby met us tonight and told us there was an emergency my first thought was that maybe Liz's symptoms were caused by some contagious illness and that one or more of you caught it and might even be dying. That's why I was so relieved that I chuckled when I saw what was going on in here. I was just so relieved it wasn't one of the truly catastrophic events I had imagined."

I paused to catch my breath, and looked around the room. Many of them avoided my eyes. Some look ashamed and embarrassed by their own behavior. I was reaching them. I wasn't talking to Joey Katz. I was speaking to each of them and it was clear I was reaching them. But I knew I had to do more than reach them. I had to convince them to abandon the course of action they had obviously decided on while I was conveniently out of the way on our hospital run. I think I had most of them, and probably should have stopped at that point, but I couldn't help myself. My pent-up emotions came spilling out.

"Which one of you wants to play God? Which one of you wants

to take full responsibility for a child's life? And which one of you feels you have the experience and knowledge to take charge of this wonderful camp and the lives of the two hundred fifty of us who live here at a time when the forces of nature have presented a challenge to our very survival? I ask you to look into your heart and see what is there. Is this something you actually want to do or is it just an exciting game? If it's just a game you picked a hell of a bad time to play it."

"Where are the kids in this plan ? Are they there at all? Is it about the kids or the camp? If you'd thought about it, I doubt you would have tried to pull a stunt like this at a time like this. I hate to say it, but you're acting like a bunch of spoiled kids. I have a feeling I know where this started. It has nothing at all to do with me changing this summer, of me being more demanding. No, I think the germination of tonight's gathering started weeks ago when some of you were all worked up about the camp rules on socializing. Are you seriously ready to take over the responsibility of running a camp because you want more time to socialize with your girlfriends? I hate to think it's that. I want to think better of you than that. I want to think this is not just a matter of all of you wanting instant gratification."

"You talk about firing me as Director. Or was I just to "retire" for the summer? I think that was the euphemism you came up with. Who endowed any of you with the right to fire me? You have no such right. You are contemplating a criminal act. Could I go to your house and tell your father to get out and assert "It's my house now?" Of course, I couldn't do that. I would have no such right any more than you have the right you are claiming, the right to fire me. It comes down to a single criminal act being proposed. I'd like you all to think about it. I would like you to be aware of criminal and civil liability if you take such an action.

"It's been a very long night and we're all tired. We can talk some more tomorrow. In the meantime, I bid you all goodnight." I picked up my flashlight and again rose and turned toward the door.

Some of the boys had started getting their things together, and were planning to follow me out the door, when Joey jumped up to renew the fray. "Thanks, Nelson, that was truly an inspiring talk. You had me spellbound and I'm sure you had many of the guys convinced, but nothing you said really changes a thing. We all understand that some of what you said was true, and we can appreciate your history here, your hard work, and how much you have done for the camp. To be fair, we have listened to you, but you have not listened to us at all. When we started to talk, your response was to cut us off dead, short circuit the meeting and end the discussion, and it almost worked. We know you're tired. We're all tired. I can only guess what you have been through tonight, but I ask you to sit back down for just a few more minutes to hear what we have to say and why we are making such an extreme proposal."

"You have questioned our motives. But I want you to think about your motives. You spoke about loving Liz Aronson tonight and that you love us all. I don't believe that, not for a minute. I do believe you care about her and you would care about any kid who was hurt or sick or in danger. We get that. It's your job to care. It's your business to care. I believe you feel responsible for us and certainly you do for the campers. I don't like to sound callous but what you love about these kids is the dollars their parents fork over for them to be here. Forgive me for even bringing that up. To us that's not the point at all. Whether you love the kids or not is not what this meeting is about. This meeting came about because of your many actions this summer."

"Do you think this is fun and games for me, some sort of an ego trip when I stand up to you and say we can't work under you any longer? That's all we're saying. We're not pointing a gun at you and saying get out. We're not stealing your camp. We're just telling you if you want to keep running the camp the rest of this summer, you'll be running it without our help and support. This is a free country. We don't have to stay and work for you if we don't want to. You are free to run the camp any way you want, but you will do it without us. We had a meeting and took a vote. That's what we decided. It was unanimous. Just give us your answer. Either you step down and allow Vico to run the camp with our help or we leave. It's as simple as that."

I hated to sit back down, knowing it would be viewed as an admission of weakness, but I felt weak and very tired. I knew I had lost much of the ground I had won with the group before Joey's latest salvo. Mixed messages were battling in my brain. Could I summon up another burst of energy to try to win them over again? Perhaps I could. But if I did, this could go on and on, back and forth for what's left of the night. I didn't think I had the strength to face that prospect. They had me in a bind. On the one hand, no matter what they say here tonight they won't all quit. On the other hand, even if it's just a big group of counselors who leave it will be very hard to have enough staff to properly take care of the kids. I don't know when or how I can get replacements for those who do choose to leave. Replacing counselors under normal circumstances is difficult enough, but under the weather and travel restrictions now, it would be quite a while before I could get a single replacement counselor. Even if the rain stops immediately, with water rising everywhere and emergencies to be met all over the Northeast and telephone lines unreliable it will be days before I can expect any new counselors to arrive and replace the cancerous group threatening to destroy the camp. I wonder if we can do it without them. If Roland, Vico, Dr. Bob and I worked with some of our oldest boys, could we do it? Could we properly take care of the kids, make sure they were all kept safe? Now I know how exhausted I am. This is crazy. Of course, we couldn't do it. There is no way we could fulfill our obligations to parents and the kids to run the camp with a skeleton staff. On the other hand, how responsible is it to allow a bunch of college kids with no real experience to take over the camp? Where would the campers be then? Who would be able to deal with emergencies? Do they have any idea of what it takes to run a camp? Well, they would have Roland on board and Vico. They are both responsible adults. What am I talking about? I can't believe I am weighing the consequences of them taking over the camp, and even considering it. But what alternative do I have? Not many. Damn Joey, I have to give him credit. He planned this well. Luck was with them for me to have to leave camp for hours at just the right time while Joey and Cozy consolidated and cajoled those who were reluctant. A new thought occurred to me.

"If I was to agree and decide to give in to your plan, what do you propose to do with me? Would you want to lock me in my house? And what about my family? And what about Roland? Have you made any plans beyond simple destruction?"

Cozy took the floor. "Of course, we've made plans. We've tried to think of everything. To answer your questions, first, it will not be necessary for you to leave camp or to be confined to your house, though you might feel it easier to stay in or close to your house. That's your choice, but we have already agreed if you are out and around camp we will ask you not to talk to any of the staff beyond saying Good Morning, hello and how are you. We are all agreed we will not get into any conversation with you about activities or dealing with kids or anything else. Second, your family should feel free to roam and do what they have always done without restriction. And as far as Roland, of course we want him to continue as Waterfront Director. He is excellent at the job. But for now, the weather being what it is and everything already having been stripped from the waterfront, there won't be much for him to do in the next few days, at least."

"Third, we plan to operate this camp on Democratic principles. We already have a constitution and bylaws. We know there has to be an executive to make decisions and we've already elected Vico to that position. His hands won't be tied. His actions won't be vetoed. He'll take care of programming and anything else he feels necessary. We will have an advisory council to work with Vico if there are matters of camp policy to determine. The council has already been elected. It will be me, Joey, Sam, Randy and Jeff. We plan on a new election every week. Is there anything else you want to know?

"What about the girls? I don't see a single member of the girls' staff in this room. Have you managed to convince them I'm such an ogre that I must be excised from the operation of their camp? It is their camp too, isn't it?"

"Yes, of course we consulted with the girls. I'm surprised Paulette didn't get up here. I guess we were supposed to call her when you got back from the hospital, but we forgot. She did not agree with us and tried hard to talk the girls into staying on no matter what. It didn't work. Every one of them is on board and ready to go if we give the word."

"All right, I have the picture. Vico, what are your plans for tomorrow?" Vico came up toward the front of the room.

"Nelson, I'm sorry. I hope you know I was not in on this. I tried to talk them out of it, but eventually I figured they were going ahead with or without me, and I thought maybe I could help keep the place sane if I agreed to act as Director."

As I listened, I knew my decision was made. It had been made years earlier when I sacrificed all of our savings and bought the camp.

"Thank you all for sharing your opinions. I'm sorry to hear you all feel the way Joey says you feel. Tomorrow is another day, and I am really too tired to continue this discussion any longer, but before I go to bed, I want to leave you with two thoughts. First, this is my camp and I am not planning to turn it over to anybody. You may think I can, but I do not have that right. I will miss any of you who leave, as will your campers. Think about them for a minute. Second, take my advice, those of you who are determined to pursue this folly and leave, wait until morning. You are all too tired to start driving now, but, even if you were wide awake, the roads are simply too dangerous to risk tonight. Gentlemen, Good night."

12

The Sun Emerges and the Terrible News

Narrator

Camp awakened with a drowsy sense of disbelief. The sun was shining. Thank God, finally! At some unknown hour the heavens had stopped pouring down upon them. The air felt lighter. The sky above was a brilliant blue, dotted with occasional white fluffy clouds. The sun celebrated its emergence in all of its brilliance. It started the formidable process of warming the soggy ground, drying the moldy cabins filled with sodden clothing. Were those last few days real or a figment of the collective imagination? What of the sickness, the constant rain and the stench? Was it all real? How could it be in the face of the beauty of this new day?

Cindy pulled the curtains apart a few inches to peak out. She looked and looked again, hardly daring to believe it was over. She opened the curtains as wide as they would go and the sun poured in on her. She could hardly believe, after the deluge last night, that it was over at last. Quietly she got dressed and tiptoed out of the room, not wanting to wake Nelson. She went to the front door to revel in the marvel of warmth and sunshine. She smiled to herself as she thought of how delighted her exhausted husband would be when he woke up and saw the sun. She was confident he must have gotten Liz safely to the hospital, and now he was home safe and sound. *I'll let him sleep for as long as he needs. Some of the others can handle whatever comes up in these few hours. He has to sleep to recoup his expended energy.* Cindy knew nothing of the events after Nelson returned from the hospital. She just knew her man was home safely.

Vico had never managed to fall asleep. In his mind, through the sleepless hours was the image of Nelson, stumbling out of the dining hall, exhausted but determined to maintain his authority and to protect his camp. *That was such a terrible ordeal we put him through. I should never have allowed it to happen. I should have stopped it somehow. I'm not sure how, but somehow I should have. I felt I had betrayed Nelson, though I knew I had not.*

He sensed rather than heard when the rain stopped. Slowly the reality asserted itself and he had hope; hope that the madness, the insanity of the black night was behind them and that somehow things would be righted by the sunshine. He checked his watch. It was six o'clock. He got out of bed, dressed and made his way to the dining hall, scene of the recent treachery. He planned to grab a cup of coffee and go down to Nelson's house to start planning for the day ahead, but he knew it was too early. Nelson would need at least another hour or so before he could get to work.

Joey awakened to silence, a strange silence. It took a few seconds for him to realize the missing sound was the patter of raindrops beating on the cabin roof above him. His campers were all still asleep, but he leaped out of bed, opened the shutters and exulted in the sheer physical joy of seeing the sun. *It's going to be a good day. We can get things dried out and start actually running activities again.* Then a second wave of consciousness hit, as he recalled the events of the night, events he had conceived and managed, but which had not ended at all as he had planned. Nelson was determined to maintain control and not a single counselor had left camp. Instead, they had all returned to their cabins and gone to bed. Joey didn't blame any of them for not following through on the threat. In fact, he recognized the folly and danger of driving in such conditions and suggested they would all be safer leaving in the morning. Suddenly the familiar sound of reveille blared forth from the speakers and, by reflex Joey shouted to his campers. "That's reveille, guys.... time to get up...assembly in twenty minutes."

Roland sensed the sun, but even its power couldn't dissipate the feeling of anger and frustration with which he had gone to bed in the early morning hours. He hadn't been at the meeting, but he knew what was planned and it made him sick. He tried to stay awake to warn Nelson, but eventually returned to his cabin because there was no way to guess how late Nelson might return from the hospital, or whether he would even be able to get back during the night. He worried about his friend and he worried about the future of the camp the counselors were trying to destroy. He worried about how it all ended last night. The sun gave him some hope. "*We'll get those bastards. Now that the rain has ended, Nelson will be able to get new counselors in and get rid of every one of those bad apples, every last one of them.*"

The bugle call announced the coming of the new day. Campers opened their eyes to sunlight streaming into their cabins. Younger campers popped out of bed, ran out of the cabins in their pajamas, cheering the return of the sun. Counselors opened their eyes to the same sunshine, but most were filled with confusion and doubts about their immediate future. Without conference or consultation, every counselor on the boys' camp staff decided to get up and continue to function as counselors for their campers, at least until somebody inspired them to a different course of action. Almost without exception, they felt guilty and unhappy with their participation in last night's nightmarish meeting. Many of them joined their campers in impromptu sun dances taking place all over camp.

Nelson Cohen's eyes were closed, but his mind was awake. He sensed Cindy's quiet moments in the room. He tried to open his eyes to look at her, but his eyelids seemed glued together. He tried to say "Good Morning" but his lips would barely part. His mind was playing tricks on him. It wasn't focusing on the movements he wanted to make. Nor would it focus on his plans or the counselor conspiracy, or the rain or the terrifying ride to the hospital. It refused all of these, but it was focusing. It was focusing on pain. There was a message, a message his brain received in waves: the message was pain. It came from his chest and spoke directly to his brain. *This awful pain, why won't it let me alone? Why won't it let me open my eyes. I have to tell Cindy. I have to tell her about the pain. I need a doctor. I have to tell her. I'll try again. I hear her tiptoe out of the room.*

"Cindy, Cindy, I need a doctor. Cindy, get doctor." *She didn't hear me. My words were trapped inside. My mouth won't open. The words can't get out. Oh, My God, this pain! They'll never know. They'll never know until it's too late. They can't hear me. I'm going to die if they don't get help.* "Cindy, Cindy, get me a doctor. Cindy, I'm having a heart attack."

Yes, that's what it is. My mind was finally able to label the pain, a heart attack. I need someone to know. When she comes back in, I'll tell her with my eyes. If I try hard enough, I should be able to open my eyes and tell her. I prayed for Cindy to come back in the room. I managed to open the lids. I can see the room and the sun streaming in. Thank God, the sun at last. I'll be all right. The sun is shining.

It's too late! I'm going to die. She won't know in time! I let my eyes close again. There, that feels better. The message from my chest isn't so strong now. The pain is easing. I knew the sun would shine today. I just knew it. I felt a trace of a smile inching across my face. I can feel it. My brain is working again, and I think of the sun, the warm happy sun, the mother of good health. Everything will be all right after all. "Let's get things going, Vico. We can't waste a minute of this good weather." That was my final thought. I was awakened a minute later by one final fearful message of pain.

Vico stood in the middle of the Assembly area. The entire camp was in their usual lines, awaiting program announcements and flag raising. Roland and Paulette were doing their best to quiet down the campers who were still exhilarated and exuberant by the appearance of the sun after the dismal days of the deluge.

"Boys and girls, I need your attention. I don't want to have to shout. I have some terrible news to convey, and I need you all to hear it." He waited for a bit until it really did get quiet.

"Some time last night while we were all sleeping, Nelson, our wonderful Camp Director, suffered a very serious heart attack, and he died."

13
The Camp Mourns

Narrator

There was shocked silence for a moment while the import of the words registered on them. There were screams and there were tears, lots of tears, and fright on the part of some younger campers who wondered what it might mean for them. Counselors comforted the campers who seemed most upset. Many of them felt guilty. Others were just sad.

"Now," said Vico, "let us all have absolute quiet as we raise our flag half way up the flagpole. It will stay at half-mast the rest of this summer to honor the memory of the great man who started and ran Camp Adventure, making it the camp we all love. After the flag-raising we'll all go in for breakfast. Further announcements about program will be made after breakfast. Paulette and I would like to meet with Unit Leaders immediately after breakfast. All right now, camp *attention!*"

Joey's shock and sorrow were profound. His sense of personal guilt and responsibility nearly overwhelmed him. *It's my father all over again. They were both unreasonable, dogmatic men from another era, who just couldn't adopt to the modern world. I beat him and now he's dead, just like my father. Why did he have to die? And why should I feel guilty? I didn't kill either of them. They didn't have to die. They could have stayed alive and continued their fight. Why must they always die and leave me feeling like this? They chose to die rather than accept reality. Why didn't they have the guts to stay alive and face defeat?*

Vico knew he shouldn't feel guilty. None of them were directly responsible. None of them caused his death. A man with a heart like that, it was bound to happen. Vico had been telling himself this for two days now, still trying, without complete success, to convince himself it was true. The feeling of ultimate responsibility was still with him; the feeling that if he had somehow been able to take charge things would never have come to a head; there would have been no rebellion, no torment and ultimately no heart attack.

It's too late to help him, but at least I can fulfill my obligation to run this camp for the rest of the summer. I'll make it the best damn camp in the country these last couple of weeks. We can't erase the past, but we can rebuild so that the kids who are here have an honest camp experience to look back on. We can't quit on them.

Roland felt shame and anger, but most of all a sense of loss. He had lost a good friend, a man with whom he had worked, confided and planned for ten years. *He was a good man. None of them will ever be the man he was.* He left *them* unnamed, but there was no doubt who he had in mind. *They didn't know they were killing him, and I'm sure they didn't mean that to happen, but that's what they did. I have to clear my mind of these angry thoughts because I know Cindy will ask me to give the eulogy. It cannot be delivered in anger. It has to be given in love.* After waging an internal war, the only emotion left was sadness. With the sadness came resolve. He resolved to do his best to finish out the summer; to save it for the kids and to save the camp for Cindy. *It's my job to protect the camp for Cindy just as I've always done for Nelson.*

14

The Funeral

Cindy

My Nelson was fifty-eight years old when he died. The shock and horror I felt when I found him that morning and realized he had died was beyond belief. He should never have died so young. We knew he had some minor heart irregularity, but his cardiologist had assured both of us that he could continue to lead a long and full life. He advised Nelson to stay in shape, watch his diet, keep regular hours and try to avoid stress. We both laughed when he said that. It was clear he had no idea what a Camp Director's life was like in the summer. I know this was a tough summer for Nelson. It was clear he was disappointed in his Head Counselor, but we had challenging summers before and plenty of stress every summer. This was really no different. I have trouble reconciling the wonderful exuberant man I've always known with his death. Paulette, Roland, and Vico and Dotty have all been wonderfully supportive, but there is just so much anyone can actually do to ease the pain. Harriett is inconsolable. She was always Daddy's little girl. Now she doesn't want to go back to her bunk. She is sticking to me, as though she thinks I might disappear too if she lets me out of her sight.

I felt relieved when the phone lines had finally started to work that day. I was able to reach Nelson's brothers and Rabbi Wolfe. Teddy and Joel are good guys. They were shocked and crying on the phone with me. They said they would make all of the other calls to family. I called my friend Judy. She'll make the calls to all of our friends. I knew none of our friends or relatives would be able to make it to a funeral, but it was a blow when the Rabbi expressed his sympathy, but explained he wouldn't be able to get there either unless they could delay the funeral for several days. Travel was at a virtual standstill throughout the Northeast. I already knew that, but I had somehow expected the Rabbi, with his connection to God, would be able to overcome that ordinary problem. I was devastated by the news. I explained through my tears we just wouldn't be able to wait that long. Electricity was still off all over camp, which meant there would be no possible way to preserve the body. The Rabbi assured me that, under the circumstances it would be acceptable from a religious standpoint for me to make whatever provisions I can for the burial to take place at camp without benefit of a Rabbi. It was, after all, an emergency situation. To have to bury him with no family or friends, other than the camp family was unthinkable, but I was getting used to the unthinkable.   .

The burial took place three days later. It was a hot sunny day. The entire camp, campers and counselors, gathered around the grave in deep right field on the Senior ball field. The giant oak tree which was Nelson's favorite, and which had always served as the right field foul pole, provided a canopy over us and the grave site. Someone had brought chairs for us. Harriett and the two boys sat with me. Roland officiated and delivered the eulogy. For a man for whom public speaking would have seemed unlikely he was wonderful. It was a moving eulogy, delivered from the heart. He loved and admired Nelson. I could see the tears in his eyes and and hear them in his voice as he spoke. He spoke about Nelson's years building the camp, the years of sweat and financial sacrifice; the wonderful camp he had produced; his years teaching and coaching; how he had dedicated his life to serving youth; and of he spoke of Nelson's love for me and for our children.

"Nelson was a man of principle," Roland said. "He was someone you could always count on to do the right thing, in good times and bad."

I listened through wracking sobs and heard with a sense of emptiness. Nelson was gone and camp is over for me. It was his dream, not mine. Once this season ends, I'll never come back to this place. They killed him. These boys he helped become men killed him with their hate just as surely as if they had taken a gun and shot him. I can't even look at them. I'll tell Roland and Vico to do whatever they think best. They won't need to consult me. I can't be around camp and even look at some of those guys again. I'll just stay in our cabin and take walks in the woods until we can finally go home and put this God-awful summer behind us.

15

Protecting the Camp

Vico

I was sitting in the office trying to work out a program for tomorrow, but it just wasn't happening. I couldn't concentrate. My thoughts kept circling back to the meeting that awful night. The scene kept playing itself over and over in my mind. *What could I have done to change the outcome? What should I have done? I just sat there and watched it happen. Enough, I had to stop torturing myself.* It was going to happen no matter what I said or did. I had to concentrate.

Let me see if I can get the weather report. That'll give me something else to worry about. I hope the battery isn't dead in my portable radio. I really don't want to go out to the car. Well, at least I know I can get the news there if I have to.

I searched the back of the closet, and finally I found the little black radio I had stuck in there when I unpacked that first night in camp. I was pleasantly surprised to discover that it was working. At first, all I could find was static. I kept moving the dial tuner slowly back and forth around 1030, hoping to catch the news on WBZ. Eventually I gave up on that and just started rotating the dial searching for voices, no matter where they came from. The station I reached came from somewhere in Maine. I was lucky to catch a complete news report from somewhere in the Southern part of the state. The news was about what I expected, but with perhaps a little optimism.

"Radio News Report: The entire Northeast is still captive to the effects of the storm. Roads are washed out in several areas and many bridges have been undermined, and declared unsafe. All six New England states have been declared a Disaster area. Federal emergency relief is on the way via helicopters dropping supplies to isolated communities. The governor has announced state highway crews are working around the clock, trying to reopen washed out roads and shore up weakened bridges. There is disturbing news of looting and pillaging. Food markets have been stripped bare, and individual famers and rural home owners have had to protect their fields and supplies. Some are standing guard with shotguns. There are reports of a few unfortunate incidents where city dwellers foraging in the countryside invaded farms protected by men with rifles and pitchforks. So far, we have received no reports of fatalities in these confrontations. We urge you all to act with restraint, and recognize that people who are creating problems for you are hungry men just trying to feed their families.

"In Boston, martial law is in effect. There is an eight p.m. curfew in the Boston area. The governor of Maine has urged his citizens to remain calm and act in a lawful manner so that he will not have to follow the example of governors and mayors with larger metropolitan areas. The first line of relief is reaching several Maine communities as I speak. The supplies are from a US Navy aircraft carrier Kitty Hawk stationed off the coast, filled with food and medical supplies. For several hours helicopters have been operating nonstop getting supplies to isolated communities as rapidly as possible. On the weather front, the storm has completely moved away from the coast, and we can look forward to several days of fine weather."

I turned off the radio, shoved my papers and partially-scribbled time schedule into my file drawer, and locked the office. Stepping out into the cool moonlit night, I paused, listened to the silence and breathed deeply. A full moon bathed the open fields of the main campus in light, while the camp buildings now appeared as dark shadows. There were flickers of candlelight showing from some of the cabins. I could see Nelson's cabin, lit more brightly than the rest. I knew Dotty was down there visiting with Cindy and I hoped there were a few others as well. The windows stood open and as I neared the cabin I stood and listened. I knew all of those voices. Dotty was still there, and I heard Paulette's and Roland's's voices too. Good, Cindy had a group. I'd finish my swing around camp, and then I'd stop back this way.

As I approached the Senior area, I could see the counselors were all up, and gathered together talking around the campfire. I really didn't want to get into a lengthy conversation with them, so as I passed, I called out "everything quiet here tonight?"

"Hi Vico, yes, all is well. The kids are all asleep."

"Good, you guys should get some sleep too. Tomorrow could be another long day." I didn't give them a chance to answer. "See you in the morning."

My next stop was the waterfront. As I made my way down the hill I was pretty sure I heard men's voices and they were unlikely to be counselors at that hour. The voices were coming from the girls' beach and I could sense the sounds were coming closer. They were coming my way. I ducked behind a prickly bush. Clearly, I picked the wrong bush. My hands and face got scratched as I ducked as close as I could, but I stayed down as they drew closer. I tried to identify the voices. They were speaking to one another barely above whisper level but in the very quiet, clear night, voices traveled well. I could hear the voices but not what they were saying. I actually held my breath because my breathing seemed to be loud enough to interfere with my own hearing. They were very close and moving closer to my uncomfortable hiding place. From my vantage point I could see four large male figures. As they passed right by me, I shifted my weight slightly and a twig snapped under my foot. I held my breath again; but they were clumping along, not so quietly, and their own sounds masked any chance they'd hear my twig. I didn't recognize any of them, but knew they definitely were not counselors, all of whose shapes I would easily recognize at that point in the season. They had to be headed toward the kitchen. Even if they didn't know the camp layout well, it wouldn't have taken them long to figure out which building was the dining hall. There were only three large buildings — dining hall, Infirmary, and rec hall — all of which were fairly close together toward the top of the hill. While they were figuring out which building they wanted, I had to get some help. I ran to the Junior unit, and rousted out Jeff, Sammy, Fred, and Mike. "Hey, guys, come with me. Very quiet now. We have trespassers and I'm sure they're headed to the kitchen looking for food. We have to get there first. Grab a flashlight, but don't turn it on. Let's go!"

We quietly made our way toward the dining hall, each taking a slightly different path until we gathered by the kitchen entrance. Near the back door, we disturbed a family of raccoons which had been attacking garbage cans. They scattered hastily into the brush. We had beaten the four intruders to their target. I quietly unlocked the kitchen door, and the five of us went in. I removed the lock from its hasp and slipped it into my pocket. Very quietly I closed the door behind us. My plan was to have things appear as normal as possible when the intruders arrived. "I want us all to make a wide semi-circle around the doorway."

During Orientation period we had discussions about nighttime intruders, but we would never have anticipated this kind of intrusion. The issue then had been the kind of oversexed teenage guys youth camps were likely to attract: Peeping Toms, vandals, kids out to cause a little trouble. We could not possibly have imagined we would be facing normally law-abiding grown men driven to steal food out of desperation to feed hungry families. I looked around the familiar kitchen to see if there were objects that could be used as weapons in a pinch. The industrial size fry pans that hung above the chef's bench could work. I ran over and grabbed one for potential use as a weapon and signaled the counselors to do the same.

It wasn't very many minutes before we heard footsteps, and then voices in the yard below. They were coming up the staircase. The back door opened, and four men came in. That was the signal for all of us to turn on our flashlights aiming directly into the eyes of the arriving men. The lights illuminated first surprise, then panic on the newcomer's faces. The two groups of men stood looking at one another. I didn't know who was more frightened, but I thought and hoped it would be the invaders who had to recover from the shock of discovery. Initiative was clearly on our side. Our flashlights in their faces gave us a major advantage. Seeing the drawn, guilty faces of the intruders was enough to make me hopeful that they'd back down without any actual physical challenge. As I swept my flashlight back and forth, I recognized Jimmy, the guy who filled my car with gas at the station in town. The others all looked familiar to me too, but I couldn't place any of them other than Jimmy, but it was clear they were all from our local area.

"You guys don't belong here. This is private property. If I were you, I would just turn around, get out and go home, and we'll forget this ever happened." Two of the men started to back toward the door, eager to get away from the unexpected opposition, but Jimmy, obviously the leader, was not so easily deterred.

"Hey, Vico, you know me. I fill your tank at least once a week. Listen, we're not here looking for trouble. We just need to get a little food to feed our families for the next few days. I know things are tough all over and you've got a lot of kids to take care of here, but is it really going to hurt you if we take just a little to feed our kids? We don't mean to harm your kids or the camp and I'm sure you wouldn't want ours to starve either. So be a decent guy. Just pretend like you've got an additional ten campers here this summer. You can spare it. We ran out of food a couple of days ago and the situation is pretty desperate. We wouldn't be here if we weren't desperate."

"Things are tough for everybody, Jimmy. I've been listening to the radio. I know what's happening out there. But you've got to understand our situation *here*. You guys aren't the only ones looking for food. They'll be others coming after the four of you. Suppose there are ten men in the next group, and five more early tomorrow and another eight hungry guys tomorrow night, all just trying to feed their families. We ran out of fresh fruit and vegetables a few days ago, and the freezer is empty. We're going to have to go out scrounging tomorrow. We'll send kids out fishing and picking berries and doing everything we can to supplement the little food we have in stock to keep our kids eating. I understand your problem, but ours is actually much bigger. That's why I just can't spare anything."

Another one of the men spoke up. "Let me talk to Cohen. My name's Landry. Tell him I'm here looking for food. He knows me and my whole family. My wife Abby was a waitress here for years, and her sister was a waitress too. He knows us. He won't say no. He won't let us starve. I know him. He's a nice guy. He's not a cold-hearted bastard like you. It's not your food. It's his. I want to talk to him."

"But Nelson is — "

"That's enough, Sammy."

I looked at Sammy, my face signaling to let me do the talking. I turned back toward the men. "I'm not going to disturb Nelson now. He's fast asleep, and he was up all last night taking a kid with an emergency to the hospital. He told me he's just got to get sleep and he put me in charge. The last thing he said to me before he went back to his cabin was 'protect our food supply.'"

"It looks like he knew what he was talking about. It needs protecting! The whole camp needs protecting so we set up a system of patrols around camp. That's how we knew you were coming before you got anywhere near the kitchen. Nelson knew our patrol system would most likely be protecting against people who know the camp, or at least know *of* the camp, men like you, people who live close enough to know we have a lot of people to feed and who are looking to find a big cache of food stored somewhere. We do have a cache of food to protect, but it's not very big and we need every bit of it. There's no point in disturbing his sleep, since Nelson knew it would be neighbors and people we know. Just do yourself and us a favor, and head right back out to the bridge. If you run into any more of our patrols along the way, just let them know we already saw you and you're on the way out."

"All right, we're going. We won't come back unless there is no other way, but if it comes down to a choice between our kids starving and coming back here to get food, you can be sure we'll return and there'll be more of us next time, so you better double those patrols you're bullshitting us about, and tell them to be on guard."

With that, Jimmy and his group trooped out the back door and down the stairs.

I looked around our circle of counselors, all with flashlights in one hand and fry pans in the other. I thought to myself if it wasn't so serious this would make quite a comical scene. As I looked around there was a collective sigh of relief. Then we were all grinning. I knew it was foolish to feel pride in this small victory, but I felt great, better than I had in a long time. I could tell the others felt the same. I sensed something else as well, the respect of those gathered around me. After savoring our triumph for a few moments, it occurred to me that my fictional patrol system should be transformed from boast to reality as rapidly as possible. If these four had come, others might indeed be on their way. I decided the members of the patrol should all be armed, but certainly not with traditional lethal weapons. The last thing we needed was to have someone shot. It was during Orientation period, I heard about the Camp Adventure Bat Patrol, which had been employed occasionally as a line of defense whenever there was word of a Peeping Tom or, some unknown intruder in the girls' section of camp.

"Jeff, I want you to go up to Senior camp and tell Joey we'll need two of his counselors on all night, one patrolling up there with a baseball bat, and one down here by the kitchen. Whoever is awake up there, you can fill them in on what went on here tonight. Make sure they understand the bats are more for psychological rather than physical use against anyone who might be coming into camp to steal food. When you're through up there, get back to your unit, let them know what is going on and assign one of your counselors to come up here in the kitchen. Make sure the rest of the boys go to bed. They'll need their sleep."

"Will do." And Jeff was on his way.

"Fred, I'll get a junior counselor to take your place in your cabin. I want you to stay here in the kitchen. You know the drill and you can fill in the others who'll be up here with you. Make sure everyone has a good flashlight and a baseball bat. I'll get someone up from the Freshman unit too. Sammy, you go to bed. Mike, I'd like you to take first shift on the path up from the girls' waterfront. If you see anyone coming, try to stay out of sight and hurry up here to warn the others. You should have a bat too. I want you all to know I really appreciate what you guys are doing tonight. I know you'll be losing a lot of sleep, so I'll try to schedule you for some sleep time tomorrow during the day. We may have to keep this up for a couple more nights before our regular food trucks are able to get through. Only then will we be able to relax and get back to normal. I can't wait for that day."

I completed the night patrol assignments, with a sense of direction and confidence in what I was doing. Despite Nelson's recent death and all of the turmoil that preceded it, I felt better about myself than I had in weeks. My mind was alive with plans as I walked briskly down toward Nelson's cabin. As I approached, I saw the candlelight still flickering, and wondered if Dotty and the others were all still there, keeping Cindy company. How much, if anything, did Roland or Paulette tell Cindy about the meeting the night of Nelson's heart attack? I hope they haven't said anything at all about it. She's had enough sadness with the death of her husband. She doesn't need her burden of grief to be complicated further by adding to it hatred for the boys and men she would then be sure had caused Nelson's death.

I entered the darkened kitchen and made my way into the living room. It felt as if the house itself had somehow relaxed in Nelson's absence. That's ridiculous. The house hadn't changed. But it *was* the first time I had ever come into this house without having to worry about my job performance or my status in his eyes. This time as I entered, still charged up with adrenalin from my recent kitchen victory, I was filled with concern for Cindy and her loss.

They were gathered around the fireplace, coffee mugs in hand.

"How did you manage coffee without electricity?"

Roland chuckled. "It's obvious you never worked in a kitchen without a coffee machine. Cindy gave me permission to go through her cupboard, and I found a long-handled pot. You insulate the handle, hold the pot over the fire and boil the water, you put your coffee in a cloth sack in the boiling pot and let it simmer for a while. When you remove the bag, what's left is a pot full of coffee. Of course, it's an art to get it exactly the way you want it, and this batch might strike you a little strong, but it's way better than no coffee."

I certainly agreed with that. After I had my coffee mug in hand and started sipping, I looked over at Dotty and silently asked my question. She understood, and shook her head, almost imperceptibly from side to side. I quickly surmised none of them told Cindy about the attempted takeover and none of them were planning to tell her.

I gave them a brief report on my recent adventure with our intruders, making the recitation as lighthearted and comical as I could. Still, it was a serious situation, and they were interested. I had to field many questions about it. The story served as a good diversion for all of them, including Cindy. Roland complimented me, telling me I had handled the situation exactly right. Dotty's face reflected pride. Cindy was interested, but it was hard to read anything from her facial expression. Paulette didn't say anything after my story, but I sensed she was worried by the reality of intruders and concerned about others who might follow.

After every possible permutation on the subject of intruders had been examined and exhausted, the conversation shifted to the morning funeral services, and the camp's reaction. We all agreed the campers and counselors had been both respectful and impressed by the solemnity of the short service and the actual burial. I doubt many of them had ever been to a funeral before, and some of the younger campers had clearly been both upset and frightened. A few had cried, but their counselors did a wonderful job of comforting them. We all agreed the camp mood will soon return to some semblance of normal. We were all sure the wonderful sunshine today would continue to lift everyone's spirits in the days ahead. The issue of food hadn't seemed to become much of an issue for the campers — not yet. Collectively there had been few complaints about the rather dramatic change in the foods that were now arriving at their tables. Pasta was now the centerpiece of most meals, and almost everybody liked pasta. We shifted from subject to subject, winding up with a conversation about the violent virus which had plagued the camp for many days, but seemed to have let up just in time for the start of the awful storm we had just survived.

It suddenly hit me how bone weary and emotionally drained I was, and I could see everyone else was beat and truly wanted to get some sleep, but nobody wanted to be the first to make the move, leaving Cindy in an empty house. After the funeral, she had sent her daughter Harriett and the boys back to their cabins to be with their friends. We could see she really didn't want to be left alone. She seemed to be forcing a smile as we said we were about ready to head to bed. Paulette stepped in and came to the rescue.

"Cindy, do you mind if I bring a sleeping bag over and sleep in one of your kid's bedrooms, just for tonight?" After a few protestations about how unnecessary it was, Cindy reluctantly but happily agreed. And we were all finally able to say goodnight.

As we left Nelson and Cindy's house, Roland called me aside. "That was good thinking, Vico, I mean how you handled the business in the kitchen. That was quick thinking. You handled it well. I thought about the decisions you made, and I agree it's a good idea to not let the outside world know Nelson is gone, not until the emergency is over and we can communicate to the parents of our campers. We don't want them getting that news second hand."

"Thanks. There didn't seem to be much I could do with the guys who came in except what I did."

"There were choices. You made the right ones. Look, Vico, I'm tired and I know you and Dotty have to get some sleep too, but I think we had better get together as early as possible to talk about how we're going to run this camp and keep things going the rest of the summer. I assume we'll get cooperation from the staff."

"How about first thing tomorrow morning before anyone else is awake. Why don't we meet in the kitchen at say, six o'clock? That will give us a few hours' sleep."

We shook hands and parted for the night as allies for the first time.

16

Feeling Guilty but Ready for a Fresh Start

Joey

We sat for hours by the fireplace, speaking in low voices, switching from topic to topic in a fruitless effort to push from our minds the enormous feelings of guilt we all shared. Our thoughts, and ultimately our conversation, drifted back to Nelson's shocking death and the solemn funeral that morning. There were long pauses as each of us privately acknowledged that nothing would change either the current reality, or our complicity in events. Cozy, seeking to elevate the pessimistic mood, retrieved and read a poem he had written. Most of his audience didn't entirely get his poetry , but we all listened silently. After Cozy's effort, our numbing sense of collective guilt made it possible for Bob Weinberg to get out his guitar. He sat on a stool in front of the fire strumming and twanging a parody of college life he had written. As I sat, half listening to both performances, it seemed to me the night of self-recrimination might last until dawn.

The solemn mood came to an abrupt end when Jeff rushed in with the shocking news of campus invaders and how the explosive situation had been successfully defused by Vico with the assistance of Jeff and his counselors. He outlined the night watch plans that had been assigned. It gave us all something real to think and talk about. Jeff sat with us for a while, relating the details of the kitchen confrontation. I was glad for the interruption, but found Jeff's obvious admiration for the way Vico handled the crisis a bit disturbing. It was a story of quick thinking, quick action and courage, qualities I had never attributed to Vico. Jeff outlined the night watch plans, dispatched Dick Reback to the kitchen, and told Major he had watch in Senior area for the rest of the night. Implicit in Jeff's recitation was that we would all be losing a lot of sleep patrolling in the coming nights. This was all we needed to give ourselves permission to use what remained of the night for sleep. Except those assigned, we all trooped off toward our own cabins.

I got into bed, and was suddenly wide awake. The long numbing conversation by the fireplace might eventually have made sleep possible, but Jeff's news and its implications for the rest of the camp season stirred up a beehive of activity in my mind. I was determined to get some sleep and tried all of my usual sleep-inducing strategies, but they all failed. Throwing game-winning touchdowns for Great Neck North didn't work because Nelson was always there on the bench ready to congratulate me. My campaign for President also failed as I saw accusing headlines flash before my eyes. "Katz indicted for double murder of Dad and Camp Director." Finally, I gave up. I simply was not going to get any sleep that night. That was when I finally closed my eyes for a minute, and seconds later the sound of Reveille came over the PA announcing the start of another day.

I woke up with renewed spirit and a sense of purpose. *I'll show him. Imagine him calling me self-centered and dishonest. I'll show him who has ideals. I'll show him how a camp should be run. I'm going to make this place the happiest camp in the country these next few weeks. We'll get a fresh start today.* I visualized myself presiding over the council that very morning where I would make brilliant program suggestions, too good to be ignored by Vico, or Roland, or anyone. They would all look to me for leadership. I would have to keep an eye on Vico. I can't believe he acted so forcefully last night. I didn't think he had it in him. I may have underestimated him, but I'll show him and all of them that they need my leadership to really make this place hum. "Okay, Kids, time to get up. Reveille sounded. Get going you lazy-heads. Time to get dressed. Breakfast in twenty minutes."

17

Working with Vico to Run the Camp

Roland

To me there was no question where my duty lay. I will run this camp as well as it can possibly be run after the emotional jolt experienced by everyone, and the loss of the man who successfully guided it for its entire existence. Cindy won't be able to run the camp alone, and I'm not sure she wants any part of running it. It's my job to salvage the camp for her. I'm sure she'll want to sell the camp, and it won't have any value as a "shell". For it to be a valuable asset it has to be sold with campers. The rest of this summer just has to produce happy campers who will to want to return in future summers. That's my job. That's my mission. I thought about the possibility of buying the camp myself, but I knew I didn't have the resources. I would never be able to accumulate sufficient funds for it to be a realistic goal. With that possibility quickly eliminated , I was rather pleased with my selfless plan to run the camp strictly for Cindy, as a kind of payback to the widow of the man I considered my closet friend. I knew the course ahead wouldn't be easy, but I was determined.

First, I'd have to establish a real relationship with Vico. It was my fault I didn't do so earlier, when I might have provided some help to him as a newcomer. Vico was my only possible reliable ally, and it would be through him I'd have to run the camp. It's a pity I couldn't do it all myself, but safety at the waterfront is just too important to be left without totally responsible and capable leadership. I can't think of another person on the staff who could possibly do the job. I just had to stay at the waterfront for the majority of every day. I could work with Vico and provide support for him every night, early mornings, and every other opportunity that presented itself.

Second, I'm either going to have to neutralize Joey Katz or send him packing. Joey is a potential cancer on the staff. He's a strong leader and can be a great big pain in the ass. If Joey decides to give Vico a hard time day after day, on issue after issue, that could destroy the rest of the camp season. If it seemed to be heading that way, Joey would simply have to go. Firing Joey while Nelson was still alive might well have provoked a great staff crisis; but now, with the guy counselors all feeling guilty about Nelson's heart attack, and knowing it was Joey who had led them on their disastrous path, firing Joey right now would be unlikely to cause a major uproar.

Third, we would have to come up with some great camp programs right away to take the minds of campers and counselors off the recent tragedy, and return them to the serious business of having fun.

Fourth, and this cannot be underrated, we were going to have to come up with some creative planning to solve the immediate food crisis, and make sure that everyone got fed and was healthy before the food trucks start rolling in.

I know, I'm doing it again, thinking of and planning for life in terms of a giant outline where I divide future time into firsts, seconds and thirds. I chuckled to myself when I realized I was at it again. I knew people might laugh me for doing this, but it's a system that works for me.

I found Vico sipping coffee, and working on program sheets when I made my way through the hazy pre-dawn light to the office. He handed me a Styrofoam cup of steaming black coffee. I could see he was in the middle of programming so I sipped in silence as he continued filling in blanks on the schedule. Vico drained the last of his cup and looked up at me with a big smile. I smiled back, and thrust my hand out toward Vico.

"Welcome to Camp Adventure, Vico. I hope you will enjoy your stay here." I couldn't hep smiling as I awaited his reaction.

"Why thank you, Mr. Samson. Everything seems to be in good order here, and I'm sure it will be a fine summer."

"Seriously, Vico, I do want to welcome you to our camp. I haven't really done that yet. Instead of welcoming you I resented you. Instead of offering friendship I just stayed out of your way, waiting for you to fail. That was my pig-headedness and my loss and I am truly sorry."

"Come on Roland, I appreciate what you are saying, but I understood. Anyone in your position would have resented a newcomer coming in and getting the job you felt should have been yours. I can't say I wasn't hurt, but I did understand. That's all in the past now, and I appreciate the welcome you just gave me. I'm looking forward to working with you. I'm going to do the best damn job I can here and I'll need your help."

"You took the words right out of my mouth. We've both got to do the best jobs we possibly can and we'll need each other's help. Titles aren't important right now. What is important is how we tackle what has to be done, and that we work together and agree on the distribution of tasks between us. I've given this some thought, and, if you agree, I think I should be considered the Director and you the Head Counselor. This isn't for publication, just between us. I don't mean this as a reflection on your ability or mine, simply a recognition that I have years of experience in this camp and I know that Cindy is relying on me to pull us through. But I also have to recognize that I will have to spend most of my daytime activity at the waterfront, and you will have to make many of the day-to-day and hour-to-hour decisions. I have complete confidence you will continue to make good decisions. I just need to be informed every night how things are going, any problems you need help with and, of course, any emergencies. What do you think Vico? Can you live with that arrangement?"

"Yup, Roland, that sounds good to me. It should work well if we can get the counselor staff to cooperate, and I think they will."

"I don't think there will be any problem at all. Joey or Cozy or possibly one or two other guys will shoot their mouths off a little, once they are past the shock of Nelson's death, but as long as we get off to a good start while they are all still pretty much in shock, it will cut the ground from under anything our friend Joseph Katz might come up with. Do you agree?"

"I agree. I think they'll be happy to forget about that Council nonsense of theirs and start thinking of their kids first."

"Good, we both agree the counselors are likely to cooperate. Let's hope we're right. The next most important item is food. Do you have anything on your activity schedule yet that relates to our food problem?"

Vico laughed.

"As a matter of fact, that's been number one on my priority list. I already had my morning chat with Bob. He figures we have enough canned fruits, vegetables, soups and sauces along with pasta and rice to feed the camp for the next couple of days. On the other hand, we are completely out of meat, fresh veggies, salad, fresh fruit, and all dairy products. He suggested we take advantage of some of our natural resources. He mentioned those giant turtles the kids are always talking about in our lake. If we can capture a few of those, he says he can make a great turtle soup. He also suggested we have kids scrounge down at the waterfront for some of those mussels that we always complain about. Interesting, he says they're not the variety of mussels you find on restaurant menus, but he thinks he can steam them, put them in a tomato sauce and they'll be a great treat for kids brave enough to try them. Take a look at this crazy program I'm concocting. It's wild. I have turtle hunting as a Senior boys' activity. The Juniors will be fishing, the Sophomores will be going on a berry-picking hike. I've got the Freshmen playing kickball. I thought I'd ask Paulette if the girls could do the mussel gathering. There are plenty of mussels on the girls' waterfront. I know this is not going to feed the camp, but every little bit counts, and think how important the kids will feel knowing they are actually contributing to our food supply."

"I'm impressed, Vico, you've done a great job thinking it through, but I wonder if there are enough fish in the lake or turtles to keep whole units of boys busy for a whole morning."

"You're right, probably not, not nearly enough and that's why I have other activities going at the same time. Take a look. While some of the Seniors are turtle hunting, others will be in arts and crafts making fishing rods and lures. The Juniors who aren't fishing will be on a nature walk learning about herbs and gathering them if there are any in our woods worth gathering. I found this old book on herbs in the nature center. I'll give it to Jeff, and I hope the pictures are good enough so they don't wind up picking anything that turns out to be poisonous. I'll have the kids switch off for second period. If they get a little bored at least they'll feel like they're doing something positive. And don't underestimate our chef! Bob is convinced that with just a few of those big snappers he can make soup for the whole camp and he's ready to make a fish stew with the fish they catch. If they don't catch enough for that he'll grill the ones they do catch. If nothing else, it will all be good for morale."

"Sounds good. Now let's just hope the supply trucks can get through to us within the next couple of days. What else did you have on the docket?"

"Just one thing. Fun! We've got to come up with some really good ideas. The tennis and basketball courts are still under water, and the soccer field is like a swamp. If the sun keeps shining the baseball and softball fields should be almost playable later today. We'll have to wait and see with all of the facilities. Just leave it to me. I'll come up with some ideas. Have faith."

After meeting with Vico, I went into the kitchen to verify his summary of the state of provisions with Bob. It was pretty much the way Vico said it was. I had my breakfast and waited for reveille. By the time the camp assembled before breakfast, the sun was shining brightly and everyone's spirits seemed to match. Everyone was dressed in shorts and T-shirts. Rain gear had all been put away or was spread out to dry all over camp. The ban against coming to the dining hall barefoot had been ignored by all as the water-logged sneakers were also set out to dry. The younger kids had enjoyed slogging through puddles in their bare feet on their way to the Assembly area. A party mood prevailed. At assembly, Vico did a mock prayer of thanksgiving to the Sun God, and everyone seemed to be with him in spirit.

Breakfast itself quickly deflated the buoyant camp. The kids were hungry, and the breakfast itself was not a great success. Bob had made some sad looking pancakes, which had neither milk nor eggs as part of the recipe. It was not great, but maple syrup rescued the dish for many of the kids. The hot chocolate, bitter and thin, was greedily gulped down. When the platters and pitchers were empty, the not-quite satisfied campers and counselors headed back toward their cabins.

Vico had asked all of the unit leaders to stay behind and meet with him after breakfast, to go over the morning program. He and I sat on one side of the office across from the counselors. We had agreed we would try to avoid getting involved in any discussion about camp organization, and keep the meeting on the business of the program for the day. I wasn't surprised to learn almost immediately that Joey's mind had also been busy planning for this meeting.

"Thanks for calling a Council meeting so soon, Vico. I was afraid we might have to remind you." That was Joey's opening gambit. I felt my facial muscles tighten and noted a sinking feeling in the region of my stomach. My God, I thought, is he really going to try to dredge up that Council business? I thought he learned his lesson by now. I wondered how Vico would handle this instant challenge. Would he make an issue of the title and let them know they were at a Unit Leader's meeting rather than a Council meeting? Or would he let Joey have his way and agree it was a Council meeting? I knew I would have to step in if it looked like Vico was going to cave.

Apparently Vico wasn't going to take either course of action. He simply ignored Joey's comment and started going over the morning program. His approach was: this is the schedule I have worked out. He was giving the orders..."The Freshmen will do such and such.... The Sophomores will.... The Juniors will....and up through the Seniors." Then he asked for comments and suggestions. That was good Head Counselor procedure and good politics. He hadn't caved and he hadn't made Joey back down either. He had just gone about the business at hand. None of them had any questions, and the comments were all agreeable. The program looked good and workable to Sammy, Randy, and Jeff. Joey didn't comment until they were through. "Thanks, Vico that was good planning. You're doing a nice job. When will we be able to have our next Council meeting?" Vico again deflected Joey's issue of the title of their meeting. Without looking directly at Joey, he said, "We'll be meeting a lot in these next few days as we work to improvise and improve on the program to meet changing circumstances. In the meantime, if any of you have suggestions, please feel free to offer them at any time." Joey looked a little disconcerted as they all got up and left. I congratulated Vico and headed down to the waterfront.

18

The Search for Food

Joey

I left the meeting with a sense of uneasiness. My two fleeting attempts to create an issue had been deftly brushed aside by Vico. I was less disconcerted that my suggestions hadn't been implemented than by the realization that the much-despised Vico might turn out to be a far more capable adversary than I had supposed. As I walked toward the Senior area, I was ambivalent about this new Vico. On the one hand, his strength might thwart my plans to take over the actual running of Camp Adventure as easily and rapidly as I envisioned. On the other hand, with Vico's newfound confidence and ability, along with his relative youth and good health, I didn't have to worry about him breaking down when I achieved effective control of the camp. It would not be my father or Nelson all over again. I didn't have to even think about that. My victory this time will not be a hollow triumph as my ultimate triumph over Nelson turned out to be. Vico would fight the good fight and lose.

I really wanted the chance to run the camp. I've loved camp and camping since I first came here when I was fourteen. Camp Adventure was my third camp and each camp had its own style, and I knew what was wrong with every one of them. I knew that I was not alone in this. I had spoken with other long-term campers from other camps. Like me, many of them were convinced they knew how to run their camps better than the professionals who were in charge when they were there as campers or counselors.

Unlike many of them, I went way beyond generalized dreams and imaginings. I had well developed ideas about how camps should be run, how my camp will be run. I felt strongly there was no need for rigid time schedules, for the intense competition that seemed to prevail at all camp activities, or for the fear of coed socialization that keeps boys and girls separate, and stands in the way of healthy camp relationships. My camp will be a camp of freedom! My campers would choose from a laundry list of activities and specialize in the things that interested them most. My campers, and counselors too, would be free to explore and marvel at the wonders of nature, and would be free from an abundance of rules and restrictions. I had visions of boys and girls working together and playing together; long lazy campfires with happy faces singing into the night; groups of campers working together under elected leaders; constructing log cabins; learning as they worked, carving camping areas out of the glorious pine forest that surrounds them. I envisioned an athletic program in which kids would want to participate just because it's fun to play, not because they have to prepare for the big game or big event looming ahead on the schedule. Certainly, I was well aware of the mechanical needs of feeding people, of making sure that needed equipment was available and in good condition, and that campers' health needs must be taken care of. Those were necessities and were not to be confused with camp goals as they have been at Camp Adventure and many other camps.

But I had to be honest with myself, I didn't just want to run a camp to put my theories into practice. I would also enjoy the sheer pleasure of having and exercising power and command. Now, with the benefit of hindsight, I know that is why I ran for office in high school and why I had taken charge of Vietnam War rallies in college. That may even have been a motivating factor in my never-ending fights with my father over Shabbos restrictions.

I wondered what my father would make of all that had gone on and was happening at Camp Adventure this summer. I'm sure I know the answer. My father and Nelson Cohen are actually one and the same. Their priorities had different labels, but were basically the same. My father had known it was God's will that allowed him to succeed in selling hospital supplies; that his new Buick was God's reward; and that it was part of God's grand design that his family give him unqualified respect and obedience. Nelson might not have ascribed it to God's will, but he would have seen his role as Head Football Coach and as Camp Director as part of the natural order of the world. In both situations they spelled it out to their followers. "I'm the boss. I've earned it. It's your job to do what I say. That's the way it is and the way it is supposed to be." I knew without a doubt that my father would have been very angry at our challenge to the Director's authority at camp. It would be contrary to God's will.

Just before arriving at the Senior area, I stopped, questioning my own motives. *Am I falling into that same trap of self-delusion and self-aggrandizement as my father and as Nelson? Well, if I am, I guess I'm at least as entitled as they were.*

"Hey guys, this should be fun. And with a little luck we'll come back with a pile of food." I led the first group of foragers. I had about half of the Senior boys with me, all of whom carried backpacks for the food they would find and bring back to camp. It was clear most of the boys looked upon our venture as a kind of comic lark, but fun just to be doing something different. I had a pocket full of petty cash in single dollar bills in case we are able to buy anything eatable. Our first stop was Don's Superette on the other side of the lake. The door was locked, but Don, the owner, came from around the back of the store. "Hey Joey, why did you bring all these kids here? We have nothing left to sell."

"Hi Don, nice to see you too. We're here because we have a serious problem over at camp. We're going everywhere to try to drum up food. We've got a lot of kids to feed, and we know you've been a good friend to the camp for years. Anything you've got left, we would appreciate it, and, of course, Nelson sent us with money. He's not looking for charity."

"Tell you what. You keep your kids in order out here, and I'll scrounge around inside and see if I've got anything at all you might want." He went back around the building, and the boys could see lights going on in the store. A few minutes later the front door opened. Don was standing there with a box filled to the brim. "You're in luck. I had a few steaks and some hamburger meat in the freezer and a few bushels of potatoes. It's all yours. Tell Nelson for me I'm giving you all I have because camp has been such a good customer for me through the years."

I thanked him profusely; and the boys, excited at the idea of steaks and hamburgers, quickly divided the food into backpacks, and started walking again south along the main road.

"We did pretty well there, didn't we? I certainly didn't think we'd be lucky enough to get steak or hamburgers. We have two more stores in easy walking distance. I don't know what to expect, if anything from either of them, but it's worth a try before we start raiding farmer's fields. We'll do that anyway on the way back." Smitty's Diner remained locked, and there were no signs of life. We plodded on until we reached the Cilleville General store, and surprisingly the doors were open. The owner was sitting inside on a stool, munching on a candy bar. "Sir, we're from the camp, and we've just about run out of food and have a lot of kids to feed. Our owner, Nelson Cohen, sent us with money to buy any kind of food we could find at any stores that were open. I'm hoping you have some stuff stored away that you can sell to us."

"Well, young fella. I sure would like to oblige, but I'm afraid all the food is gone. In fact, just about everything is gone. I still have magazines and corn cob pipes, but I don't suppose either of those will help your food situation any. I wish you boys luck, and I hope everyone stays healthy at the camp. I was over there once, years ago, when it was owned by Beaupre. Nice layout there. I think he told me he had about seventy-five campers there that summer. I understand it's a Jew camp now. How many kids you got there this summer?"

"We have about 200 campers and another ninety people who live and work there."

"Well, I see you really do have a big problem. I wish you well. Nobody should be allowed to starve in this country. Sorry I can't do anything to help."

I led the boys out, but instead of going back via the road, we were going to take to the fields and paths in the woods. "There are two or three farms just off the back path between camp and Cilleville. We'll walk along the edges of their fields and see what we can find." We grabbed a few dozen ears of corn from one field before a large dog came charging at us, loudly expressing his displeasure. At the next farm, the garden was close behind the family home, and it would be foolish to attempt to steal. Instead, I went to the garden door and knocked. I explained our predicament to Mrs. Courtney, who was very generous. "Come out back with me, and I'll show you what you can pick." It was amazing. She let us take all of her carrots, beets and string beans. When we came to the rows of tomatoes, she let us take everything from one whole row. She also let us strip a few strawberry bushes. The boys enjoyed the picking, and were both very polite and thankful. Then we started back to camp.

Vico and Bob greeted us as we arrived at the kitchen with our haul. They were amazed we had been so successful. While we were still standing around the kitchen, we were joined by triumphant fishermen, displaying their meager catches, as excited as sport fishermen might display their prized trophies. Four boys came through dragging a fifty-five-gallon barrel with difficulty. There were two gigantic turtles angrily thrashing away in the barrel. A minute later another barrel half rolled and half dragged in again by four boys with two more gigantic snapping turtles. "I hate to think we've been swimming with these guys in the lake."

Bob was even more excited to see the turtle catch, and told us he would take care of them and we could look forward to our first ever turtle soup. He tugged one of the turtles out by the tail, and held it up for everyone's inspection. Kids ran back to their cabins for cameras. All of us from the three groups were in a state of heady enthusiasm from our morning adventures. I don't think any of us expected to be as successful as we were.

Lunch was late that day, but it was a huge success when it finally came. Everything that was brought to the table was food we had caught, won, or stolen during our morning activities. The turtle soup was a great hit all around. Most of the kids decided it tasted like beef stew, just missing the beef. Kids who had never eaten fish before were delighted at their new culinary discovery. No matter that the fish were scrawny, boney and not very tasty. It was *their* fish. The small supply of fresh vegetables was nibbled in small bites to make the meager portions larger in their minds, mouths, and stomachs. Everyone lolled through the meal, making it last as long as possible. My boys who had come back with steak and hamburger meat were promised they would see their prize catch at another meal, either that night or the next day. Vico and Roland walked the aisles between tables, big smiles on their faces. They stopped here and there, checking on how the kids were enjoying their very special meal. On the way back to their own table, Vico stopped at my table and informed me there would be another program meeting after lunch. I watched as Vico made similar stops for Jeff, Randy and Sam. Round two coming up. I wasn't going to waste any time challenging him on the name of the meeting. I would meet his afternoon program head on. Whatever Vico had planned, I'd be ready to argue for a different course of action. This was going to be a test of wills, and I bet my will was stronger. After lunch, on my way to the office, I invited Cozy to join us.

19

Taking Charge

Vico

I was mildly surprised but hardly shocked to see Cozy at this small meeting, but I didn't say a word about it. The meeting started peacefully and happily, with all of us congratulating ourselves and one another on the success of the morning and the pleasure of eating fresh food again. Then I took out my schedule and got to the substance of the meeting. I had made a decision that most of the afternoon would be normal activities, or as close to normal as possible, only modified where necessary to take account of the underwater fields, tennis courts, etc. The kids needed a change of pace and would soon get tired of food gathering if that was all they did. I also introduced some program items which benefited from the small lakes which had accumulated on low spots around the campus ... A tug of war where the losers would be dragged through the water was a sure winner ... A laundry-washing contest was a little more questionable ... Volleyball played in deep water on the soccer field was bound to be a hit at least until they got too wet and too cold. Jeff suggested raft building as a project since there was so much dead wood brought down onto campus from the torrential rains. I thought that was a great suggestion and wrote that in for the Junior program. Tubby and Randy were happy with the programs for their campers. Joey had kept silent through the whole presentation. But I could tell he appeared ready to launch an attack.

"Vico, your program looks good, but I don't think we're ready for it yet. We really should keep working to get more food in here. I know supplies are supposed to be on the way, but nobody knows when they will get here. And we have no idea how much of our normal supplies will get through. We can't risk waiting until we're down to nothing. There might even be another storm, and that will complicate the supply line still further before anything gets through to us. We should take advantage of the good weather while we have it, and see if we can accumulate enough additional food to supplement what we have and give us an extra day or two of food we may need later."

We were all listening, and he was making a strong case. It is hard to argue against the reasonable and cautious approach Joey advocated. In fact, before finalizing the schedule for the afternoon, I had given serious consideration to a program that continued the search for food, but had rejected it. I let him go on and spell out his plan.

"I think we should pretty much run the morning program again only changing the units around so everyone is doing something different than they did in the morning. We could even add to it by having some of the seniors go hunting for some game in the woods."

Jeff interrupted. "Come off it Joey. What the hell are you talking about? Hunting? Kids with rifles? What are they going to shoot, a few squirrels and chipmunks? More likely they'll wind up shooting one another." I thought Jeff's point was irrefutable, but it was good to let them all give their opinions.

"Some of the kids are pretty good shots", said Sammy, who doubled as the camp riflery instructor. "I could pick out the few who are the best shots and I'll bet they'd come back with something. It might be worthwhile."

As the discussion continued on the pros and cons of hunting, which was plainly ridiculous, it was accompanied by a lot of off-the-wall suggestions and much laughter ... Joey had made a mistake and he knew it. Before it went on too long he interrupted.

"I'm withdrawing my hunting suggestion. Jeff was right. It's not worth gambling. The safety of the campers comes first. That's exactly my point, Vico. Having the kids do a tug of war, play deep water volleyball and build rafts may be fun, but anything that takes away from food gathering is a gamble on our very survival. There's plenty of time for play when we have enough food."

"Thank you Joey, you've made your point, and it's a legitimate point. I think we all understand and appreciate your view. I certainly wouldn't do anything I thought was risky for our kids, but I don't see a half a day of play time as a risk. If any of the rest of you have anything further you want to say, speak up."

"Joey's right. We ought to stock up more." This was from Cozy. "I think we should take a vote."

"A vote will accomplish nothing, Cozy. I made up the program and it is my responsibility. It's my job as Head Counselor to make the daily schedules. Right now, in Nelson's absence, I'm running the camp. I don't want to be dictatorial, and I don't think I have been. You've all had the opportunity to speak up, and you have all spoken up at this morning's meeting and again now. That's the way I'll run the meetings. Nobody will be shut off, but a formal vote is not called for at all. I consulted with Roland before this meeting. He agrees with this program and three of you Unit Leaders think it looks good for the afternoon. So that's the program we're going to run. As for the Seniors, Joey. If you think they can stand a little more food gathering without becoming too bored or demoralized I authorize you to vary the program for your boys in any reasonable way, provided only there is no hunting, and that you keep me informed so I know what everyone is doing and where they are. Just send word to the office if anybody is leaving camp as part of food gathering. That's it for now, guys ; I think you should all get back with your kids for what's left of rest period."

20

Joey's Program Falters

Joey

I fumed silently as Cozy and I left the meeting. Somehow Vico had managed to sidestep the issue and leave me feeling isolated from the other Unit Leaders and without a viable cause. Almost worse is the fact I was stuck with my own program option; the Seniors were going to have to attempt more gathering that afternoon. I didn't really have a choice. That's what I had been advocating for everyone.

It didn't take long for me to recognize what a bad idea it was. At the end of rest period, when I announced the program, my announcement was greeted by a chorus of groans and even sporadic boos from the campers, and a less vocal but equally unenthusiastic response from my counselors. But I couldn't backtrack.

As I led my resentful troops into the swamps, and down to the water attempting to gather food, it was clear that nobody had his heart in it. The morning's enthusiasm had not survived lunch and rest period. It didn't help that our kids had to pass all of the other groups in camp playing, laughing, and clearly having fun. My counselors were looking on this as some kind of punishment, and they blamed me for it. I understood since I felt pretty much the same. This was a new and uncomfortable reality for me. They usually just did whatever I asked without question. I gave up trying to justify the decision to them because I was having enough trouble convincing myself. Help would be on its way in a day or two and the food shortage would be over. Certainly, having our kids sacrifice the afternoon, creating an unhappy situation wouldn't be worth much in terms of satisfying actual food needs. By mid-afternoon, the kids and counselors had more than enough. That was obvious from all of the grumbling and the lackluster attempts they were making. I called it quits and gave the kids the chance to run and play ball. My announcement of suspension of food gathering was met by cheers that seemed genuinely enthusiastic. Their cheers were far better than the boos and groans I heard earlier,

21

Relief Arrives but a New Problem Emerges

Vico

I heard the clatter overhead and raced out the door to see how close they were. The helicopter was just across the lake and headed our way. It seemed everyone in camp heard the clatter at once. Kids and counselors came streaming from all directions running toward the Senior ball field, the largest flat area in camp. There was joy on their faces and I could hear laughter as they started to run up to the Senior ball field. I did my best to get ahead of the running, jumping, skipping, happy throng of kids and counselors on their way to deliverance. By the time I got to the Senior field, Joey had things under control. I have to give him credit. He had set out traffic cones, leaving a large central area with Senior boys forming safety lines to keep younger campers from getting too close to the landing copters.

Our campers were literally screaming their excitement to one another as the helicopter slowly lowered into the middle of the opening. When it finally landed, our kids knew to stay back until the props stopped swirling. As soon as they were still, the poor pilot was surrounded and overwhelmed. He was used to delivering supplies, but I don't think he had ever been involved in a scene like this one. He laughed and looked just as happy as the campers. I made my way through, and with some help, managed to get the kids quiet.

"Hi, I'm Vico, and I'm sure glad to see you. I think you can tell from what's going on around you that we are *all* very happy to see you. I'm not sure what you have on board, but whatever you've brought it will be very welcome."

The pilot looked like one of the good guys in a John Wayne movie and sounded like an American Airlines pilot. He returned my greeting with an appropriate Texas twang.

"Well, looking at your crowd of young folk I have the feeling they're going to be just a tiny bit disappointed when you all see what I have. I'm number one of the rescue resupply group. My chopper is filled with what they call survival food. There'll be two more coming behind me. Your kiddos are probably looking for hamburgers and fries. They'll be coming, probably by chopper number three. They'll just have to be a little patient. You want to explain to the kids before we start unloading?"

Roland had come up by then and he took charge of the actual unloading operation. He asked Cozy to help and the two of them and the pilot unloaded sacks of flour and sugar first, then cases of canned fruit and finally cereals. The crowd was mostly silent during the unloading until the first giant carton of Frosted Flakes was unloaded. That was met by a roar of approval and was followed by another almost immediately after as Sugar Pops emerged. The entire unloading took a very few minutes, and the pilot closed his supply hatch.

"I've got to be on my way now. Those kids need to move back farther away from here. You know these machines don't always go straight up. Sometimes when I start the rotors we move sideways a little before we start moving up. Just give me plenty of clearance. We'd hate to have an accident. You can keep your kids handy up here if you like. There should be another chopper here in a half hour or so with more for your camp. Good luck."

The next helicopter didn't create nearly as much excitement among the campers, but they all gathered once again to see what new goodies might arrive. They watched as cases of milk, margarine, and soybeans came out of the hatch, followed by cases of fresh melons, plums, peaches, and finally, corn. A great cheer went up, and, though the shipment didn't have meats and poultry, it contained items that would satisfy lots of cravings and would go a long way toward making most of our population content with the meals. It was better and more than I had expected. The mission of the Navy was to prevent starvation, not to pamper the sons and daughters of the rich with roast beef and steak. Certainly, they had fulfilled their mission nobly.

I took stock of our situation, and it looked like the food crisis could be over. In general, things were looking much better! The sun was shining and the water level was going down. Roland told me it dropped a full foot since yesterday. The major roads would be reopening soon, maybe as soon as the next day. True the waterfront was still a mess, with dock sections and boats strewn all over the lake. But later the counselors could form a safe circle around kids in the water to give them a General Swim. Some land activities were running even though many of the fields were still like bogs. Fortunately, there are enough high spots for many of the field sports to adapt and get games in. Walking around that morning, I saw that the kids seemed to be enjoying the improvised games. They were just happy to be out and playing again.

The staff mood was also much improved. From my standpoint, Roland was playing just the role I hoped he would play, advisor and backup. I had feared that he might have planned to actually take over. The Unit Leaders, even Joey, appeared to be working enthusiastically with their kids. I was right to feel pleased with the situation, and optimistic about having a really good final two weeks, sending our kids home happy with camp and eager to return next year. Knowing something intellectually is one thing, emotionally another. There was a warning voice inside that told me not to relax; not to get too comfortable, smug, or even happy. Something could easily come along to throw us all into turmoil all over again. The other shoe could drop.

It didn't take long. Late that afternoon, Jeff Saunders came into my office. "Vico, we have a problem. It hasn't affected my kids directly, but it affects camp, and it's something I'm sure you'll want to take care of as soon as possible."

Whatever Jeff was about to tell me I was sure I would prefer not to have to hear it. My God, with all we had been through this summer, we didn't need any new problems. Of course, I had to hear it, and I had to deal with the bad news, whatever it was. "OK, Jeff, what's the problem?"

"I don't like to talk about other counselors, but our responsibility is to the kids first and foremost. Dick Reback has been getting physical with his kids. It's probably been going on for some time now, but I didn't want to say anything unless I was sure. You know what a noogie is, right?" I nodded yes. I knew where this was going, but I didn't want to cut Jeff off until he told me the whole story.

"Well, at first, I thought a noogie or two was all there was to it, and I thought I nipped it in the bud a while back. Early in the summer, we were at the waterfront one day and I saw him give

Stevie Himmelman a hard punch on his left shoulder. Roland saw it too, and he shouted at Reback. I didn't know if anything else was going to happen to Reback and I wanted to make sure he wouldn't be tempted to do it again, so I went to talk to him. I told him he'd better not do that again or he'd wind up being sent home. I reminded him that hitting a kid or any physical punishment of a camper was totally prohibited and a firing offense, and he was lucky he got off so light that time. He told me he would never do anything like that again ever, and sounded sincere."

"You know, with all that's been going on this summer I haven't paid that much attention to Reback or his campers until recently. He and his kids aren't part of my unit. For the few days when it was raining, we never saw kids with their shirts off, but when the sun came out and we were able to get back outside, at least half the time the boys were either in tee shirts or had no shirts on at all. Today we had our first general swim since before the rain. The kids were all excited to go swimming, and just about everybody was in having fun except Reback's kids. All six of them were on the benches above the swim area and they all had shirts on with sleeves that covered their upper arms, which was kinda strange. I went over to them and asked Billy Massotti why he and the others weren't swimming. I picked Billy because he's a 'perfect camper'. He was in my group last year and I know him really well. He never does anything wrong, so I didn't think he would be sitting up there as a punishment, but I had no idea what else it could be. Reluctantly, he told me their counselor was punishing the whole cabin, and part of the punishment was no swimming for the next three days. *We finally have beautiful sunny weather and he won't let his campers go swimming?* What could they have done that was so bad? Then I remembered that punch I saw at the beginning of the summer. I called Stevie Himmelman aside to try to get the story from him. I'm going to paraphrase what he said, but it'll be pretty close to his exact words.

" 'We were noisy after taps last night, and we took too long to quiet down so he got mad at us and said no swimming. But he was just looking for an excuse. He didn't want everyone in camp to see we all had black and blue arms from the noogies. We all have them. They're starting to change color and fade a little now. I guess he figured in three days the evidence will be gone.'

"I ended the conversation then and there, and I knew you would want to be the one to deal with it."

"Thanks, Jeff. You were right to bring it to me. This sounds pretty bad. Was there anything else?" Jeff shook his head 'no'. Listening to Jeff's account I knew how this had to end. I just had to think through just how to go about what had to be done.

"Thank you, Jeff. This can't be allowed to go on, and you were right to come to me. I'll handle it from here, but do me a favor and don't discuss this with anyone else today. A lot of conversation traveling around camp won't help those boys, or the camp."

Before dinner, Roland stopped by the office, as was now his routine, to get a rundown on how the afternoon went, the parts he couldn't see from the waterfront. I'm sure he was assuming there was nothing terribly eventful, and we could have our assembly followed by dinner and call it a great day. I told him about what Jeff reported, and how upset he was. We both agreed that if the story was true, Dick Reback would have to be fired, but first he was entitled to tell his side. We couldn't just assume that everything the kids told Jeff was accurate, although since it was the entire cabin, I would tend to believe them. We might even have to speak with some of the kids ourselves, but I hoped that wouldn't be necessary. We asked Dick to come into the office right after dinner.

When he did he didn't deny a thing. He did try to explain himself, thinking we might agree that he was somehow justified in his actions. "I tried hard", he said. "After that incident the first week of camp I knew I wasn't supposed to ever hit them, even in fun; but you have to admit, Nelson gave me the worst group of kids in camp. They never stop yammering and complaining and disagreeing about everything. All those days we couldn't get out because of the rain we spent way too many hours together indoors every day, and they got impossible! So, yeah, I worked out a punishment system. One noogie for not shutting up when I told them to, two noogies for talking back and giving me lip, and three noogies for anyone whose voice woke me up in the morning before reveille. None of the kids complained. They didn't mind. They seemed to enjoy it. It was like a game where they earned points."

"You think they didn't mind? They hated it! And it's not because they're bad kids. You may have thought of it as a game, but they didn't.

"You know that hitting kids is absolutely forbidden in the camp rules. You just can't seem to get it. It is wrong to hit kids. It is forbidden to hit kids. It is spelled out as a cause for immediate dismissal, and we discussed it over and over again during orientation period. It's also simple common sense. Your way of dealing with your campers leaves us no choice. A long rainy spell is no excuse. Dick, your little game is going to cost you an immediate ride home.

"I want you out of here as soon as possible. You may not realize it, but your kids are afraid of you. You can't be with them one more minute than it takes for you to pack and get out. This is non-negotiable. Do you have a car here?"

"No, I wish I did."

"Then we'll get you to town in time to catch the 9:30 bus back to Boston. I just want to make sure your parents know you're coming. Fortunately, our phones are working again. Make that call right now. I don't care what reason you give them for coming home, but it has to be clear to them that you are coming home. You understand that, don't you?"

I sat there while he dialed, and listened as he told his mother he was coming home. I didn't stick around for his explanation. My next concern now was picking the right Junior Counselor to promote to replace him as cabin counselor for the rest of the summer and to pick a cover story to explain to his campers why he suddenly decided he had to go home.

22

Joey Proposes to Replace Green & Brown with a New Program

Joey

In bed that night, I thought about what had happened, the camp's newest cause célèbre. I wasn't surprised Dick turned out to be a loser. Thinking back on the summer, I couldn't remember seeing him socializing in any way with any other member of the staff. He always struck me as kind of a loner. But it was more than that. He was just an odd guy. It's easy to believe he could pick on young kids that way. He had no business working with children. He should never have been hired. Vico didn't have a choice. He's handling this just the way I would. Normally I would try to rally support for a guy getting fired, but not for this guy. Not for what he did! Good riddance!

Once I decided I didn't want to do anything about it, I fell asleep rather easily, and woke up the next morning with renewed energy, fired up to give my kids their best day of the summer. It was a great day too. We played Watermelon League with the teams alternating between softball and volleyball in the morning. It was fun, like old times. Then we went down to the waterfront. Regular swim was impossible, but Roland asked if some of us would like to round up dock sections, which had floated all over the lake, and paddle them back to the swim area. My kids loved doing it. It was fun, and they got a sense of accomplishment from it. We retrieved about half of the dock sections and lined them up on the beach. Roland said he would get them in order so that in the afternoon we could reset some of them in the swim area where they belonged. After lunch, we played touch football and a new game called Scatteration Ball, which the kids seemed to like. Then we went back and helped Roland and Bob Weinberg put the docks together. The afternoon wound up with a big water splash fight, and it was altogether the best day of the summer for my boys. I loved it too. That night we had our first real dinner in a long time. We had roast beef, mashed potatoes and bowls of the gravy the kids love. And the ice cream with fudge sauce and whipped cream. It would be hard to beat that.

It was my turn for a night out after taps. Kerri and I left camp for the first time in a very long time. We went to the Gray House, which was filled with counselors from other camps, all out celebrating the end of universally enforced isolation. Kerri and I had cantaloupe sundaes, danced together, and did a lot of laughing. At about eleven-thirty we drove back to camp and sat in the car making out. It was a great night to top off a perfect day.

That night as I lay in bed, I couldn't get to sleep, again. I always had so much on my mind. What was keeping me awake this time? After such a good day I should have slept like a baby. Why am I having a problem? Camp seems to be going well, maybe too well. Maybe that's the problem. I tossed and turned for a long time until my body finally took command and insisted my mind should turn off for the night. It worked, but it was not a cure for my disquiet.

After a too-short night's sleep, I woke up feeling lethargic. I went through the motions and did everything I was supposed to do. I got my campers moving, said the right words and announced a fun schedule for the day, but I knew I was going on autopilot. My body was going on muscle memory, but my brain was not fully engaged.

It was busy with its own machinations.

Finally, it dawned on me what was eating at me. I missed politics. And I missed the intrigue, and the power I had enjoyed from it in the past. Once I acknowledged the cause of my upset, or unrest, or whatever it was, I got really angry with myself. The intense political schemes I had been involved with at school for all those months were precisely what I had wanted to avoid when I decided to leave student protests behind me in Boston for the summer, and come to camp. Sure, we had some political battles at the start of the summer, and those ended with Nelson's death. It's only been a few days, but I have to admit I miss the rough and tumble of politics. Its absence has left me feeling unfulfilled. I miss the fun of planning, particularly planning for how a camp should run.

Since Nelson's death, things were running too smoothly. Vico seemed to be running the camp well, and there had been no big screw-ups. The other Unit Leaders were content to go along with the programs as presented. My Council idea was a dead issue. I had to give the guy credit. He outmaneuvered me on that, and his UL meetings were well run. He was even being democratic. Nothing to complain about. So why was I aggravating myself? Was I so crazy for power and politics that I wanted to upset a smoothly running apple cart? I had a good case against Cohen, but it would be tough to fault Vico, since Cohen died. And yet, there was one remaining serious issue to be addressed before the camp season was over. It was the issue of basic camp philosophy.

Later that day, without me having to stir up anything, the cause fell into my lap. Vico called for a very brief meeting after lunch. He wanted to remind us that at the Sunday night counselor meeting, we would be picking teams for Green and Brown, camp's Color

War. He wanted us to think about who we would honor as Captains in each of our units, and to think about how we would match up the campers for competition in everything from archery and baseball to spelling bees and softball.

On Sunday night I had to be ready, prepared not only with the strong arguments against the camp's tradition of Color War, but also with a truly attractive alternative special event for the last week of the camp season. I was lying in bed working through alternatives when suddenly the idea came to me, the big idea, the idea I needed to knock that meeting on its ass. They're going to love it. I just needed to work through enough details to make a killer presentation. I sat up in bed, grabbed my clipboard, and started making notes. The ideas came tumbling out faster than I could write them down. The more I got on paper, the more excited I became at the prospect of my sensational New Program in action. I kept writing and reading, scratching out and re-writing and re-reading. It had to be perfect. It had to make sense. It had to be magical, to capture their imagination. It had captured mine! With enough on my clipboard, I was finally ready to make a presentation as soon as the occasion presented itself. There were three more days to get ready, to work out the kinks, and then, *look-out, Vico. You'll be knocked out of the box by this one.* I wondered if I should try it out on Cozy. No, I wanted to surprise them all, Cozy included.

The Sunday night meeting started as such meetings always start. The Director and Head Counselor (Vico held both roles) made his opening remarks, complimenting the staff about all of the things that went right that week and then suggesting a number of small items that could and should be improved in the week to come. He did it well. His compliments were obviously sincere. He handled the meeting with confidence and skill, far better than he had managed similar meetings in the early part of the summer. I sat listening, waiting for the preliminaries to end. Vico finally shifted from general counselor matters to the approach of Color War.

"I know you old timers know all about Green and Brown, but before we break up into groups to make up the teams, I want any of the counselors who have never experienced a camp color war to feel free to ask any questions about how it goes. If there are no questions, we can start working on teams right now."

That was my cue. I raised my hand, stood up, and walked from my seat in the back to about the middle of the seated counselors. I didn't want to invade Vico's territory in the front. It was important I not give the impression I wanted to take over the meeting, though, of course, this is exactly what I planned to do.

"It seems to me when we all agreed to relieve Nelson of his directing duties ..."

There was an audible gasp as I mentioned the unmentionable. I waited for a minute for it to quiet down again ... "one of the things we all agreed about was that many of the concepts and long-standing policies that Camp Adventure lived by were out of date. Remember, it wasn't really the man we wanted to get rid of. It was his 1920s ideas. Now Nelson is gone. Not the way you would have liked and certainly not the way I would have liked, but he is gone."

They were all still unsettled by me mentioning Nelson. I paused to let them settle down.

"But camp policies have not changed in any way since his death. Please don't take this the wrong way, Vico. I think you have done a great job dealing with things during the emergency, and have been doing a great job running the camp since, but we all know camp is running now exactly as if Nelson was still with us. We have a little less than two weeks left in the camp season, and we have the opportunity that most of us will never again experience, the opportunity to create innovative program changes to replace outdated ones. We have the chance to fashion a new concept and put it into practice. That is what I propose to you tonight."

I could sense they were uneasy, but they were listening and interested. That was all I needed. It was time to shock them with my program.

"If there is one program that is absolutely typical of the outdated concepts on which this camp has been run it is *Color War*. I know it is not real warfare, but it is an insidious competition: the kind of competition that grooms boys to become the warriors of the future. Our world is filled with more than enough warriors. Those of us who have lived through Color War in the past know it creates a degree of hostility and disrupts harmony within each cabin group. It sets friend against friend, and carries some campers and even counselors into insane behavior. If there is one camp program we should do away with it is Color War."

I looked around the room for reactions. Cozy was nodding agreement. Bob Weinberg and Major Michaelson looked as though they also agreed. I tried to avoid looking at the other Unit Leaders. Fred Sweeney and Jeff Sealy were receptive, while Tubby Brown had a hurt look on his face. Vico did not look happy. He was turning red in the ears the way he always did when he was upset. Roland looked as though he was ready to explode. It was time to survey the ULs. Jeff Saunders seemed to be listening, while Randy and Sam looked antagonistic. Everyone was shocked to a certain extent but, other than Roland and Vico, who were understandably upset, I think the rest of the staff looked interested. There was no doubt I had their attention.

Fred Sweeney's hand went up. "It's all well and good to talk about doing away with Green and Brown, but that's the most exciting event of the whole summer for most of the campers; the one that sends them home high as a kite and filled with positive feelings about the summer and about camp. If we did away with Color War, we would have to invent an incredibly good alternative. So far, you've just presented the negative. Let's hear what you have up your sleeve?"

"You're perfectly right Fred. There has to be an exciting event to end the summer, one good enough to replace Color War. I've given a great deal of thought to that and have come up with a very strong program to propose. I suggest a week with an American Indian theme. This event will include everyone in camp, boys and girls. It will last as long as five or six days and will represent a complete departure from past programming at Camp Adventure. It will combine a study of American Indian culture with nature, campcraft, and some mild competition."

I certainly had their attention. Even Vico and Roland looked curious. It was time for me to paint the picture.

"Imagine this. We plan for a week of American Indian activities. We divide into six tribes, boys and girls on the same teams. Each tribe will have a home territory. The physical layout would be something like this. We can subdivide the woods on the other side of the road into two distinct homelands for two of our tribes. Another tribe can have the land by the Millstream as their home area. A fourth tribe can occupy the island on the far side of the lake and two tribes can actually stay on the main campus. We will have to divide this area into two equal sections. The tribes whose homes are on the campus will have to understand they cannot use any of the buildings. Each tribe will have a camper chief, warriors, braves, and a council of elders. That's the counselors' role, tribal elders."

I saw heads shaking as I went on. I didn't exactly have them with me yet, but I would.

"The first two days of the program will be devoted to the tribes physically setting up camp. Their job is to make their area livable for their tribe. They have to improvise shelters, protect sleeping areas against animals, and find a way to secure their food supplies. The Council of Elders on each team will help them develop a history and customs consistent with the history of the actual tribes. I discovered that our camp library has several books on American Indian tribes of New England. These will be helpful for the Council of Elders. As part of each tribe's customs, they will have created and learned dances and chants."

Somebody was groaning. I couldn't see who it was, but that was a bad sign.

"On the final night, each tribe will demonstrate both their dances and their chants to the entire Council which will include all of the tribes. They will have to do a lot of rehearsing to prepare for that grand finale.

"As part of the first day of activity, each tribe will have to cultivate the land, send out a team hunting with the bows and arrows, slingshots, and anything else they are able to fashion. Some of them will forage for roots and berries. On each team there will be a group in charge of cooking. Of course, we will have to supply each tribe with additional real food from the kitchen, but they will have to manage to cook it. They will have to get water from the lake and streams, transport it to their areas and boil it before they can drink it. They will have to figure out and set up toilet facilities, separate for the braves and squaws. Incidentally, that is the only place where we will differentiate activities based on sex. By the third day they should be ready for tribal games. We'll have two days of tribal games. One game could be a huge Capture the Flag game covering the entire camp property and the surrounding woods. That can be a daylong event. All throughout, the tribes will spend time getting ready for the final day's activities, with a variety of games of strength by champions from each tribe. There are literally hundreds of games we can draw upon. I know there are still a few loose ends, but I've worked out most of the problems, and I am convinced if we set our minds to it, we will have one truly great event."

I was reasonably sure I'd done more than simply get their attention. I thought they were intrigued and most of them were with me.

"Any comments?" I smiled as I looked around the room.

"Sounds good, Joey," Cozy chimed in. Roland stood up, and I knew he would be less than enthusiastic. I was not disappointed.

"Joey, if you wanted to question Color War you could have brought it up at one of the Unit Leader meetings rather than waiting for *this* meeting, which you knew would be devoted to making up teams for Green and Brown. Your suggestion is out of order. I don't happen to think much of your substitute program, but even if I did, this is clearly not the time or the place for a proposal like that.

"Vico, why don't we just get on with making up the teams. That's the way it's going to wind up anyway, and this meeting will be long enough without going off on Joey's tangent."

As Roland sat down, I was ready to respond, but I held back waiting for Vico's response. Everyone's eyes were on Vico, and I wondered if he would fight, or cave in. I kind of hoped he'd fight. Then it would be a showdown between us, and I was willing to bet I'd come out on top. Vico hesitated for a moment, and then he turned toward Roland.

"Where's your sense of democracy, Roland? Everyone has a right to say his piece. Shouldn't we consider a good idea no matter where it comes from or when? I don't think we should rule anything out on a technicality, or refuse to hear it because it comes too late. Joey, tell us more. Let us in on all of the details so we can properly judge the merits of your proposal."

I didn't know whether he was mocking me or not, but I was not pleased with his attitude of sweet reasonableness. I expected him to either fight or give in. Did he really want to leave it up to the counselors to decide the merits of my proposal, or was he just making fun of it? Asking me for details? He knew perfectly well that details are ironed out at a desk, with a lot of thought and consideration for every aspect of the decisions. That couldn't be recreated in a meeting like this. I will say he sounded like he believed in democracy. I think the counselors might have been swallowing his line. I would have to cover myself, but couldn't get too bogged down in details in that moment. I think he knew that.

"Vico, I've given you the essence of my proposal. It seems to me the question is not one of getting into details at this time, but deciding whether people like my basic idea. If you all like it, we can work out the details later in a quiet place where there will be time to consider the ramifications of anything we decide."

I saw Roland pop up again. He clearly did not want to let this happen.

"I think your idea stinks to high heaven! Not only does it stink. It is a potential disaster. You spoke of the kids winding up high from this event. I think they would wind up so low from your brainstorm they would never want to set foot in this camp ever again. Not only that, but we would probably wind up sending a bunch of sick kids home from exposure, injuries, or poor nutrition. You know how cold the nights can get here in late August. The campers are looking forward to Green and Brown. For most of them, it's the best activity of the whole summer. The campers who come back every year, came this year expecting Green and Brown at the end of the summer. This has been a tough enough summer for them without eliminating the one program that might leave them with happy and positive memories. You're a great speaker, Joey, better than me, but all of your fancy talk comes down to a bunch of words. You talk about changing the camp. You've already changed it plenty when you took control of camp and broke Nelson's heart. I hope you're satisfied with the mischief some of you have already caused. You destroyed Nelson and put the very future of this wonderful camp in doubt. At least you should have the decency not to destroy the rest of the summer for the kids. There's only a little time left. Think about them for a change instead of your own agenda."

When he sat down some of the veteran counselors smiled knowingly. This was the Roland they all knew so well. Some were smiling because they agreed with him. Others because they weren't about to cross him. Others looked shocked. They listened to his rude assessment and kept their mouths shut. The fact that he was implying I was responsible for Nelson's death didn't occur to them, but I admit his attack left me momentarily speechless. I hoped the violence and unfairness of his attack would hit them soon and it would rebound against him. Did they realize he had just accused all of us of killing Nelson? I didn't answer him back, but surprisingly Vico did.

"I know how much Camp Adventure means to you, Roland, and I'm sure you got carried away because of the unfortunate events of this summer rather than because of Joey's suggestion. Let's get away from trying to assign blame for an unfortunate tragedy, and get back to the merits of Joey's proposal rather than discussing his motives. I would like to assume that Joey and you and everyone who speaks tonight has our campers' best interests at heart."

He was being reasonable and clearly attempting to lessen the tension in the room. Interestingly, he was splitting the establishment in the eyes of most of the counselors.

I could see that as he listened to Vico, Roland was relieved. He could see Vico was doing exactly what he had to do to prevent Roland's venom from making reasonable discussion impossible. It was certainly clear to me, Vico was bailing him out. This guy is turning out to be a way cooler cucumber than any of us had given him credit for being. He had figured out just the right tactic to reverse the mood in the room. When Roland finished ranting, I thought I had them. Then Vico put us right back where we were. They were going to discuss this thing and analyze it to death unless I could do something. I underestimated the bastard again. I was about to get up and thank Vico, but didn't get the chance. Jeff was on his feet with his hand raised. Vico called on Jeff before I got a chance.

"Joey, I know you don't want to get down to every last detail, but I want to ask a few practical questions that require answers before we can go much further. I hope you have some good answers. I'm not worried about how we would divide up the tribes. That's a logistical problem we could work out. I'm worried about what happens when we are out there in the woods. You implied we'd be digging latrines, but really, what would we do for toilet facilities? Even assuming we did a decent job locating and digging them, nobody would be happy using latrines, certainly not the girls."

"Why not? They do it in the army all the time, and there are women in the army these days."

"Joey, these are kids. They aren't army recruits. By the way, do we take toilet paper with us or do we make do with dried leaves? What if they ended up using poison ivy?"

This brought a tension-relieving laugh.

"Of course, we would have a supply of toilet paper for each tribe."

"What about sleeping and changing clothes? These tribes are going to be coed, and the kids and counselors are going to need their privacy."

"You're right, of course, each tribe will have a few tents along with them for changing. The tents will be used both for changing and as emergency shelters in case of a heavy rain storm. As for sleeping, I don't see any harm if boys and girls are sleeping outdoors, in their sleeping bags, in the same general area. We would designate separate sleeping areas for boys and girls."

I didn't know what had gotten into Jeff, but he just wouldn't let go.

"I'm sure those areas would wind up very flexible and I'm sure you and Kerri wouldn't mind that either."

Once again, Jeff got a laugh from the group. "Seriously Joey, what about those separate sleeping areas for boys and girls? That might get tough to enforce. It's not hard to imagine some of the Senior boys and girls would find a way to get together. It would be very difficult to prevent that happening in the dark. There's no telling how far this could lead."

"Come off it, Jeff. Now you're looking for trouble. If you are seriously worried about these kids having sex, we could make sure when we divide the senior teams that boys and girls who are established boyfriends and girlfriends would wind up on different tribes."

"Joey, be honest with yourself. The sleeping areas for boys and girls would have to be really far apart. If they were within range of each other, it would be trouble. If I was out there lying in the woods knowing Gloria was in a sleeping bag a short distance away, I suspect I would have trouble keeping my mind and attention on my kids and what they were doing."

"Maybe, but that is not something we have to decide this minute. Do you have any other questions?" I hoped Jeff was through, but my hope was not realized.

"I've saved the really important question for last. What on earth are the kids going to actually do for activities during those long days in the woods? I know what you said, but all of that together doesn't really add up to one good day of activity. I know my kids. They need action."

I heard a buzz of agreement with Jeff's last comment and I had to reverse that immediately. "They'd have plenty to do! It wouldn't be the same old stuff they've been doing all summer. If you mean baseball and soccer are action and nothing else is, then I would agree, but it'll take a lot more time, energy and imagination than you think to do the things I have outlined. We've had some experience with food gathering and fishing. You know how much time that can take. Making lean-tos, storage areas, and campfires would keep them busy for at least a couple of days. Then the big Capture the Flag games will take a whole day. The day before the final challenge matches, each tribe will have preliminary trials and tests to determine who their champions are for each activity. It will take a lot of time to teach the kids their tribal songs and dances. You know how long it used to take to teach and rehearse songs and cheers for Color War. This would be similar, only not a competition, just a matter of pride to perform well. Cooking will take hours every day for some of them. Don't' worry, they'll be plenty to do."

Jeff broke in again. "I was hoping you would have more to add. Those things don't begin to add up to enough activity. My kids would be bored to tears after the first day. They'd be driving me crazy to get them some real activities. Joey, I hate to say it, but I for one will be voting against your proposal." There was a smattering of applause. But there were other hands going up. Cozy, Randy, and Major all had hands in the air. Vico gave Cozy the nod.

"I'm not worried about them having enough to do. Jeff, use your imagination. If worse comes to worst, we can rig volleyball nets between the trees. We can take some balls along with us to our various area. With branches all over the place the kids can make lacrosse sticks and they can learn a real game the Indians invented. I think it's a great idea, Joey. I'm all for it."

Tubby Brown spoke up next. "I'm not for it at all. My kids don't want anything to do with girls, but more important, they love

Green and Brown."

I looked around the room. There were no more hands. I thought it should be my turn to respond, but Vico stood up and once again I had lost the moment. Judging the current mood of the group, there was no way I was going to interrupt Vico. He had come across as remarkably evenhanded on the subject.

"Joey, I'm afraid I'm opposed to your suggestion. First, I disagree with you strongly about the merits of Green and Brown. True, I have never seen it in action here, but I have been to other camps where they have Color War, and in every case it was the highlight of the camp season, generating terrific excitement like nothing else ever did. I see it as a grand game. The kids who have been here before know Green and Brown and they apparently love it. They've been driving me crazy all summer chanting 'Let it rain, let it pour, all we want is Color War!' There is no doubt in my mind that they look forward to this as the highlight of the entire camp season. Second, there is the legitimate procedural objection that Roland voiced. If you wanted to bring up something as serious as a fundamental program change like this we should have heard about it long before now. We've had at least a half dozen Unit Leader meetings in the past couple of weeks. You could have brought this up then. Broaching it at the last minute is both rude and inconsiderate. You knew we would be dividing up teams tonight. I'm sure you didn't bring this up now to disrupt our plans, but if we spend much more time on your suggestion, it will have that effect. I think the subject is closed. We will have Green and Brown this summer. And this is the night you all have to choose up teams."

"When I said we should listen to new ideas and suggestions I was serious, and I have been listening. Joey, I've been thinking about your program, not instead of Green and Brown, but as a possible additional activity, a filler for the important few days between now and the start of Green and Brown. Actually, your idea sounded pretty good until I started to think of the ramifications. Some of them are pretty major and cannot just be brushed aside or ignored. First is the expectation of our campers' parents. When they sent their kids here, it was with the understanding that it was a boys' camp and a girls' camp and not a coed camp. They were told the activities would all be separate for boys and girls. Many of them, particularly parents of teenage girls, would be up in arms if they thought their girls would be sleeping in the woods with the boys. And they would be justified. As Jeff said, if Gloria was lying there in the woods near him, he would probably not be paying complete attention to his campers. Jeff happens to be one of the most responsible counselors in camp and clearly one of the most honest with himself. If you all look at this clearly, I'm sure you will appreciate the point he made. We wouldn't be fulfilling our most basic responsibility, paying attention to the needs and behavior of our campers. Next, the issue of hunting. We've been through that before and simply changing from guns to bows and arrows may reduce the danger slightly, but does not eliminate it. And it makes the chance of successful hunting even less likely. Our kids can't even hit the targets that are standing still, never mind fast moving tiny targets like chipmunks and squirrels, the only animals they might not frighten away with their noise. I also have to agree with Jeff that at least the younger kids would be bored. Joey, if you would like to respond you are welcome to do so, but after that, I'm willing to have a vote to see whether enough counselors think your idea is worthwhile for us to use as a filler for a few days the week before the start of Green and Brown. I won't consider using it as a replacement for Green and Brown. It's too late for that."

I know when I'm licked. I could see from their faces he had most of the counselors with him on Green and Brown. *The question was whether it was worth the effort to get them to consider my Indian week before Green and Brown. The whole point was to get rid of Color War.* I should save my energy for more important issues that may come along between now and the end of camp, and withdraw my idea now rather than lose by a vote. I can't believe I let this one get away. If I could beat Nelson Cohen, who was a powerhouse, how could I lose to Vico? Vico! I had to rethink what I wanted to accomplish for the rest of this camp season. In the meantime, Vico was waiting for my response.

"You've all heard my program plan. I don't want to belabor the issue. With a little imagination I'm sure you can see how this could have captured the kids and be a positive program. But I will withdraw my suggestion now. I think a vote will be pointless."

23

A Few Boys Want Out of Color War

Vico

He's lost them and he knows it. Two weeks ago, he had them solid, and it wouldn't have mattered what he came up with. They would have gone along. Still, I'd have to be on my toes with him, he was a powerful character. I guess the real goal would be to see if I could actually get him on my side. If I could somehow do *that*, the rest of the summer would be a breeze.

Time to get on with why we are here, "I'm pleased to announce the Head Coach of the Green team is Cozy Martin." There was restrained applause from the counselors. Nobody was surprised. The rumor mills around camp had already picked him. The identity of the other Head Coach was more of a mystery. "Head Coach of the Brown team is Tubby Brown." This time there was real applause and people went over to congratulate him and slap him on the back. I then announced which Unit Leaders and specialty counselors would serve as judges and who would be coaches for the two teams.

The formal meeting was adjourned, and it was time to split up to evaluate the kids for teams. As my counselors moved off by unit to occupy different sections of the dining hall, I motioned to Roland, and the two of us went out the door. The Unit Leaders would get back to me with their team lists much later in the evening.

"Thanks, Vico. I almost blew it in there. That kid really gets under my skin. But I think you may have finally shut him up for good, hopefully for the rest of the summer. I don't know what's eating him. He has more leadership potential than any other kid on the staff. I think his pride was hurt when he saw he couldn't win this one. I don't think he will give us any more grief this summer. What do you think? I'll trust your judgment better than my own at this point. Man, you've changed a lot these last couple of weeks. I'm sure the whole staff has noticed it, but I'm the only one likely to tell you. You've been making choices and decisions every waking hour these last weeks, most of which would have left you in a daze earlier in the summer."

"Thanks, but getting to Joey. He is really an enigma to me. Why would a kid as bright as he is be expending so much time and energy dreaming up ways to make trouble? That's clearly what this Indian business was all about. He obviously spent a lot of time on plans for that, and convinced himself he had a great idea. But was his motivation simply to throw a monkey wrench into our plans? Well, he lost this round, but in his mind the battle may still be on. He can still do lots of damage."

"I'm going to go back in and watch what's happening with his Senior group dividing up teams. Just for sour grapes, he may do everything he can to create a mismatch that will sabotage the balance in Green and Brown for our oldest kids. I'm going to have to keep an eye on our two head coaches too. Cozy and Tubby may be flattered now that they were named Head Coaches, but it won't take much for Joey to get at least Cozy way off track. It will be our job to keep them fully engaged with their teams."

I said goodnight to Roland, and circled through the dining hall, checking on each unit's progress with dividing the teams. They all seemed to be working in earnest. This was particularly true with the

Senior counselors. They were battling one another over the team placement of each camper. Joey seemed detached from the process. He just sat back and watched. The other counselors, sensing his abdication of responsibility, put in the time and effort and were doing a great job. I was proud of them. The picture left me wondering if Joey really had decided to totally withdraw from participation, or if this was just a temporary setback, with him licking his emotional wounds before he regrouped. It was hard for me to read what was going on in that devious mind. I stayed and listened for a while as the counselors in his unit debated on their placements. They finally wrapped it up at around 1:30, and trooped off, exhausted, to the Senior area. I took all of the secret team lists they had created and locked them away in my file cabinet. I indulged myself for a few minutes to think over the events of the evening, before I also headed for bed.

During the next few days, activities appeared to be truly back to normal. I didn't see much of Roland because he had to spend all of the activity time at the waterfront, trying to push kids through swim courses, stealing extra time to make up for the time lost during the flood. I didn't see much of Joey, either, during this period. He seemed to be fulfilling his UL duties and otherwise minding his own business. I couldn't ask for or expect more. The few days flew swiftly and happily by. Suddenly it was upon us. The start of Green and Brown was the next day. Both Head Coaches had prepared their staffs and had opening rallies planned for their teams. The camp was at a fever pitch of excitement in anticipation.

Joey knocked on the office door. "Can we come in?"

"Sure, come ahead." Then I looked up and saw that "we" meant

Joey and the six campers in his cabin, the oldest boys in camp, two of whom didn't know it yet, but had been picked as the camper Captains of the two teams. As I saw them squeeze through the door I said, "wait a minute. I didn't know there were so many of you. Let's go out on the porch where there is a lot more room." We walked out to the porch, and the seven of them sat down. "Okay, what's up?" They all sat stonily quiet. I saw Joey nudging Jake Newman. He was apparently the designated spokesperson for the group. Finally, and somewhat tremulously his spoke up.

"We decided we're not going to be in Green and Brown this year. We've had enough of intense competition. We came to camp to relax. We're all old friends and have been coming for years. We don't want to wind up our camp years angry with one another and enemies, even for a few days." I was taken aback and momentarily speechless at this unexpected turn of events. I had no doubt where the sentiments behind Jake's speech had originated, but I had to address the boys. I would get to Joey later.

"Jake, you know what happens here when it's Green and Brown. That's all that happens. Nothing else is going on anywhere in camp. If you weren't in Green and Brown, there wouldn't be another thing for you to do. The six of you can't just sit around and do nothing for a week. That's not what your parents are paying for and certainly not what they expect. If you're going to be in camp during Green and Brown, you're going to be in Green and Brown."

Bobby Nason piped up. He was one of the strong camper leaders and, though he didn't know it, was slated to be the Brown team Camper Captain. "We don't want to disrupt Green and Brown. We just don't want to be in it. Can't we use whatever ballfields or courts aren't used for Green and Brown activities at each period and use those for ourselves? We don't want to be in Green and Brown, but we also don't want to just sit around doing nothing. We would stay out of the way so we wouldn't interfere with Green and Brown in any way."

"You know, you guys are the leaders of camp. If you're not participating, it won't be the same for the other kids in camp. I probably shouldn't tell you this, but two of you have been named team captains for this year's competition. That's quite an honor and a responsibility. Are any of you certain you want to give up the possibility of being captain and leading half of the camp for a week? You know we count on the captains as song leaders, and as leaders of all the important events. And as the person most important in providing spirit for the whole team when your team gets together for rallies. It's an experience you will remember for the rest of your life.

"Two of you have been chosen to take on that responsibility, but you *all* are the leaders who the younger campers look up to. It would be a shame to disappoint everyone and miss this opportunity. That's quite an honor you're planning to give up. Boys, I want you to understand the situation. We want you to stay and fully enjoy your final summer as campers, but if you refuse to participate in Green and Brown we cannot allow you to stay in camp. You will have to go home. As I said, when Green and Brown is on that is all that is happening in camp.

"We can call your parents right now, and you can discuss it with them. They know you better than anybody. Let them help you decide whether you want to go home now or be in Green and Brown." I could see this came as an unpleasant surprise to them. It was not in their play book. That's when Joey stepped in and spoke for the first time.

"Thanks, Vico. I can't do a thing with them. I've been talking to them until I'm blue in the face. They just don't want to listen to reason." I was surprised by his duplicity. He was undoubtedly the one who inspired this unprecedented camper rebellion.

"That's right, Joey's been trying to get us to go along. We told him early in the summer that we didn't want to be in Green and Brown this year, and he's been trying to convince us that we should, but we've had it with Green and Brown."

That was Danny Sundberg speaking, and he was one of the pleasantest, most agreeable kids in camp. The whole thing would be incomprehensible if I believed them and thought it was all their own idea. However, I had a high degree of confidence this was not the case. This was an idea Joey had somehow planted with them and convinced them it was their own. It was clear what he had been doing these past days when he had appeared to be so cooperative. I had deluded myself into thinking he was through making trouble for the summer. I could see it for what it was. If he hadn't been able to get his way with the counselors, he was going to manipulate the campers, an unpleasant new chapter in an old story with Joey Katz. I should have been prepared. Very early in the summer there had been that counselor protest meeting I was sure he had engineered, and that was followed by the morning when the entire camp of campers and counselors had disappeared before breakfast. That was Joey's doing. Then there was that nightmare meeting when they confronted Nelson. That was Joey's doing too, no doubt about it. Yes, this was quintessential Joey, but this time he was more subtle in his maneuvering. He got the kids to do his bidding, and even convinced them the idea originated with them. What an incredible manipulator! But this I would never understand: What motivated such incredibly destructive behavior? Enough of this.

"Okay, kids, why don't the six of you go back to your cabin for a while and think it over while Joey and I have a chat. Then we'll all talk again. If you still want to skip Green and Brown, we'll call your parents and apprise them of the situation. Head back to your cabin now. Joey will be up in a few minutes and I'll see you again in half an hour or so." The kids seemed reluctant to leave and a good deal less certain of what they wanted to do than when they came in. They must have been pretty sure they could hang around here during Green and Brown, and looked shocked when I said they would have to go home. I watched them head toward the Senior area.

I sat there with Joey. We sat staring at one another. I felt almost certain that this whole thing was his idea. I couldn't tell what was going through his mind, but I thought it might be a sense of satisfaction. On the other hand, he had also looked surprised when I said the kids couldn't stay in camp as spectators. My first inclination was to fire Joey on the spot. Probably, it would be better to deal with the campers first so that their ultimate decision wouldn't be influenced by sympathy for, or out of a sense of loyalty to Joey. I waited to hear what he was going to say. I think he was waiting for me to speak first, but eventually he gave in.

"Vico, do they really have to go home if they don't want to participate?"

"That's what I said, and I meant it. We can't have them here, sitting around displaying contempt for the camp program and all the participants. It would create problems with other campers. I don't want to have to deal with that. I'd like you to go back now, wait a few minutes, and then send them back here two at a time, fifteen or twenty minutes between. When they get here, If they still say they want to miss Green and Brown we'll be placing calls to their parents."

Half an hour later, the first two boys joined me in the office. It was Jake Newman and Russ Segal.

"Welcome back, boys. Which one of you would like to call his parents first?"

"Do we have to call our parents?"

"Yes, of course you do. If you are not going to be in Green and Brown, they are going to have to agree that you can come home, and be prepared to come and get you. I'll let you explain the situation to them. Be sure to tell them why you want to miss the most exciting week of the camp season. You don't have to convince me. You have to convince your parents that this is what you really want to do. Now who wants to go first? I'll stay here in the office with you in case they have questions for me, but I won't say a word unless they ask to speak with me."

Russ Segal spoke up first. "You can call my Mom. She should be at home. I know what my Dad will say if you call him."

"You're sure you want to make the call?"

"Yes, I'll make it."

"Here's the phone. You call your Mom and tell her about your decision. Just dial the number. Don't worry about making it collect. This is camp business."

Russ dialed the number, and I think he was hoping she wouldn't be home. But she answered, and he started pleading his case. He didn't get very far. I could hear her screaming at him over the phone. "What kind of nonsense is this! You always love Green and

Brown! You come home singing the songs, and when you talk to your friends at home that's all you talk about. Where did you ever get such an idea? No, you cannot come home. You do what Vico says, and you'll have a good time. It's a good thing you didn't call your father. He'd be very upset with you."

He hung up the phone looking slightly shell shocked at his Mother's vehemence, but when he spoke up, he looked me straight in the eye, smiled and said, "I'll be here for Green and Brown. Can I go back to the cabin now? I'll tell the others my decision is to stay."

"Sure, go ahead. Jake, it's your turn. Pick up the phone and dial whichever parent you want." He got through on the first ring. I couldn't hear anything his father had to say. I did hear Jake's end of the conversation. He started by telling his father why he wanted to come home. "Yes, Vico says we have to be in it or we have to go home ... I just think I had enough competition already. I don't need more this summer...I understand competition may be good for me.......Yes, I always liked it in the past ... Yes, it was my own idea ... The whole bunk decided ... No, nobody influenced us ... Joey said he didn't agree with us, but I'm pretty sure he's on our side. We've overheard him talking to other counselors right from the start of camp about how everything is bad this summer and how Color War will be the worst ... Okay, I get it. You want me to stay and be in Green and Brown. Okay, I'll do it, but I won't be happy ... Yes, I'll do it right. I'll have a good attitude. Who knows, I might even be a team captain ... Vico told us two of us from our cabin will be team captains ... Yes, I suppose that will be fun ... Yes. I'll have a good time ... Okay, Dad, goodbye ... It's all over ... I'll do what I said ... Yes, I'll play hard."

He hung up.

"Well, you heard it. I'll be in Green and Brown and I will play hard. I have a feeling some of the other guys may change their minds about calling home when they hear how the calls went with Russ and me."

He left the office and I waited, wondering whether two more would be coming. Half an hour later Joey strolled in with the news that the boys had all changed their minds. They would all be in Green and Brown. I thanked him for the information. Later that night when I relayed the entire episode to Roland, he asked, "So what are you going to do with him? It was obviously his idea all along."

"I agree. I intend to fire him tomorrow morning."

Morning came, and with it an exciting break out for Green and Brown. Spirits were high all through camp at assembly time. It took a while for the teams to line up in their Color War configuration, and while they lined up I was pleased to see that the six who had said they wanted to drop out were enthusiastically helping get the younger kids on their teams in order.

I had no doubt their positive spirits would continue throughout. And unlike with Joey, I trusted my judgment on this. We eventually got everybody into the dining hall, seated by teams; one half of the dining hall now Green and the other half Brown. After breakfast, both teams left for spirit rallies on opposite ends of camp. The counselors who were judges held a meeting in the dining hall so they could be assigned to their morning activities where each was to referee that morning. I asked Joey to excuse himself from the meeting and join me in the office.

"Vico, I should be out there now, helping to get the judges lined up. Some of these guys are new and don't know the ropes."

"That may be true, Joey, but they're going to have to learn how to function without you. Joey, we've come to a parting of the ways. This last stunt you pulled was inexcusable." He looked stunned.

"I don't know what you're talking about, what stunt?"

"Joey, this is beneath you. If there is one thing you are not, it's dumb. You know exactly what I am talking about. Your fingerprints have been all over every protest, every meeting, every kind of disruption this summer, and until now you've always used fellow staff members as accessories. But to plant this idea with the kids, to plot to have them miss the best activity in camp and destroy their summer in the process, that is a degree of callousness I didn't think you had in you. Joey, you are a brilliant guy, and I hope that someday you will make peace with yourself, and you can afford to be decent to the people around you. Nelson had a long history with you, and he was willing to overlook things, but we don't, and I'm not. Nor is Roland. We want you out of here. In fact, we want you out of here before noon today. I made up your final check last night. I wrote a final check for Kerri too, in case she chooses to leave with you. I discussed it with Paulette and she and I are agreed that we'd be happy to have Kerri stay, but we understand she might want to leave with you. You made a good choice with her. She's nowhere near the counselor you are, but she is sweet and kind and cares about her girls. No matter what's happened here this summer, I always thought you truly cared about your campers, that is until you pulled this stunt. I wonder if you care about anyone but yourself. Joey, there is nothing further to say. You should just go back to Senior Camp and start packing. When you're done, you can come and pick up your check."

I could see the anger rising and I certainly understood it. It must be a shock to him to actually have to pay a price for his hateful behavior. I waited for his explosion. It was immediate.

"Vico, if you fire me now, you'll be sorry. I'll take the rest of the staff with me. You'll have fun trying to run the camp with a bunch of junior counselors. All the big guys will follow me."

"Joey, get out! Get out now! If you seriously think anyone will follow you, you're a fool, and I never took you for a fool. The other counselors have had enough politicking already. They just want to be left alone to finish the camp season and enjoy the fun and excitement of Green and Brown with their campers. When they learn you tried to manipulate your campers to ruin Green and Brown, after all that has gone on this summer and after our long staff discussion about Color War, I doubt if anyone will follow you, even Cozy. Right now, just get out of my sight."

24

Joey Counts on Support From His Friends

Joey

I was so angry I felt like taking a swing at him. That might make me feel good in the moment, but it wouldn't change the situation and might even make it worse. I got up slowly and went toward the Rec Hall, where Cozy's team was holding a rally. I planned to catch him as soon as the rally broke. My timing was good. I listened as he gave a pep talk to his boys.

"Now, I want you all to run back to your cabins, make the best beds you've ever made, do your cabin cleanup the best you've ever done it, and when the bugle blows for activity, I want you to run out to the area with your team, bringing all the equipment you will need with you, ready to kick butt! You all got that? Whose gonna win?"

"We are!"

"Who is gonna win?"

"We are!" .....

"Louder...Who's gonna win?"

"WE ARE!"

"Now you've got it. We'll kick their butts!....How we gonna win?

"We'll kick their butts!"

"Good! Let's get out and do it."

The campers and counselors piled out of the Rec Hall and raced back to their cabins. Cozy and I were alone. I told him what just happened and that the bastard had actually fired me.

"We're not going to stand for this. I want you to get all of your coaches on board. Meet me at his office at high noon. All of you will stand there threatening to resign if he fires me. How does that sound?"

"Actually Joey, I'd like to help, but the timing is terrible. I just got my team started. The kids and all of the counselors are raring to go. None of us really want to leave now. And at noon time I'll be running our next rally."

"None of you will have to really leave. Just say you're *going* to leave. That will get him. I'm going to talk to Tubby about his coaches too, and I'll get all the judges in on it. The whole boys' staff will be there, telling him you're leaving. He won't have any choice. He'll have to back down."

"Joey, I can't do it. I hate to say it, but you're wrong this time. The word is out that you tried to get those kids to back out on Green and Brown, and an awful lot of people are upset with you. We're not going to back you this time Joey. We're just not."

I was shocked by Cozy's reaction, but there didn't seem to be anything I could do about it. If I got that from Cozy, there was no point in talking to Tubby. He loves Green and Brown. He'd never want to leave no matter what.

"Cozy, I'm really disappointed in you. There is such a thing as loyalty. When you get home after all this is over, don't bother calling me. I'm sure I'll be too busy taking care of important matters."

I wasn't sure what to do about Kerri. She didn't really fit into my future plans. But I guess until I figured out what I was doing next, I'd better include her. I'd go talk with her and tell her we're leaving camp.

25

A Memorable Camp Season Ends

Vico

I was surprised Joey didn't attempt a final dramatic scene. He came and picked up their paychecks, while the whole camp was in the dining hall singing and cheering for their teams. Hardly anybody noticed when Joey ambled down the office steps, climbed into the driver's seat, and drove out of the parking lot. I could see Kerri sitting, dabbing her eyes as they drove away.

That final week of camp was glorious. The Color Wars for both the girls and the boys were close from start to finish. The winners were determined in both contests by the Song and Cheer contests on the last night. After all of the tears, hugs and reconciliations between old friends, Green and Brown was over. That left us with the breathtaking task of getting all of the campers and most of the staff, packed up, and ready to go home in one day. It was a tough day, but we did it.

The buses rolled in by 6:30 that final morning. The campers boarded buses heading in different directions after tearful goodbyes to friends they might not see again until next summer. As the buses rumbled down the road, I was relieved to know that everyone made it onto the correct bus, and that they were on their way. But my biggest sigh of relief came a few hours later when I got the phone call from the last of the bus trip leaders, who had accompanied the homebound campers. That was the call that told me all of our campers had been successfully reunited with their parents.

That night we had a Chinese banquet for all of the staff who remained in camp. A few counselors who had been asked to accompany our campers home on the buses missed that final treat of the season. The following morning, the counselors all drifted out, some in groups, others one by one. By three-thirty camp was empty. The only ones left were Dotty and me, Roland, Paulette, Cindy, and our children. We gathered together at Nelson and Cindy's house for a final wrap-up conference. Collectively we celebrated the successful conclusion of a difficult and painful camp season. An overwhelming melancholy pervaded our discussion. The inescapable tragedy of the summer was the death of Nelson, the guiding hand of Camp Adventure. We all understood the overwhelming weight and sorrow of this loss to Cindy and her children, and I marveled privately at her composure. We laughed and we cried as we spoke of Nelson, recalling his strengths and his many eccentricities. In deference to Cindy, we recalled him primarily with words of praise.

Roland offered to remain in camp a few days to help Cindy close up camp. I agreed I would help too, but I knew I only had a very few days before I was due back at school. We talked on and on well into the evening, barely taking time out for sandwiches and coffee. Cindy debated with herself whether she wanted to hold onto the camp and continue to run it, or if she should be looking for a buyer. We all agreed she didn't have to make that decision immediately, and should give herself a little time and distance to recover from this very tough summer before making a final determination. Roland volunteered to help her for another year whether she decided to stay in business or was in the process of selling.

That night, Dotty and I discussed the past summer and the

future. Strangely, despite the intense agony I experienced at times, I had a yen to see if I could take this place and make it work as it should. Dotty was very supportive, but we both asked the question: Could we afford to gamble all of our savings and incur a big debt to buy the camp? We batted every aspect of the issues back and forth until the early hours of the morning. But before we turned out the lights, a decision was made. In the morning I went to Cindy, and told her if her eventual decision was to sell, we would like to be considered as potential buyers.

"I understand this was Nelson's world and yours as well. I know how difficult it will be if you decide to give it up. But I assure you, if Dotty and I are running the camp you and your family will be forever welcome to spend all of your summers at Camp Adventure."

"You're very kind, Vico and very polite too. But the way I feel about camp after this summer, I won't mind if I never step a foot back here ever again."

We left camp not knowing what the future would hold for us, but hopeful.

We signed a purchase and sale agreement the day after Thanksgiving. Camp Adventure was ours and our lives were changed forever.

26
Epilogue: Fall 1990

Vico

I was in the boathouse helping Jim stow the kayaks and canoes for the winter when the intercom buzzed. It was my secretary Karen. "Vico, there's a guy here looking for you." I was a little annoyed at the interruption. I was hoping to finish up this final physical task of the summer. "Karen, who is it? Did you get his name?"

"He didn't give me a name. Said he wanted to surprise you. He used to be a counselor here a long time ago. He said you'd remember him."

"Okay, send him down here. If he's an old counselor he can help us finish putting these boats away."

I spotted him as he walked across the beach toward me, He looked familiar, but I couldn't immediately identify him. When he was perhaps twenty-five yards away there was no longer any doubt. Despite his graying hair, the handsome athletic looking man who approached me with his hand outstretched and broad smile on his face was Joey Katz. I could see the years had treated him kindly. I hadn't thought about him in a very long time, but was interested to see if he had mellowed.

"Hello Vico, it's been twenty years, but you look the same. You look great."

"Joey Katz, it has been a long time, but I would know you anywhere. I could never forget you. You were one of a kind." He nodded his head up and down in agreement and chuckled.

"I know what you mean, and I don't blame you. I apologize."

"I heard you bought the camp right after my last summer here. I've been meaning to get back for a visit for a long time now, but this is my first time on the East Coast in years. Camp looks good, lots of new buildings and the old ones look spruced up. I'm impressed to see you actually have a boat house. That's pretty fancy for a camp in New England. I remember how we used to lug the boats down from the Rec Hall to the waterfront at the start of the season. That was actually fun, but a boathouse certainly makes sense. Camp must be doing well."

"Yes, we are. I'm happy to say we're in good shape."

"Congratulations! I never doubted you would be successful. Getting rid of me that summer was proof enough of your good judgment. For months after you fired me, I was angry at you, but eventually I understood why you had to do it. For years now I've intended to call or write to say thank you for firing me and to apologize for my part in the problems here that summer. I had to be in Boston on business this week, and a figured I might never be this close again. This was my chance. So, I picked a day, rented a car and here I am. I want you to know when you fired me that day it was probably the best thing that ever happened to me. Thank you." And he held his hand out again. We shook hands for a second time, and then he continued.

"When you fired me, it was quite a slap in the face, which I richly deserved, but it also served as a wakeup call. That morning when I left camp, I wasn't sure where I was going or what I would be doing. I moved back in with my mother for a few days to give me time to figure things out. I reviewed the summer and thought about why you fired me. After I got past my hurt feelings, I admitted that I did it to myself. I had asked for it. Once I acknowledged that, it led me to the bigger question. What was driving me to act that way? What the hell was I doing with my life. My only purpose seemed to be to prove that I was some sort of superior being, that I was a winner and I could always get my way. It took me a while to understand that winning wasn't everything; that I needed something more than that. I needed to build something positive with my life. I needed a worthwhile goal.

"I had no plans and lots of time to reflect and think. Eventually, I came around to connecting my Dad to Nelson, two men who, on the surface, had nothing in common. But I was wrong. They had the most important thing in common, a sense of who they were. My Dad came to this country as a kid, and had nothing. From nothing he built a successful business. He accomplished something with his life and he was proud of what he did, but I never appreciated it. As a kid I was embarrassed that his business was selling adult diapers and rubber sheets to hospitals. But in that week, while I sat around at home trying to figure out who I was, I came to appreciate who he was. My father fulfilled a purpose and he was satisfied with what he had accomplished. I finally came to understand, even though it was a little late, my father was a successful human being.

"Then my thoughts turned to Nelson. As a young man he had a goal and he went out and made it happen. First his goal was to become a teacher and a football coach and he was able to do both well. Then he had a dream. Camp Adventure was that dream and the big goal of his life. He accomplished what he set out to do. The camp was his pride and joy. He was so proud of what he had built and how much good he could do for kids. When I looked at him through my new lens it became obvious to me that, in the same sense as my father, Nelson Cohen was very much a successful human being.

"Then I took a good look at who *I* was and what I had accomplished. I had an epiphany. I didn't like what I saw. I was ashamed when I thought about the way I manipulated and schemed at camp that summer. It seemed all I had ever done was talk and prove I could create turmoil. From that day, my goal in life has been to accomplish something real for myself and my family, just as this camp was Nelson's legacy and now it is yours, I had to build something of value. I still didn't know where I was going or what I would do, but I knew whatever I did I would be striving toward a positive goal."

I was beginning to like this new Joey Katz. "I often wondered what you would wind up doing. You had so much potential and were so sharp. Despite all of the aggravation you caused me that summer, I had confidence you would not continue to waste your life creating problems for others."

"I'll tell you what I've been doing, but first I would love to play catch up with you on some of the people who were here at camp with me all those years ago. The only one I know about is Jeff. He and I have been working together for years. I haven't had contact with anyone from that summer until I wrote to Nelson's wife Cindy a few years ago. I wanted her to know how much I admired her husband, how he and my Dad were the most important influences in my life, and how I always thought of Nelson as my second Dad after my own father died. She wrote back to thank me. I didn't mention you in my letter to Cindy because I only knew you that one summer of my life, but I can tell you now, you also played an important role in my life by forcing me to really look at myself."

As we walked up toward the dining hall, I started to fill him in a little on my family.

"My wife Dotty is out doing errands, but she'll be back soon and I know she'd love to see you. She is the camp's financial watch dog. She keeps me from spending too much. During the camp season she is also our trouble shooter, working with girls who are having problems adjusting to living with others. We always have a few of those. You'll meet my daughter Celia who is up in the dining hall now. She'll put up some coffee for us. She was just a very little girl when you were here. She's all grown up now and I'm proud of my girl. She's a school teacher and here at camp, our girls' Head Counselor. She's a great girl. The kids all love her, and she's a very effective leader with the staff. You just missed meeting our son Ron. He's a Junior at Harvard and is already back at school. He has your old job, Senior Unit Leader, and he loves it."

"Are there any other people still in camp I might remember from way back?"

"No, they're all long gone now. A few key people stayed on to help us run this place those first few years. Roland came back for two more summers and he was a huge help educating me on the hidden aspects of taking care of a camp. He works for the Red Cross full time now. He is their head of the water safety program for all of Long Island. Paulette was with us for four summers, and truly ran the girls' side without much help from me. When she married, she and her husband moved to California and that was the end of camp for her. We're in touch occasionally. She has three kids now and seems to be happily married. Tubby Brown was with us for a couple of years. He's a very successful Wall Street lawyer. The only other one I can think of who stayed on for a while was Jeff Saunders. He was a wonderful and talented young man. I'm glad to hear the two of you are working together. Every so often I see Cozy Martin's name in the paper. He was recently named Poet Laureate for the state of Maine. I have a couple of his books of poetry in our library at home. Other than the ones I mentioned, I have lost track of the other counselors from that far back."

"Now it's your turn. Are you a lawyer or a doctor or in business?"

"I'm in show business."

"That covers a lot of ground. Tell me what it is you actually do. Whatever it is I know it obviously gives you pleasure and a sense of accomplishment." We both laughed.

"I run Empire Studios. You must have heard of us."

"Of course, I've heard of Empire Studios. Everyone knows Empire Studios. Is that really your company?"

"No. It's not my company, but I am the CEO so it's fair to say I run the place. Actually, Jeff and I run the place. Together, we started Empire, struggled financially for a couple of years, but things started going well and we were bought out by a big conglomerate. We are both employees. Jeff is in charge of theme parks. He's done a terrific job there. We passed Universal in daily admissions this year. We're still a long way behind Disney World, and it's unlikely we will ever catch up, but what Jeff's accomplished has been amazing. I've stuck with our original business, producing movies and TV programs.

"I'm impressed. I guess you have accomplished something these past twenty years. How did you ever get into that?"

"Once I decided it was time to grow up, I took a leave from

college, got into my car and started driving. I didn't know where I was going, but I was looking for my thing, whatever it would turn out to be. I drifted westward, taking all sorts of odd jobs as I crossed the country. I was a waiter in several different states, became a backhoe operator in Iowa, and was actually a cowhand in Nebraska. If you remember that Billy Crystal movie, *City Slickers*, where he and his friends became cowboys, let me tell you it was nothing like that. There were very few laughs. It was damn hard work. That trip across the country was quite an education. I think it took me about six months."

"It was early Spring when I reached Los Angeles. Shortly after I got there, I bumped into a friend from college. He and I had spent a lot of time together back in college. We had met as Freshmen, and worked together organizing student protests against the Vietnam War. When I met up with him, I asked him what he was doing in LA. He said he worked for his father, who turned out to be a movie producer. My friend talked his dad into giving me a job as a studio gopher. A few months later I became an Assistant Director. I was still really a glorified gopher. But one day I got the classic Hollywood break. The Director I was working with got sick in the middle of the picture, and I was given the job of finishing it. The film was a success, and that led to me directing another movie. After that, one movie led to another and another. It evolved, with lots of hard work, and a lot of politics too."

"Forgive me for rambling on. I didn't come here to brag about myself. I came here today with just one purpose, to apologize for my behavior that summer and to say thank you for what you did for me, all of those years ago, forcing me to look at myself seriously for the first time and to finally grow up."

"I'm happy to learn some good came out of that camp season for you. You were so sharp as a young man it would have been a shame if you had never capitalized on that intelligence. It's also reassuring to have you tell me that when I fired you it was a positive turning point in your life. All of this is good, and I congratulate you. But I wonder if Cindy or her children will ever really be able to forgive you. Maybe she has or she will. After all, you were just a kid. Still, it is hard to forgive or forget your activities that summer. It's almost impossible to think about Nelson's death without assigning at least partial blame to those of you who were the architects of turmoil. Verbally you have taken responsibility for your behavior. I hope for your sake it goes further than that."

"For me, the memories of that camp season will never be pleasant ones. It was a season filled with turmoil, irresponsibility from people who should have known better, constant tension all summer long, culminating in Nelson's death. It was an awful summer, but it was also a major turning point in my life as well."

"Nelson's death, the most terrible thing that could possibly have occurred, was what made it possible for me to buy the camp, a decision for which I have congratulated myself ever since. Camp has been wonderful for me and for our whole family. Equally important for me as a human being were the lessons I learned that summer, lessons that have been guiding principles ever since. Nelson Cohen may have been stubborn and abrasive, but he was a great teacher. In my mind, he was the embodiment of the word integrity. I always believed in honor, but I had never been tested; not the way Nelson's was tested that summer. For him there was no end to how far he was willing to go to support his beliefs. His example is never far from my consciousness whenever I am faced with a challenge. The lessons I learned have guided how I deal with the world, and particularly the wonderful world of camp. And, happily, I have never been tested to the degree we all were that summer."

About the Author

Arthur Sharenow spent sixty summers of his life in camp. He started as a camper at a very young age and continued on in camp until his retirement. He experienced every aspect of camp life, from camper to counselor, to Unit Leader, to Head Counselor, and finally to Owner/Director. After selling the camp to one of his former outstanding long-term camper-counselors, he stayed on for an additional eight summers so he could continue to enjoy the sheer joy of being at camp, a place always alive with the excitement of childhood and youth.

"I loved being a camp director. How many people are ever given the opportunity to try to create a perfect world. We Camp Directors have that opportunity every summer. A perfect world for our campers was always my goal. Many summers we came very close. Other years we fell somewhat short. The summers that stand out in my mind as most collectively challenging were the last three summers of the 1960s, where the national turmoil associated with the Vietnam War spilled over into summer camps. Happily, the mood of the country changed in the following years, and we experienced decades of wonderful camp seasons.

"After my retirement from summer camping, two new interests became prominent in my life. I took a number of writing courses, several of which were writing memoirs. Many of my memoirs turned out to be camp stories. My writing instructor encouraged me to turn those stories into a book, which I did. *37 Summers: My Years as a Camp Director*, is a collection of memoirs, all from the pages of my camp memory. My current book, *The Summer Camp Uprising* is a novel and comes from the same memory source, but is entirely fictional.

"My second new area of concentration was photography, re-awakening an interest from my early teen years. I worked hard at photography, learning and doing. Eventually I started exhibiting and selling the photos I considered my best. Along the way I started teaching photography, and have been doing so over the past dozen years. What I like most about teaching photo classes is that it reminds me of coaching kids in softball and baseball, something I loved doing all of my adult years at camp."

About Zorba Press

Enchanted by the gorgeous gorges of Ithaca, New York (USA), Zorba Press is an independent publisher of paper books, ebooks, audiobooks (forthcoming), and films.

Zorba's mission is to promote the innovative ideas and the daring books that inspire creativity, nourish children and childhood, humanize technology, point the way to a renewed culture of love and kindness, courage and freedom, sincerity and peace.

For more information and a complete list of our current published works, visit Zorba Press online at

https://ZorbaPress.com

Also Published by Zorba Press

37 Summers: My Years as a Camp Director
a memoir by Arthur Sharenow [ISBN: 9780927379373]

The Summer Camp Uprising
a novel by Arthur Sharenow [ISBN: 9780927379526]

Camp Counselor Smart Guide:
How to Work With and Play With Kids at Summer Camp
by Michael Pastore [ISBN: 9780927379427]

Lark's Magic: a funny novel for children
by Michael Pastore [ISBN: 9780927379076]

Child Maintenance:
How to Respond to Misbehavior Without Force, Rewards, or
Punishments
by Michael Pastore [ISBN: 9780927379434]

101 Problems in Child Maintenance:
Real-Life Training Situations for Everyone Who Works With
Kids   by Micahel Pastore [ISBN: 9780927379380]

101 Answers in Child Maintenance:
Answer Guide to 101 Problems in Child Maintenance
by Micahel Pastore [ISBN: 9780927379410]

Visit Zorba Press online at https://ZorbaPress.com

Made in the USA
Columbia, SC
02 July 2021